OUR
OPTIONS
have
CHANGED

(On Hold Series Book #1)

JULIA KENT
and ELISA REED

1329802

Julia Kent

Elisa Reed ♡

Learn more about Julia Kent and join her newsletter at:
www.jkentauthor.com

Learn more about Elisa Reed at:
www.facebook.com/elisareedauthor

Interior Design & Formatting by:
Christine Borgford, Perfectly Publishable
www.perfectlypublishable.com

Having it all is a fantasy, right?

Chloe Browne knows all about fantasy. Fantasy is her job.

And she's very, very good at what she does.

As director of design for the O Spa chain, a sophisticated women's club that is trending its way into being the Next Big Thing, Chloe's ready to take on the world.

One baby at a time.

Her home study's done, and she's about to adopt, a thirty-something single mother by choice. Who needs to put her life on hold for the right guy when the right baby is waiting for her?

Besides, talk about fantasy.

The right guy?

Pfft. *Right.*

And then in walks Nick Grafton, with those commanding sapphire eyes and wavy blonde hair and a sophisticated mouth that only smiles for her.

He's perfect.

But the last thing Nick wants is to start fresh with a new baby as his college-age kids fly the coop. A single father for more than fifteen years after his wife walked out on her family, Nick finally tastes freedom.

But he likes the taste of Chloe more.

♥ ♥ ♥

Our Options Have Changed is a standalone contemporary romance, the first in the On Hold series by *New York Times* and *USA Today* bestselling author Julia Kent and journalist-turned-fiction-writer Elisa Reed. The characters in the On Hold series are part of the O Spa, a location that appears in Julia Kent's Shopping for a Billionaire series. Cameo appearances from that series are in this spinoff, so readers who love Declan, Shannon, Andrew, Amanda, Marie, Chuckles and more can enjoy a new series while experiencing visits from old book friends.

ACKNOWLEDGEMENTS

To Elisa, who came to me with this idea and all it took was pixie dust and cat herding to make it happen. Note: I am the cat. Meow.

To my husband, who reads all my books first and declared this one "the best book ever." But he says that about all of them, so I am suspicious, though grateful. I think he has an agenda.

To unnamed people who helped with the adoption issues that arise in this book. This is a sensitive topic, and I hope we've addressed it with grace.

To all the people who decide to be an adult, even when it's not fun. You deserve to be acknowledged.

~JK

To Julia, for making my dream come true. Most. Fun. Job. Ever.

To every reader with a dream, *never* give up.

To my 'booster rocket,' never fall away.

~ER

CHAPTER ONE

Chloe

MY DESK AT work is one smooth sheet of inch-thick glass. It's called a waterfall. It's utterly simple and uncomplicated, and every night when I leave my office, I leave that surface perfectly clear. Free of stress.

Gleaming.

So when I walk in this morning and see what appears to be a bound report lying open on my otherwise beautifully empty desktop, I am not happy.

There goes my chi. And it's only seven a.m.

I can tell from across the room that the page has been highlighted in a shade of day-glo pink so bright it hurts my eyes.

It *still* hurts my eyes.

Whatever this document is, someone has helpfully previewed the contents for me.

I stow my tote bag in the closet, pulling out my laptop, cell phone, and my heels.

I push my empty cardboard container of coffee far down in the small rattan wastebasket. At O, the women's spa (and so much more) where I am director of design, visual clutter is *not* in keeping with corporate standards. My next coffee this morning will be sipped from company china: a white mug outlined with a pale grey rim. O.

Just . . . O.

Sitting in my chair, I squint at the alarmingly pink page. It's the color of Pepto-Bismol. I doubt that's a coincidence.

Access: The Consolidated Evalu-shop team conducted its initial assessment of O's flagship location in downtown Boston at 11:30 am on a weekday. As our vehicle approached the retail shop, it became apparent that neither street parking spaces nor garage facilities were available within an easy walk of the entrance. Investigators were forced to park two blocks away in a metered space requiring $2 in quarters for two hours, with no refill option after time expired. Grade: C.

Recommendation: Complimentary valet parking service should be instituted at the door immediately.

Sigh.

Okay, the good news: Operations at O are not my area of responsibility. The not-so-good news: Presentation is. Once you enter our door, if you can see it, I am responsible for it. And now it seems that my spa—my career baby—has been deemed average.

Average. Grade C. Middle of the bell curve.

I flip quickly to Section 3 and skim down the page. Thankfully, no highlighter. I can open my eyes. A random paragraph reads:

Staff Attire: Servers (Male) Our team unanimously awarded very high marks in this area. The male thongs were clearly custom-made, and without exception, well-fitting. They were constructed in such a way as to reveal the positive attributes of each server, at the same time leaving the most intimate details to the club member's imagination until intentionally revealed. The servers' short kimono jackets were chic and serviceable; the motion of the fabric and open style of the jacket captured and held the viewer's interest. Very high-quality materials. Grade: A.

Great. Let's translate this, shall we? The nearly-naked men get an A, the facilities get a C. Sex sells. Parking doesn't.

And there's more. Over one hundred pages more.

We've been mystery-shopped.

Being the subject of a mystery shop evaluation is like standing naked in front of your future in-laws with your credit report taped all over your body and lie-detector tests from all your exes being read over an intercom. In the middle of church.

While standing in a pool of sharks.

Or maybe it just seems that bad. I'm not sure. But I do know there's no way I can read this much pink without more coffee.

And some Xanax-flavored creamer.

A C? I'm that kid who never earned a C in her life. Failure starts with C!

Okay, so, technically it starts with F, and right now, another word that starts with F is coming out of my mouth as I read this secret shopper evaluation that is longer than my college senior honors thesis.

I live for O.

Don't misunderstand. You've heard of O, right?

We've been written up in every lifestyle publication from A to Z. Boston trendsetter Jessica Coffin Instagrams about us regularly—although I'm never quite sure whether she's being sincere or snarky, and sometimes I suspect she's on retainer. This is from yesterday's feed from Jessica: *Standing O.*

O is a twenty-first century club for sophisticated women. A fourth space for women of a discerning taste.

Home is the first space. Work is the second space. Third spaces are locations like coffee shops and malls.

O is the fourth space. The space where you can arrive. Rest. Relax. Indulge. Be someone you can't be in the other three spaces.

Based on our membership rates, we're onto something. Our investors are, shall we say, pleased.

O does have a public presence, thanks to our retail environments. In Boston, Chicago, San Francisco, and soon in New Orleans, sophisticated consumers can spend hours—and hundreds of dollars—browsing our selection of "elegant accessories for intimate pleasure."

That's right—sex toys. That's what the masses call them. Except at O, we cater to a clientele that doesn't want to be one of the *hoi polloi.* They want to be unique. In the know. Enlightened and cosmopolitan on the surface.

But a wildcat down . . . below.

Which makes a Grade C unacceptable. No one wants to be average.

Especially down below.

"'Trying too hard'?" I read aloud, my words coming out like a bark, my fingernails curling and biting into my palms. "How dare they!"

The last time we were mystery shopped, the review began with superlatives that turned my ego into a hot air balloon.

This new eval? More like a Patriots football.

I read on for a very long time, forcing my face to relax.

Every O has its levels. We begin with apparel. Think of it as gift-wrapping—who doesn't love to unwrap a beautiful package? Gently tugging off the ribbon, sliding a fingernail underneath the glossy paper, slowly lifting the lid and spreading open the rustling layers of tissue paper to reveal the delicious surprise beneath. We offer both lingerie and street-wear boutiques.

"The clothing seems a bit out of date and not accessible to the average woman," I whisper-read, wondering who wrote that? There was that word again. *Average.* We don't cater to the average woman! Our boutiques carry every size fathomable, and designers from Milan you've never heard of (but will next season) have exclusive pre-season visits with us to make decisions about their lines. We don't follow trends.

We *set* them.

But it's not just about merchandise. O is a destination. All our retail spaces include stylish bookstore cafés, where our clientele can sip espresso with a twist of lemon peel from tiny cups while reading masterpieces of erotic literature. Famous authors spend nearly a year on our bookstore signing wait lists to get a crack at access to our members (and their purchasing power and buzz).

O's clients enjoy meeting a friend here after work for a sparkling glass of prosecco, and sparkling conversation about who gets to use that new toy on whom tonight, without the annoying meat-market feel of a bar.

And if you happen to want a little meat? We have another bar on site for that, except this meat doesn't hit on you.

It *serves* you.

That white china cup of black coffee descends onto my desk as if delivered from a crane. I look up, and up, at a wall of flesh that makes my morning just a little more tolerable.

"Oh, Henry, thank you. I really need this."

"I can see that. You look a little frazzled. And it's only nine o'clock." He lowers himself into a white upholstered armchair facing my desk, his brow wrinkled with concern, as I blink. I've been mired in all the ways O disappointed a mystery shopping team for the past two hours. No wonder I'm exhausted.

Henry Holliday is seriously seven feet tall. He is my 'work husband.' Ginger hair, green eyes, and the muscular physique that his somewhat unique job requires. Henry is a master masseur in the O Club spa, and fills in occasionally as a performer for private parties. Dancing is in his body and soul. And it pays the tuition for his brain: Henry is working on his master's degree in public health at Harvard.

In a roundabout way, working at O is a form of public service.

See what I mean? At O, you're here to be served.

From the moment you step into an O property, you enter a different world. A world of serenity, where your senses are first lulled, then stimulated.

A world designed by me.

Chloe Browne.

Who has just been given her first C.

CHAPTER TWO

Chloe

"**W**E'VE BEEN MYSTERY-SHOPPED. I found the report on my desk this morning. Anterdec is watching us closely—I guess that's what comes after a ten-million-dollar investment," I explain to Henry as he watches me intently. I'd invite him to get his own cup, but I know Henry hates coffee, which makes him part cyborg.

He tenses visibly. It's a sight. Henry has more muscles than the average person.

There's that damn word again.

Average.

"And? Anything I should know? What did they say about the spa? You know I need this job, Chloe. It pays well *and* fits my class schedule."

"Not sure yet, it's over a hundred pages long, but so far it seems fairly neutral."

He sucks in his breath as if scandalized.

Neutral. Average.

The overachiever's biggest fear.

"I know." I shake my head sadly. "Do you have any idea who it could have been? I filled in giving some of the tours last month, but no one seemed like they were evaluating us. Everyone I saw honestly seemed to be enjoying themselves. And enjoying you." I smile.

He doesn't smile back.

"There are no more services that I can provide for our clients and still be faithful to Jemma. None. Thank god I have an understanding wife. I am giving my all, thanks to your uniform design."

"Which, by the way, got very high marks," I say cheerfully. "Who knew shoelaces could be so popular?"

He gives me an arched eyebrow and leans forward. "Let's see that report."

I hold it away from him just as my phone buzzes with a text.

"Don't answer that!" he snaps. I wince. Henry's not just an employee. He's a good friend, and he knows why I want to look.

I look.

"It might be the adoption agency," I protest. "I have to take it." I'm waiting to hear whether I've been cleared after my home study for adoption. Nearly a year since I started the process, and I'm finally in the home stretch.

Henry groans.

The text says, *Hey beautiful.*

Not the adoption agency, unless part of their services now includes self-esteem building for prospective mothers.

It's Joe. My boyfriend of three years.

I tell myself not to reply.

I can't help myself. I reply. *Hey.*

How's your morning? he writes back quickly.

It's had its highlights. Too much to text. One hundred and twenty-five pages too much.

Tell me tonight? Your place?

I tell myself to say no. I do. I really do.

"Chloe." Henry's voice holds a low warning, like he's defending me from myself.

Yes, I text back.

Great 6:30

Self-loathing is an art. I should be pinned to a wall at the Institute of Contemporary Art.

I met Joe at my last job. He was the chief legal counsel. I was a project manager. One of our vendors failed to deliver a $40,000 conference table to Joe's legal firm, and we sued. Joe got the table, and earned a bonus.

When the table finally arrived on site, Joe and I immediately used it to conduct a late-night intimate meeting—and a very satisfying meeting it was, too. That table was fabulous for spreading out and getting the job done under tight circumstances.

;)

Joe is my greatest supporter, my confidante, my tender lover. And due to some rather unfortunate timing, still someone else's husband.

I know, I know, don't even say it. It's such a cliché, right? They grew apart, they haven't slept together in years, the divorce will be final any day now . . . and we fell in love.

A familiar story, so contrived, but when it happens to you, it feels painfully real.

At least at first. Lately, it's just painful.

And Joe needs to get real.

"I can't believe you're caving in," Henry says with a sigh. Henry and his wife are not Joe fans, to say the least. He plucks the thick report out of my hands deftly and maneuvers away, like he's practicing a dance move. His ginger waves have tightened with summer humidity, and curls ring his forehead. They bounce as he shakes his head.

"I can't show you the whole thing, Henry. You know I have a non-disclosure agreement on things like this! Let me find the spa section, and the private entertainment review."

Henry is a rule follower at heart, so he returns the report.

I check the index, and pull out a highlighter of my own. Orange.

"Okay, here it is . . ." I hand him the report and watch his eyes scan the pages.

"Think, Henry." I lean forward. "Do you remember anyone who seemed to know a little too much about your services, or asked too many questions?"

He frowns. "There was one woman—you know, when I enter the room, the client is always lying on the table, under the cover, as instructed."

I wish he hadn't mentioned lying on a table. Joe. Technically, I wasn't lying on the table. I was bent over it. Well, the first time, at least . . .

"Chloe?" Henry waves his hand in front of my face. "Earth to Chloe! You listening?"

"Um, right. Yes." I will away the memory with a sigh and a sip of my coffee.

"But this woman had the linen sheet wrapped around her, and she was looking at my framed diplomas on the wall."

"Anything else?"

"Well, yeah, now that I think about it . . . she was older. Blonde. Kind of wild. Ditzy, but I got a sense it was an act. She came here with a younger woman, and later mentioned her daughter was getting married. She drank a shot out of my navel."

"How is that memorable?" I tease. "Every woman who sets foot in O does that." I pause and think. "Hell, so have I."

"I think it was a requirement during my interview," he says dryly.

Everyone working at O has some pretty good stories. We have a very appealing staff of men and women, all highly trained to provide the ultimate release from stressful reality. O space is carefully designed to encourage escapism. But Henry is on the frontlines of funny. As he says, it's lucky he has an understanding wife. Actually, Jemma is one of my closest friends.

Technically, we're not supposed to talk about clients, ever, but when the three of us have dinner, it's confidential.

And hilarious. I'd write a book if my employment contract didn't specifically prohibit it.

"Not sure I want the details." I pause. "Yet. Do you remember her name?"

He snorts. "No, are you kidding? I don't even see client names. I just see their membership number. But if I recall correctly, her number should have been sixty-nine."

I burst out laughing. "We didn't assign sixty-nine to anyone! Sort of like high-rise buildings that don't have a thirteenth floor. It would be tempting fate."

He stands to leave, glances at my phone, then looks at me closely. "Is the mystery shop the only thing on your mind?"

Unexpectedly, my eyes fill up with tears.

I'm *not* a crier.

I am cool. I am collected. I hate crying.

"Dammit, Chloe." He knows. We all know.

Joe.

"Henry, do NOT make a Joe Blow joke." We've been down this road before.

Henry leans down, and I stand up for his hug, but forget I'm holding the orange marker. Which somehow highlights the front of his grey gym shorts.

Perfect. But at least we're laughing now.

"Better highlighter than lipstick, I guess," I offer.

"Only until Mystery Shopper #69 comes back," he says ruefully.

My phone buzzes with a text.

He snatches it away from me.

"It could be the adoption agency!" I protest weakly. I don't even reach for it.

Henry looks. His head recoils. "It is."

"It is?" I gasp, grabbing the phone.

Home study cleared, Chloe. Please call me when you can. Congratulations, Yvonne.

Henry and Jemma have been my staunchest supporters through my adoption process. They came over and helped me install child-proof locks on all my cabinets before the home study. Have given tips and hints, listened and held me, parsed through logical issues and irrational state requirements.

"Yes. It says *yes*. Home study cleared," I say in wonderment.

His face splits with a huge grin, his white teeth shining, the former tense lines between his eyes gone. "I knew it." He pulls me into a hug. "You're going to be a mom soon."

Mom.

The phone buzzes again. I look behind Henry's shoulder at the phone in my hand.

And buy a fifth of Tito's, Joe texts. *You can drive me home.*

"You are getting what you deserve, Chloe," Henry says. "Everything you've ever wanted."

I turn my phone off.

Right.

♥ ♥ ♥

COFFEE HAS DIMINISHING returns, and by two in the afternoon, I am a rat pushing the caffeine lever over and over without receiving the desired effect. All I can think about is babies. My computer screen has twelve tabs open, one to PoshTots, one to Babycenter, one to Dr. Sears, one to the CDC guidelines for cribs, and the rest are for baby clothing sites. I don't know why they make shoes for babies who can't even stand up, much less walk, but they are ridiculously cute.

Hey—priorities.

"Chloe? Must have been a good night if you're still wearing hangover glasses after lunch."

Carrie is O's junior designer, though she's only a year younger than me. We're opposites. I'm darker-skinned with dark, straight hair, while Carrie looks like someone dropped her out of an Amazonian cornfield in Iowa. Her long, wavy strawberry blonde hair hangs over one shoulder in a loose ponytail, like a witness to the awful mystery shop report.

She drops a bunch of new fabric samples in the basket next to my desk, towering over me. "Are those the new J.Crew sunglasses?"

Well, yes, they are. I take them off and rub my eyes.

"Worse than a hangover. I've been reading hot pink criticism for four hours. I needed protection," I explain.

She gives me a polite, soft laugh.

"Carrie, how are we doing with the voice response system? We've reached a point where we need to get the computer system in place for customer service calls and reservations."

"I'm on it, Chloe." Carrie reaches for a folder and slides out a piece of paper. "Our only obstacle now is the service request menu."

I look at the list.

Press 1 to schedule a massage appointment

Press 2 to request a master masseur

Press 3 to speak with a coordinator about divorce parties

Press 4 to purchase merchandise

Press 5 to—

I squint. "Does that say what I think it says?"

Carrie laughs. "Yes."

"We can't have an option to speak directly with one of the masseurs. They'll be inundated!"

"It's a new idea from the business development office. Customer-driven. They want 'phone sessions' with the guys."

"Paid phone sessions?" My jaw drops. I've seen a lot here, but this takes the cake.

"Right."

"That's phone sex!"

Carrie squirms, her face reddening. "Ah, technically, it's a half-hour consultation with the guys to discuss self care." I can tell that is a very well-rehearsed euphemism written by a marketing team via focus group input, all right.

"How much?"

We often speak in shorthand. Carrie knows what I mean. "One eighty."

"For a half hour?"

"Focus groups. Marketing priced it with focus groups." See?

Called it.

"Was there a beta test?"

"Yes." Carrie bites her lower lip. "Revenue from each customer jumped like crazy. They want the personal touch. One woman set up a recurring appointment."

"I'm surprised Henry didn't mention this to me."

Carrie lights up. "Do you think you could convince him? He was the most requested consultant and he refused."

I'll bet his wife *Jemma* refused.

"And the guys . . . they're okay with this?"

Carrie chortles. "Ryan's loving it. Says he makes more money talking to women about their hot flashes and uptight husbands than he does when his hands are on them. They just want someone to listen."

"For one eighty a half hour, Ryan better be a damn good listener." Ryan is one of the tatted-up male employees. The women love him.

Carrie's face softens, eyes going unfocused. "He is."

"You can handle the phone tree people? I don't have to add this to my plate?"

"Sure. No problem. It's all about getting people to put themselves on hold when they need to be patient, and to learn to press the right buttons to get what they want."

"Just like sex," I note.

We share a laugh.

Just like life, I think. Someday, maybe my options will change, and I can just press zero for help.

If only life were so simple.

A message window pops open on my computer screen:

HELP GET ME OUT OF HERE NOW

It's the cool and unflappable Henry.

What's wrong? I type back.

CLIENTPROFNAKED!!

Professional naked? Your client is a stripper?

This would be highly unusual for an O client—our members might enjoy watching a show, but they don't typically perform in it—but it's certainly nothing to panic over.

PROFESSOR!

NAKED!

HELPOUTNOW!

I'll get Zeke, I type. Zeke's our other master-level masseur. He has brown hair halfway down his back, pulled up in a trendy man bun right now, blonde streaks a sign of his addiction to outdoor life. Tanned, with strange scars dotting his thighs, and a tattoo of a mandala on one ass cheek (hey—I can't help but look—it's my job) in vibrant colors. Zeke's a great asset to O.

Not quite as experienced as Henry, and lacking his way with words . . . although judging by this message, Henry's way with words has just escaped him.

I check the daily appointments screen and see that Henry's in the Sage Room, on the spa level, second floor. Then I'm out the door, running for the elevator.

In four-inch heels, this is more like speed-walking on tiptoe.

As I "run," I call the spa manager and explain the situation. Not that I *understand* the situation.

Zeke and I arrive at the door of the Sage Room at the same moment. He taps gently, giving me a look with green eyes that glitter with mirth. After a slight pause, the sliding door opens and Henry slips out.

Poor Henry has a towel wrapped around his head like a turban, hiding his curly ginger hair. Although the treatment rooms are maintained at the optimal temperature, he is sweating profusely.

"What's wrong?" Zeke asks urgently. "Should we call security?" I love his English accent. So do the clients.

"Barnacle!" Henry hisses.

Zeke and I exchange a glance.

"A skin condition?" I am at a loss.

"Professor Barnacle! My bio-ethics professor! Naked!

Moaning!" Henry is distraught.

"Zeke, are you free now? Can you take over?" I ask. "Her information should be on the iPad screen, right?"

He nods and disappears into the darkened room, the music pulsing and then silenced as the door slides open and closed.

Inside the staff lounge, I pour Henry a glass of O's signature passionflower-infused iced tea. Counter-intuitively, passionflower is supposed to be calming. With a shot of vodka, it might be. Members can order it that way, too, but of course the O team must not indulge. Until their shift is over, that is.

"When I entered the room, I smelled a familiar perfume, but that happens all the time. And the lights were low, and she was lying face down, covered with the sheet. The client info screen showed that she requested the Tantric Touch massage, ninety minutes. I put my music on, and I started warming and mixing the oils. Then I noticed the wild black hair." He shudders. "And that purple nail polish she wears. But still I wasn't sure."

"Did you say anything?" I ask because Henry has a distinctive voice, surprisingly soft for a man of his power and size. That voice would identify him, even in the dark.

"No, the idea is to be as silent as possible. As if my hands were unconnected to anyone. Just floating touch."

I reflect on this for a brief moment. Money actually *can* buy happiness.

"So I began the massage," he continues. "In Tantric practice, everything proceeds very slowly. Thank god for that. If it went any faster, I'd have violated every faculty-student interaction policy on record by now. It wasn't until she turned over that I knew for sure it was Professor Barnacle. And by then she was begging me to 'move to the center of her chakra' and 'release her inner flood.'"

"That's a new phrase for female ejaculation," I mutter.

"I thought that was a myth?"

I don't even dignify that with a response.

"Poor Zeke." Henry shudders and motions for me to make

another cup of tea. This is a role reversal. Part of his job is to serve me. But we're friends, and I'm compassionate, and I'm curious.

I want to know what the hell happened in the Sage Room, and if I'm already being nice, I might as well pump him for info.

"Did she touch you?"

Before Henry can answer, a loud moan that rises along three octaves takes up all the available decibels in the room.

"Oh, dear," I whisper. We do have some rather enthusiastic clients who fully embrace their sexuality and aren't inhibited in expressing pleasure. Generally, though, they manage not to shatter all the wine glasses in the tasting room.

"I hope she tips well," Henry mumbles, then looks at me. "And I swear, if it were anyone but my advisor, I'd be fine with the basics."

Another moan.

"Is that what Zeke's doing? *Basic* Tantric Massage?" If that's "the basics," we need to up our prices.

Henry shrugs.

"We do need to walk a fine line. I'm sure Zeke's not crossing it."

"Oh, God," Henry's professor cries out. "You have divine hands."

"That's it," Henry announces, elbows on his knees, fingers threading through his hair in frustration. "I can't continue working here. This was way too close a call."

An alarm buzzes through me. Clients request Henry at a rate three times higher than our other masseurs. That's why his fee is so much higher, and the profit margins are fabulous. With a presentation for investors coming up this week, I have to have the financials in a solid place.

Henry's too valuable to let a horny barnacle scare him off.

"Go home. I'll talk to management and make sure they'll cover your base pay for the day. You're rattled. *Understandably* rattled," I add, as Henry glares at me.

"Can you imagine finding someone from your personal life

suddenly invading your work space?"

"No." I shudder. I have one rule: no mixing business with pleasure. Okay, so I broke that when I met Joe, but that was it. One time only. Joe was the exception.

"Who's the moaner?" asks Ryan, walking into the lounge carrying a Kylo Ren costume and a light saber. He hangs the costume in the staff closet and turns around, hands on hips, ears perked.

"Client," Henry snaps.

"Duh, it's a client." Ryan shoots him a pissed-off look. Ryan is our resident "Bad Boy" masseur. Liberally covered in real tattoos, he's sleeved and looks just enough like Charlie Hunnam when he dyes his hair blonde to make him the second most popular masseur at the spa. "But damn, she's wicked loud. Chloe, you need to upgrade the soundproofing in those massage rooms."

"Duly noted." Now *that* is one operations item a mystery shopper would never, ever document.

"Why the hell are you sitting in the lounge sipping tea in your shoelace?" Ryan asks Henry. His hair is his natural chestnut brown, short but longer at the bangs, and he wears a slight beard, just scraggly enough to make him look dirty, but not so long as to evoke *Duck Dynasty*. Like all the O men, he's tall, muscular, and makes Joe Manganiello's abs look like Pillsbury biscuits.

Note to self: O Spa calendar series photography needs to be booked. Stat.

Henry stands abruptly, abandoning his tea. He gives me a savage look and says, "I'll take you up on the offer to go home," his butt-flossed ass the last we see of him as he storms out.

"What the hell's wrong with him?"

"The moaner is one of his professors."

Ryan lets out a low whistle. "No shit?" Like all the other employees at O, Ryan knows how aggressively Henry separates his personal and professional lives. "No wonder he's upset. She recognized him?" Women love Ryan's Southie accent, which becomes more pronounced when he talks about drama.

"It's all fine now," I say. Ryan has a tendency to hoard gossip, and I am not going to be his supplier.

One of the cleaning staff enters the room, dressed in the O signature kimono but with a zipper instead of a tie to hold it closed, and swiftly removes Henry's cup of tea.

"Hey, Chloe, I think payroll screwed up last week. I was shorted about eighty bucks on my paycheck," Ryan says.

My turn to groan. "Again?"

"Corporate never makes mistakes in my favor."

I pat his forearm as I walk out of the lounge. "File a ticket in the new accounting system. CC me on it. I'll make sure it's caught up next week." I don't handle operations, but with O poised to expand into new franchises after my upcoming presentation with Anterdec, I troubleshoot every issue these days.

He flashes me a brilliant, grateful smile. If I didn't have a strict "No Fraternizing" rule with the employees, I'd be so tempted.

"Thanks. You're the best."

"Oh, God!" the professor screams. *Screams.*

"I think Zeke's the best," I say out of the corner of my mouth, as Ryan bursts into laughter.

Just another day at work, and it's not even half over.

CHAPTER THREE

Chloe

I WAS BORN without abdominal muscles.

This has never been confirmed by any medical professional, but it's the only possible reason why I have executed tens of thousands of curl-ups in my lifetime with no visible result.

None.

Jemma is lying on the mat next to mine, cradling a two-pound weight on her chest. She's not even pretending to move. If we pulled the mats outdoors on the roof deck, people would think we were tanning.

Hmm, not a bad idea. At least we would be accomplishing something.

One of the perks of working at O Club is that we get to use Oxygen. Not the breathing apparatus. The fitness studio. Although there *is* a special room here where members can inhale concentrated oxygen in special scents.

We offer Summer in Provence, Colorado Evergreen, Caribbean Spice. For non-vegans, we have Ferrari Leather. I have suggested Warm Balls—more than once—but it never appears. Am I the only one who finds that scent delicious? And for some of us, it's scarcer than Southern Oleander.

We're in product development for a new scent: Jamie Fraser. The focus group marketing companies have been inundated with volunteers to test-smell *that* one.

Jemma turns on her side and does a few leg lifts. Like, three. In the middle of my work day, I can take an hour and join any class with an open spot. In fact, I'm encouraged to join a class every workday. It helps me stay in touch with the business and the clientele.

Maybe once I adopt, we can add Baby and Me yoga classes.

Scratch that. Definitely out of the scope of O's branding.

But I can't stop thinking about babies.

"It's a good thing you decided to adopt instead of doing IVF, Chloe. I can't really see you doing a strict daily routine of Kegel exercises. Unless lululemon introduces a maternity line with super cute yoga pants." Jemma's comment about adoption jars me out of my reverie.

"Oh, lots of benefits to adoption. Like, I don't have to worry about my water breaking in public. And I'll definitely take the baby home wearing my pre-motherhood jeans." No one has openly asked, but I'm adopting for reasons that are no one else's business anyway, so the lack of questions has been fabulous. It's complicated, but the bottom line is, I have always wanted this baby.

Jemma sticks her tongue out at me, just a little. It's cute. "You would anyway. Your size never changes. My closet has every size from 2 to 14. I've shopped in major department stores that don't carry that many sizes."

"My size never changes because I am a contentment eater."

"A *what?*" Jemma laughs.

"A contentment eater. I'm not hungry when I'm deliriously happy, and I can't even look at food when I'm sad or upset. Or stressed. When I'm perfectly content, and everything is smooth, *then* I will polish off a pizza. By myself. But since I've almost never been perfectly content . . . size four." Okay, six. But who's checking?

"And anyway," I continue, "you have a husband who finds you dead sexy no matter what you're wearing." And he should. Jemma's gorgeous.

"I do," she agrees, smiling to herself. She runs her hand along her own curvy hip. "Maybe when your baby comes, contentment will be easier to find. How much longer now?"

"The birth mom is due in twelve weeks. After all this time, I can't believe the baby is almost here. I'm so excited, Jem. And terrified. I keep wondering if this is how my mom felt when she adopted me."

"How is Li?" Li is a sixteen-year-old homeless street kid I met a few months ago while doing philanthropic work for a charity attached to Anterdec, the parent company of the O Spa chain. Through a series of still bizarre events that I am amazed ever happened, she came to me, confessing her pregnancy, and asking me to adopt the baby.

Unreal.

Even my adoption lawyer said she'd never heard of such a thing.

Yet here we are, months later, on track. I go with Li to the downtown health clinic for her monthly checkups. Baby's fine. Li's getting social services, refusing help from me other than some shopping sprees, and determined as ever to have me adopt.

Unreal, all right.

If it weren't happening to me, I wouldn't believe it, either.

"Li's fine. A trooper."

"You realize she still might . . . this could be . . ."

I place my hand on her arm. She stops her leg lefts. I'm not sure if she stops out of compassion for me, or relief that she has an excuse to stop.

"I know, Jem. You and Henry and the social worker and my lawyer don't have to remind me constantly. I'll support Li if she changes her mind. I really will. I'll just go back to the more traditional route I was in before she came along. It's okay."

"Sorry."

We share a smile that manages to mix excitement, wistfulness, and pain.

"Not content yet?"

"Nope. I'm the only expectant mother ever to lose three pounds."

"What's Joe saying about this? It's going to change a lot of things. You're not going to be able to meet him at odd hours, or on a moment's notice." Jemma looks at me carefully. "Or bail him out of jail when he gets a DUI and doesn't want his wife to know."

"That only happened once!"

She gives me a look that manages to mix pained pity with drill-sergeant grit.

I look away. "I have a meeting in twenty minutes, gotta go."

And I roll up my mat. I'm never going to have abs.

It's hopeless.

♥ ♥ ♥

5:30. I'VE GOT TO leave work now if I'm going to meet Joe at my apartment in an hour. There's plenty of wine, and vodka in the freezer if he wants his favorite martini. But I need to stop at the Broadway Market for olives, some chèvre, and those little toast crackers he likes.

And I need to do a little picking up before he gets there. Joe doesn't like disorder, and there's a black lace bra drip-drying in the bathroom. A wine glass and a coffee cup in the kitchen sink.

And oh my god, I left my swan charging on the bedside table. Joe may be my boyfriend, but every woman needs a battery-operated backup, right?

Jemma's words haunt me. She's right. Joe has zero interest in kids. I know this.

Yet I'm adopting anyhow.

I admit it: I have a paradoxical inner life. I own it.

I am stuffing the mystery shop report into my bag when my phone screen lights up with a text coming in.

Joe: *I can't believe this, have to cancel tonight*

Shit.

Shit, I type.

I know, SO sorry, have to work late. This acquisition. Joe is representing a company that's buying an Italian textile factory, and the international laws are complicated.

I text back a frown.

But the divorce lawyer said there's been movement, he replied. *Honey, I'm so close.*

I smile. He can't see it, of course, but I do. *No worries. Poor you, don't stay too late. Call me later,* I answer.

Damn it. He's been doing this lately. That acquisition might be great for his client's bottom line, but it's been hell on my libido.

At least I don't have to race to the market. But I was *really* looking forward to seeing him.

And feeling him.

And him feeling me.

And who knows when he'll have another free evening.

Henry and Jemma's gentle (and not-so-gentle) chiding runs through my mind. I know I should dump him. I know I cater to him. I know I accept less. But I've invested all these years in him. You don't spend three years fighting your own instincts and giving in to this kind of passion only to walk away, never knowing if you were almost across the finish line.

He showed me more divorce paperwork last week. Well, a blurry photo of papers on his phone, at least. He's so close.

Poor Joe, working so hard, and now I have nothing to do tonight. I wonder if my swan is done charging?

He might be working late, but surely he has time for a quickie. Everyone has time for a quickie, right? That's why they're called quickies. Short, hot, sweet—

And *something.*

Something is always better than nothing.

I'll stop at the market anyway, and get him some lovely things to eat. Cheese and crackers, some fruit maybe, and one or two of those chocolate shortbread cookies he loves. I'll make a basket, how fun! Maybe I'll put in an IPA or two, and I can buy a little vase with a huge Gerbera daisy . . .

His office is closed by the time I get there, but the security guard remembers me from my days as a client. He smiles and waves me in.

I stop in the ladies' room in the lobby. Brush my hair, add fresh lipstick.

Idea: private label lipstick line for O. Color names like cOral Sex. Branded line of lubes with hot names like O Now!

I add a spray of my lemon verbena perfume at the base of my neck, and on both wrists. I change from my street shoes into heels and smooth the tops of my thigh highs. I slip off my thong and put it in my bag.

One more spritz of perfume, under my skirt. Just in case.

And up in the elevator, to the fourteenth floor.

The door slides open. I have always loved after-hours offices. Most of the offices dark, no phones ringing or machines running, the view of city lights below. No one watching me.

Creative freedom.

Picnic basket over my arm, I head down the hall to Joe's office, my hips swinging like a runway model. My high heels make no sound on the grey carpet. This will be a total surprise. Arousal twins with anticipation. My thighs buzz and I am so ready. As I get closer, I can hear faint music, that jazz station he loves. Another bonus of working after everyone else has gone home is putting on your own music.

My pulse races now. I love to create special moments, and this feels so much like our first time, all that desire built up for so long and finally, unexpectedly, released.

And released.

And, if all goes well . . . *released again.*

The memory of our first time seizes me as I finish the long walk down the hallway.

So beautiful it was worth waiting for. That's what he told me.

Pretty much every sexual fantasy I ever had came true in that one unforgettable hour. Until he had to leave for a business dinner. I was the appetizer.

That was three years ago. Sex has never been quite that hot since. But tonight . . .

I slow as I get closer to his office, my pulse throbbing between my legs, a smile on my face as I imagine his delight at my little surprise.

Hmm. There's a black sweater slung over the side of a cubicle. Someone must have gone home and forgotten it.

And oh, that's odd, one black high heel. In the doorway to the conference room.

Then I'm in the doorway, peering in.

At Joe, leaning back against the enormous limed oak table. *Our* table.

And the girl on her knees in front of him, her head moving up and down, her hands on his hips, pulling him in, head bobbing in an all-too-familiar rhythm.

He gasps, "Honey, I'm so close."

I can't move.

"Baby, this was worth waiting for," he groans.

Then he looks up and sees me, and there's a strange kind of pause as we both process what's happening.

I've had better days. The day I totaled my car in my senior year of high school? Better.

The winter day six years ago when my wallet was stolen and all my credit cards were used to buy Vuitton luggage and plane tickets to Tahiti? Better.

Every single day of my life up till today?

Better.

CHAPTER FOUR

Chloe

ONE MONTH LATER

CARRIE WALKS BY my office door, then backs up and asks, "Hangover glasses two days in a row?"

"They are *not* hangover glasses, Carrie, there's just a lot of glare in here. Morning sun."

"Okay, whatever. Looking good, Chloe." She moves on.

Today all of O's corporate management team will be meeting with the investment team from Anterdec. They're all coming here, on site, to check out the place in person and make decisions. In Boston, Anterdec is the biggest player in hospitality properties, ranging from international hotel chains to restaurants and so much more. I have to impress them. My career depends on it.

And so does impending motherhood. I've built up a ton of paid time off, and when the adoption goes through I'll need all the maternity leave and flexible schedule time I can get.

If the adoption goes through, I chide myself. If.

If I just keep these sunglasses on, maybe they'll think it's a fashion statement? Because my eyes are so puffy, I look like Ronda Rousey after fighting Holly Holm. Worse, actually. Last night was another bad one, flashbacks and bitter tears.

And I'm slated to present the design scheme for O's newest location in New Orleans, when all I can think about is Joe, that blonde head bobbing between his knees, and how he looked at me. A month has passed, a month of shame and anger, of self-flagellation and fury. I let myself be deluded because it was easier than facing the truth.

Which makes me human, I guess.

I still can't believe it. He gave me a blank look, and then said one word to me. One.

"Oh."

Just . . ."Oh." Irony can be a real bitch.

It's been a busy month, between social workers and lawyers and adoption agency workers arranging for paperwork for the adoption, and Joe turning into Joe Blow, for real.

I have accomplished a lot.

Block Joe on my cell? *Done*

Block Joe on Facebook? *Done*

Block Joe on email? *Done*

Call locksmith to change locks on my apartment? *Done*

Those were easy. Done on day one. He spent the next three weeks creating ways to contact me, from new accounts on OKCupid (yes, my profile's still there . . .) to leaving messages for me at work. Carrie's a reliable gatekeeper, though she's recently taken to answering the phone in fake foreign languages whenever "Private Number" appears on caller ID.

One hundred percent success rate in guessing the caller's identity.

Joe tweets, Instagrams, Facebooks under false names, calls my office, texts, and tries every way he can to weasel his way back in. Why wouldn't he? It always worked before. Can't blame him for that.

But I can blame him for plenty of other behavior.

The hard part came later, though, when the shock wore off and the anger really set in.

I couldn't sleep last night, so at three a.m. I got up and collected the following items:

- Tee shirts, 3 (two Princeton, one Coldplay concert which we attended together but he couldn't take the souvenir home)

- Boxer shorts, 3 pair

- Princeton sweatshirt (okay, you went to an elite school, enough already). Here I had a weak moment. I admit it. A whiff of his French cologne made me bury my face in the sweatshirt and sob. The moment passed.

- Running shorts, one pair

- Nike running shoes, one pair

- Socks, two pair

- Shaving kit

- One tube of athlete's foot cream

- One half-used bag of floss wand picks. Joe was obsessed with periodontal disease. He would pick his teeth after every meal, even if we were watching a show.

- All the carefully chosen birthday and Christmas gifts I have given him that of course he couldn't take home, including the small, signed Picasso etching of a cat that was his Valentine in February. Joe gave me my cat last year. He said she reminded him of me because she was so sleek.

I took a long, hard look at the cat. No, she stays. It's the boy-friend that has to go.

It all made quite a big pile.

On second thought, I put the Picasso etching back on the wall. Let's not be crazy.

There is an actual service that will come to your home and just get rid of it all for you. If you can't bring yourself to part with his frayed boxer shorts—because he used to do that adorable little dance in them, or because you are hoping he will come back for them and suddenly realize you are his One True Love—you (or your best friends) can hire a team to come to your house and exorcise the demon.

NeverEver will go through your closets with you, gently pull each object from your clenched fingers, pack it up, remove it, and burn the appropriate herbs afterwards. If they could prescribe Xanax, I would have called them.

I did briefly consider selling some of it on Never Liked It Anyway, which I never thought I'd have a reason to use. After a breakup, you can go to their website and sell the crap your ex gave you. It's monetized revenge *and* purging. A client told me about it.

It's brilliant. But who would want Joe's half-used bag of floss wands?

Don't answer that.

Instead, when I felt myself losing heart, I just whispered, *"This was worth waiting for . . ."*

Except it wasn't.

"Oh." He really just said that.

Asshole.

I took the box of Joe's crap and mailed it to his house this morning on my way to work. Now I have more closet space. Good.

All good.

No—not good.

Better.

♥ ♥ ♥

IF I NEVER see another conference table, it will be too soon.

Much of my job requires me to stand in front of small groups of people and present my ideas for environments that are appropriate, completely unique, and undeniably beautiful. Spaces that no one could have imagined and no one ever wants to leave. Spaces that can be created on-time and on-budget. And thanks to O's enlightened mission, spaces that are environmentally sustainable, actually contributing to our natural resources.

All while being sensual, female-empowered, and high-value. (That's O, not me, although I'd like to think the same descriptions apply.)

These presentations almost always take place around conference tables.

Sigh.

Seated around O's table right now is Anterdec's investment team, along with O's directors and senior managers. Their meeting will last all day. According to the agenda, I am here to walk them through the concept for O NOLA. But I also have a short pitch of my own to make. A way for O to bring pleasure to women who deserve more of it. gO Spa.

"Good morning. I'm Chloe Browne, design director for O. This is Carrie, our junior designer. She'll be helping me today. Carrie, could you start by lowering the shades a bit? It's very bright in here, and I want to be sure everyone sees our vision clearly."

I also want to be sure no one sees *me* too clearly.

Have I told you my theory of successful design presentations?

First rule: be absolutely confident in the work you are showing. The design is the star.

In keeping with this idea, I am wearing a sleeveless black linen shirtdress. Silver hoop earrings, silver bracelets. My hair is tied back. Simple and neutral, nothing to distract from the work.

Second rule: be absolutely confident in yourself.

So I am wearing my power underwear. Does that make you think of Wonder Woman? Supergirl maybe? Their superpowers are different.

What I have under my dress now gives me the delicious power of knowing a secret. No one else in this room would guess that I am wearing a black mesh corset, structured with boning that holds me tight and pushes my breasts against my dress. They can't see the tiny matching thong, or feel how it runs between my legs and up. Only I know.

Joe used to know, too. Which made it so much hotter.

No no no! I can't think about that!

I look around the table. Some familiar faces, some new.

Andrew McCormick is here, and oh *my*. He's the new CEO of Anterdec, and O has been one of his special projects since the beginning. I wouldn't mind being *his* special project, but . . .

Amanda Warrick. She just joined Anterdec as assistant marketing director. She was here once before, unofficially, shopping us for a bachelorette party for her friend. I gave her group their tour. I've heard rumors that she is Andrew's girlfriend, but if so, they're keeping it very quiet.

Wait. Amanda . . . here before . . . shopping us . . . that mystery shop report . . .

Alarm bells begin dinging.

"Hey, Chloe," she says with a wink. I smile back, projecting serenity.

To the right of Amanda is a seriously handsome man. Serious, and handsome. He looks the tiniest bit familiar? A bit older than me? I meet his eye and smile.

In a purely professional way, of course.

He looks down at his phone, frowning slightly.

Hmm. Usually when I smile at a guy, he smiles back. But usually my eyes are not swollen to the size of hard-boiled eggs.

Sigh.

I turn to my presentation. Everything was pinned up before I left the office yesterday. One long wall of this room is covered in white linen, just for this purpose. All the fabrics we've selected for O NOLA, the samples of wood finishes and paint colors, squares of carpet, and photos of furniture options are displayed in groups.

And I immediately see that two of the fabric samples have been pinned in the wrong groups. I step over to the wall and re-pin them, reaching up high over my head.

Glad I caught that before I started presenting.

A side table holds materials too big or heavy to pin up, like stone and marble samples, ceramic tile, a faucet, a sconce. There is a stack of folders for everyone, with floor and furniture plans and of course all the estimates, budget sheets, and timelines.

Carrie distributes the folders, and they automatically open them and begin flipping through. All except The Frowner. He's looking at my chest.

So I look at my chest.

Which, of course, makes everyone watching me look at my chest.

My secret power isn't secret anymore . . . two buttons of my shirtdress have come open.

Black mesh corset on full display, one pink nipple fully visible.

I pull my dress together. I wish I could pull myself together. My face is bright red, and red is not in the O corporate color palette.

"This is not the presentation I had in mind," I blurt out. "Normally, when I set out to give clients something they've never seen before, it's not quite like this."

Amanda starts to giggle, so infectiously that I have to join her. Everyone else follows, and the formality in the room evaporates. Suddenly they're all on my side, except for The Frowner.

Is the guy made of stone?

"Did you get that corset here?" asks a blonde woman. Diane. Diane . . . something. She's in accounting. Severe face, hair pulled back in a tight bun, smile twitching her nose.

Amanda asks, through laughter, "Does it come in large?"

Of course I did. Of course it does.

One hour later I have finished giving my virtual tour of the new O. I have passed around fabric samples so that everyone could feel for themselves just how luxuriant a fire-retardant material can be. I have given a very short course in sustainable woods, and explained that the ash for O's custom cabinetry is sourced only from accredited plantations. And, of course, I have justified every dollar to be spent.

Everyone seemed to love it. Except The Frowner, who now clears his throat.

"Chloe, I'm Nick Grafton. I handle branding for Anterdec properties. It's critically important for a new brand like O to carry the same recognizable image throughout all locations. Can you tell us a bit more about how your design will do this while at the same time bringing in the unique atmosphere of New Orleans?"

Even seated, I can tell he's a tall man. All the time I spend with seven-foot-tall Henry has skewed my perspective a bit, but Nick must be over six feet. His hair is thick and a little on the long side for a corporate guy, light brown with a hint of silver. I admit it: I have a total weakness for long hair. Not man buns, but a little over the collar . . . something to grab and maybe pull at intimate times . . .

Ice blue eyes.

But what really gets my attention is his dark navy blue suit. Crisp shirt. Cotton madras plaid tie. When you spend every work day surrounded by mostly naked men, a fully-dressed guy gets your attention.

Sexy. Makes you wonder what's underneath.

Not that I'm objectifying him. Ahem.

Did he say his last name is *Grafton*? My turn to look closely at him. My first boyfriend—we're talking age fifteen here—was Charlie Grafton. Not an unusual last name, though, right?

His question is easy, really. I answer, he thanks me, no one else has a question.

I signal Carrie to lower the room lights. Showtime.

"O is never ordinary," I begin. "We've created another O for you, and I think it's our most exciting space yet." The faces around the table are mildly surprised, not expecting anything else from me.

I click a button to lower the screen and another to start the slideshow.

"This is our first gO Spa." I flash to a picture of a full-size RV. "This vehicle could be the beginning of a fleet. In every city where O has a presence, the gO Spa can go beyond the physical location. The gO Spa can be booked for private parties and weddings. It can travel to concert venues and theaters for services to big-name performers."

The next slide is an interior view of the gO Spa. Three small showers. A bank of four hair washing and styling stations. Small closets filled with curated professional clothing.

"But it has another important purpose. The gO Spa is how O will give back to the communities that have welcomed us and made our success possible. A way to demonstrate our commitment to the idea that peace and pleasure are vital to everyone."

Nick Grafton is giving me his full attention. I like it. I could get used to it.

"In inner cities, classes in self-care and stress management can be offered to high school seniors, or new mothers. Mini spa services could be provided for a reduced fee, or even on a complimentary basis in areas of need."

I've been keeping one eye on Andrew McCormick, but I can't read his face.

"And we have already implemented a pilot project in Cambridge with homeless teens. I have personally gone on weekly ventures for the past five months. The PR coverage has been extraordinary." I nod at the report I've handed each of them. "Metrics are all laid out in there."

Silence around the table. Although I imagine I hear gears shifting in fourteen brains.

"Metrics aside," I add, "This outreach project changes lives. I've seen it." My voice grows passionate. "The women and girls who show up at gO have dreams and aspirations of a better life. They know it's out there, but they have no idea how to get to it. O can show them. It's O's mission to empower women. I take that mission very, very seriously."

I don't mention meeting Li on my first gO Spa homeless trip. I don't mention how she cried in my arms after her shower, hair cut, facial and mani-pedi. I don't mention how on my second trip she told me she was pregnant, and how our on-site social worker helped her get medical care and government assistance.

I definitely don't mention how she asked me to adopt her baby. None of those details matter in a conference room.

This is all about money. Not mercy.

But money allows for more merciful acts.

Reaching down, I pull out a soft grey t-shirt with orange letters that read "you gO girl."

"Every visitor to gO Spa receives one of these."

A bald man at the end of the table clears his throat. "This is a big investment," he begins, but Amanda jumps in.

"The PR from this would be worth a fortune," she says excitedly. "It would pay for itself."

Already has, I think to myself.

And gO Spa has already helped one special young girl find a way out of trouble.

Already helped a new baby find a secure life.

And helped my greatest dream come true.

Nick nods slowly, brow knit in concentration. Those arctic eyes meet mine and he asks, "How does this mobile RV spa fit in with brand expansion? Seems risky. Doing well by doing good is a great concept, but I want to know how this ties in with deeper corporate identity issues."

And suddenly, Nick Grafton just flipped every switch inside me.

He's a handsome guy. I wonder if he ever smiles.

CHAPTER FIVE

Nick

I T TAKES EVERYTHING in me not to smile at her.

Everything.

She's a pro. Sophisticated and smooth, gracious and composed, well-versed and well-informed. Chloe Browne moves with a confidence that gives the air in this stuffy conference room an erotic charge. Her dark hair, so smooth it must be soft. A body that doesn't quit. Those brown eyes—tilted slightly, yet paradoxically round. Alert and intelligent, they take in the room.

I'm watching her. It's my job to watch her.

And she's watching me.

Days like this make me love my job.

Her mouth stretches with a delighted precision, as if she were waiting for someone to ask my question. Electricity shoots through me. She's four steps ahead of the rest of us, a chess player who thinks in dimensions, not boards.

One corner of my mouth rebels and rises.

"A great question, Nick." Her lips part slightly. The tip of her tongue slowly touches the edge of her top teeth. Then she gives me a sultry half-grin and says, "Integrating new positions into our body has been so exciting."

I did not imagine that.

Chloe's flushes. "I mean, integrating new *locations* into our body *of work* has been exciting." She clears her throat, squares her shoulders, and continues. "New Orleans is the prototype. O's brand ties in to Anterdec's brand as a luxury option for insiders. People in the know."

"Your maiden voyage." Not smiling is impossible.

Her lip curls up, a mirror image of my own. "This is virgin territory, yes."

Andrew McCormick's eyebrow shoots up as Amanda Warrick's face goes deceptively blank.

"Love the innuendo. Fits nicely with the sensual branding that O cultivates," Andrew says, his words snapping like the sound of buttons on a tailored woman's shirt popping off, as I tear it open in the throes of passion.

Or something like that.

"The Big Easy." Chloe lets that hang in the air, her eyes opening just slightly, then narrowing.

We're playing a game. I don't know the rules, but I sure do like handling the pieces.

"How easy?"

Andrew happens to be drinking from his coffee cup as Amanda asks *that* question, his throat spasming with the kind of hacking that provokes a sympathetic wince from the rest of us.

He glares in response.

At *me*.

There is a moment when you look at a woman for the first time. It's an up or down moment. Thumbs up: yes, I'll sleep with her. Thumbs down: she never enters my consciousness again sexually.

Chloe gets considerably more than a thumb's-worth of *up* from me.

I shift uncomfortably in my chair and try to wrest control back from the strange tension that has infused the room.

This is a business meeting. Branding. My specialty is branding, and on paper, Chloe's spa line has some serious weaknesses. Significant investment in an unproven market means that high risk needs to pay off.

You can't put that kind of trust in just anyone.

"Very easy," Chloe replies, reaching for a clicker and pulling up a PowerPoint spreadsheet. "Take a look at O Boston. Here's the initial investment. Here's the profit and loss statement."

"Seventy-three percent growth in Year Two?" Andrew lets out a low whistle. My shoulders relax. I had no idea they were tight.

My pants are tighter.

Why am I invested in whether the CEO of Anterdec buys into the O Spa expansion? Until three minutes ago, this was just another pitch.

"Hold on," Amanda interrupts. "That line for marketing and advertising. That figure is impossibly small. Did you forget a digit?"

Andrew gives Amanda a satisfied smirk. "A typo would explain that crazy profitability." He leans back and reaches for his phone.

When Andrew McCormick reaches for his phone in a meeting, it's over.

"No."

Chloe's single word rings out like a gunshot.

Andrew's hand freezes.

"That is not a mistake. Word of mouth is our primary form of advertisement."

Andrew makes a grunt I know too well. It's the sound I make when one of my college-age kids asks to borrow the car for a week. In Mexico.

"Isn't that a little too 1990s?"

"Every customer who walks through our doors converts."

"One hundred percent?" Andrew's eyes telescope. "You're certain?"

Click. A new graph appears.

"And each of those customers brings in an average of 3.8 new clients?" Amanda says, reading the slide.

"And that's without paid advertising?" Andrew says skeptically.

Chloe remains unflappable as they read and analyze, talking

about O as if she weren't the expert. "Yes. In fact, our business model is counter-intuitive. The more we advertise, the less we sell."

I frown. "That's impossible."

"No, Nick," she says, her voice like velvet and chocolate. "That's O."

"You're saying there's some disconnect between paid ads and foot traffic?" Amanda asks.

"It's lifestyle," I murmur. "The advertising taints the allure. The appeal is in the secrecy. In being told by someone in the know. Women want to be part of the exclusivity, and it's not special if everyone knows about it."

Chloe studies me.

"Like an affair?" Andrew asks. Amanda glares at him.

Chloe pales. It's the first hint of insecurity in her, and it intrigues me. This is a complicated woman.

She recovers quickly. "No. This is nothing like an affair. An affair is a secret because of shame. O is a secret because of *pride*." She squares her shoulders and blinks exactly once, mouth slack and flat, devoid of emotion.

Andrew's voice goes tight. "This is also nothing like any profit and loss statement I've ever read. It's either brilliant or a giant waste of money."

"Brilliant." The word's out of my mouth before I even decide to say it. Our business meeting has lost all pretense of being a corporate affair. Chloe's chest rises and falls rapidly, yet her breath makes no sound.

"You're telling me that Anterdec should make a significant investment in a subsector of the spa industry by trying an unproven and sweeping lifestyle niche—the fourth space—based on a blip in a spreadsheet and promises that word-of-mouth marketing is superior to data analytics we can track on paid ads?" Andrew makes a dismissive noise in the back of his throat.

"No," Chloe says, before I can blurt out the opposite. "We have data analytics as well."

Click.

"Does that column actually say 'sex toys'?" Andrew asks, giving Amanda an arched eyebrow. "You didn't tell me that they—"

"The average client owns 3.2 devices."

"Only 3.2?" Amanda mumbles.

Did Andrew just kick her under the table?

I don't care who is screwing whom at the company, but *knowing* who is screwing whom is strategically important. Catalogue *that.*

"Before they begin patronizing O, that was the figure. After two months of membership, that average increases to 7.9," Chloe explains.

Amanda interrupts her. "Do we sell batteries and chargers on-site at the O spas? If not, we need to."

Andrew raises an eyebrow and tents his hands, index fingers pressed against his lips. "Good point."

What's next? An O Spa porn channel? I almost open my mouth, but stop.

Because they might take me seriously.

"I will add batteries and chargers to our inventory. Great suggestion. All devices purchased on-site," Chloe says to Amanda. "All via careful customer relations management that allows staff to learn their preferences and anticipate their . . ."

"Kinks?" I ask helpfully.

"*Preferences* is the term I would use," Chloe says, her voice smooth as silk. "We optimize our device sales. Private label, all made in the USA, no BPA—"

It occurs to me that this is the first professional meeting I've ever attended where the casual discussion of sex toys as a profit-making venture has been a primary topic. Staying cool is key. The CEO acts like we're discussing cars or magazines or lamps.

I wonder what Chloe's *preferences* are.

All 7.9 of them.

Then again, she's hardly average. Bet her number is higher.

That mesh corset, after all.

Down, boy.

I raise my hand to a spot above my ear and run a tense hand through my hair. Across the table from me, Andrew McCormick does the same. With great concentration, I return my attention to the screen, where it should be, and not on Chloe Browne's cleavage.

Where it wants to be.

Through the next ten slides, Chloe shows us exactly how brilliant she is, while I struggle to grasp the landscape of the meeting. She walked in here with a fringe idea and a slim chance of convincing Andrew McCormick to invest on the scale she wants.

And now they're talking New Orleans, San Francisco, and—

"Rio would be a great target for 2018," Chloe says, sitting down across from Andrew, tapping the end of a pen against the front of her teeth. "What about Tokyo for 2020?"

"The Olympics!" Andrew and Amanda say at the same time, then laugh.

"We're getting ahead of ourselves," I declare.

"You're not convinced I'm worth taking a chance?" Chloe asks, her nose twitching with amusement, that curled lip driving me mad.

"You've convinced me," Andrew says, standing and finally looking at his phone. "Nick, make it happen."

"What?"

"Give Chloe whatever she needs."

"Whatever she needs?" I choke out in surprise. Quickly, I recover, face showing no emotion, even if my pulse and half the blood in my body has migrated below my belt and I can't stop wondering what's under that corset. One peek of a nipple is like being given a single sip of Hennessy cognac.

It's great, but you want the whole thing in your mouth eventually.

God help me, her eyes meet mine and her smile widens.

Best. Job. Ever.

"Right. Chloe, why don't you go back to your office for an

hour or so, while Nick and Amanda and I hash out some details in the conference room. We'll call you," Andrew says, standing and reaching for her hand. The only hint of emotion in Chloe's face comes from the micro-movements in her eyes. She is pleased.

I want to please her. And not just with Anterdec's money.

In this business setting, she *should* be pleased. Sharp and perceptive, she's turned the meeting around. A green light from Andrew McCormick isn't easy to obtain, and she marched right in here in secret dominatrix lingerie and she did it. I am intrigued and a little spellbound.

Maybe I'm just lightheaded from the lack of blood flow to the brain.

She unmoors me, turning back decades, making me feel like an awkward, uncoordinated teen.

But with a man's appreciation for all that goes into making her *her.*

"Nick?" Andrew's clipped tone makes me realize I'm in my own head. Chloe's standing before me, her nose twitching with amusement, the rest of her face revealing nothing.

"Great presentation," I say, shaking her hand. My eyes float down to her rack.

"It's an eyeful, isn't it?" she jokes.

"Certainly impressive," I confirm. "The *graphs.*" I need to dial this down. Andrew's giving me looks that could peel paint. "You give great data."

"I aim to be Good, Giving, and Game."

"Isn't that what Dan Savage says about sex?"

"It applies to business, too."

"A universal set of tools."

She shrugs. "Everyone can have the same tools, Nick. Tool acquisition? Anyone can do that. The real skill is in implementation."

With that, Chloe Browne leaves me speechless, hard as a rock, and the object of my boss's ire.

One hell of a hat trick.

"Coffee?" Andrew's admin, Gina, appears with a smartphone in hand, an app for a local coffee shop open.

Grateful for the save, I give her my order and will myself to think about subjects that deflate. She takes Amanda and Andrew's requests and disappears with quick, nervous steps.

"Didn't know Anterdec added a dating service to our portfolio. Cut it out, Nick," Andrew says with a warning tone as he settles back into his chair.

Amanda snorts.

Catalogue *that*, too.

I say nothing. Eyebrows up, eye contact with my boss, but no words. I don't challenge.

But I don't back down.

"Oh, good Lord," Amanda finally says with a sigh, reaching for Andrew's hand. "*We're* together. Nick can flirt."

Before I can reply, Andrew leads her into the room we're using here at O. I follow, loving the hypocrite he's become in the course of three sentences. We settle around the table, Amanda perched on the edge, Andrew in his chair, me in the chair with the view behind him, the Financial District spread out for us, the ocean stretching behind him as if it were there for his pleasure alone.

It's good to be the king.

"She's good, isn't she?" Andrew says.

And giving and game, apparently.

I give Amanda a look. She shrugs.

"Chloe?" I ask.

"Right. Smart, intuitive, an eye for design, and a great presenter. Gets three layers deeper than anyone in the room ever considered. She's strategic and composed. Perfect face of O."

Her O face sure does come to mind.

Damn it.

"You want to fund her?"

"The RV spa thing seems farfetched, but figures don't lie."

Chloe's figure, bent over the edge of a bed, that sweet ass—

"Nick?" Andrew snaps his fingers. I shake myself like a wet dog.

"Right. How much should I put in her?"

Andrew's jaw grinds, but before he can answer my garbled question, we're interrupted.

Thank God.

"Twelve inches!" Gina exclaims from the doorway.

Timing really is everything.

"What?" Andrew sputters.

She's holding a tray with three enormous white coffee cups in it.

"Twelve inches! The size of these coffees from downstairs. They're so big!" As she hands out the coffee, Amanda stifles a giggle. Sunlight bounces off her ring. A wave of memory pours through me, lightning fast, like a retracting cable that snaps hard at the end, leaving marks.

Simone. Our engagement. Working nights through undergrad to pay for her little diamond chip of a ring . . .

The same ring she mailed back to me from France, along with her signed divorce papers.

"Jesus, Nick, what is wrong?" Andrew's gone from anger to a furious concern, the irritated worry radiating off of him with a masculine sense that triggers my testosterone, sending me into high alert. We're playing male hormone ping-pong, only without the paddles.

Paddles.

Chloe and a paddle. . . .

"You're not like this. You're the focus man."

"The what?"

"That's what people call you behind your back," Amanda explains cheerfully, her big eyes wide and friendly. They're the color of mink, with lashes so long the bottom layer sticks to the top, making her reach up with a finger and rub.

"People talk about me behind my back? What do they talk about?"

"Your nickname—pun intended—is Focus Man. Now live up to it," Andrew says sourly.

Damn. I've only been with Anterdec for a year, and so far, so good. After they acquired my firm, my prospects weren't exactly certain. With three kids in college, this needs to last. Just long enough to have an empty nest, and then . . .

And then no one depends on me. I'm free. Free to pursue whatever I want for the first time in my life.

A flash of mesh corset fills my free mind.

"Focus Man?" I laugh. "I can think of worse names to call me."

We all take a sip of our gigantic coffees and sit in silence for a moment. Andrew types on his computer, drinking more, then looks at me.

"Done. Gina can take care of specifics, but I green-lighted another gO Spa RV and two more locations for new, full-service spas."

"Do I get to help hire the staff?" Amanda asks Andrew with a wink.

"You," he says archly, his voice going low and dark, "are staying at HQ with me."

She gives him a wicked smile.

I miss having a woman smile at me like that.

I wonder if Chloe's free for dinner.

If I'm Focus Man, I can be focused in more ways than one.

CHAPTER SIX

Chloe

CARRIE IS RIGHT behind me as we head for our post-mortem in my office. That presentation went well. Better than well. My skin buzzes with triumph.

And maybe—just maybe—from being once-overed by a man with eyes the color of the sky.

"Oh my God, who died?" she gasps, pulling me out of my mini-fantasy.

There are roses in my office.

A lot of white roses. Six or eight dozen, by my guess.

Presentations like the one I just completed fill me with a weird mix of warrior-induced adrenaline and terror-induced cortisol. I'm primed for battle. This pathetic attempt to make up for what I saw that night—for what Joe did to me a month ago—has the opposite effect of what he intended.

The asshole just won't let it go.

Won't let *me* go.

Fury sears me from the inside out.

"Carrie, here, take some for your desk," I say, grabbing the biggest vase and thrusting it at her. "Actually, take some for everyone. Take them all. They make my eyes water." That's a lie. My eyes aren't blurring from rose fever. My vision is distorted by rage.

"Seriously, Chloe? Thanks!" It takes her three trips, but she gets them all out.

On her third go-around, she frowns. "Who are these from?"

"An old colleague."

"He must really like you."

"He used to," I say faintly, my voice tinny, like I'm whispering through a pipe.

A sewer pipe.

Does Joe really think that eight dozen roses from Montelcini Flowers will magically erase the memory of *his* long stem in someone else's mouth?

"What happened?"

What happened? *What happened?* The words spin through my mind, untethered and dangerous, like a pain-covered boomerang. None of this is Carrie's fault, and I can't get the image of Nick Grafton out of my head.

Any more than I can stop seeing the back of Joe's blonde bunny's head.

"Chloe?"

I steel myself and give her a neutral look. "Nothing. His tastes didn't align with mine. He decided to go for a younger look."

"That blows."

Oh, if only you knew.

And with that, she's gone. Carrie can take a hint.

I take out the mystery shop report and my Costco-sized bottle of aspirin, sit down at my desk, and do not move for the next hour.

Every ten minutes or so, the receptionist looks in and gives me an update. Joe has called six times. She wants to know when I am going to take his call.

NeverEver. Taylor Swift could not have said it better.

Deep in the details of an eviscerating—but accurate—mystery shop analysis, I don't notice the man in the doorway until Carrie says, in a stage voice, "Her office is right here."

"Chloe, that was a great presentation." It's The Frowner. Nick Grafton. Damn, I should have googled him but I forgot. "I'd like to talk more about your ideas for carrying the O brand through all levels of design. Things like that grey O border on the china—the client almost doesn't even notice, but it's always in view. Very smart. Would you have your admin call my assistant and set up a meeting for next week?"

"Of course. Thank you." I'm flustered, surprised by his sudden appearance, and a little shaken. One sandal is off, and I'm frantically feeling around for it with my foot so I can stand up properly. And my lipstick is completely worn off . . . but that reminds me: "I have some thoughts about a line of private-label O cosmetics. I'd love your opinion."

"Interesting. Next week then." He hesitates. "A bit of a personal question—did you by any chance grow up around here?"

"Across the river, in Cambridge." I look at him curiously.

"I have a younger brother, Charlie, and you look just like one of his friends. Any chance . . . ?"

"Oh my god, Charlie Grafton!" I laugh. "I thought I recognized your last name. How is Charlie? We have totally lost touch."

"Charlie's, well, . . ." he starts, when my desk phone buzzes. I look down at it, but before I can pick up the receiver, the intercom starts, "Code Seven, Code Seven."

We both stare at the phone, perplexed.

This is the call for security. Something is *wrong* at the front desk.

A business like O requires first-rate security 24/7. So much can go wrong, internally or externally, online or physically.

Privacy is paramount at O. Our cybersecurity is the tightest available. The last thing O needs is public exposure of our clients' names.

Or their preferences.

We're also on alert at all times for crazies.

Sometimes it seems like we're a magnet for crazies. Conservative protestors pop up once in a while and need to be convinced that we really aren't the place for protests. Generally, sending the g-stringed, all-male revue out to the protestors with boxes of donuts does the trick, but security is always there for backup.

And every once in a while, an O client confuses a staff member's professional attention to physical pampering with True Love. Those situations can be tricky. Henry gets at least one proposition a week, and some of them are quite insistent.

What we offer our club members is relaxation and serenity. Our mission you might say, is inner peace. Our security team is invisible, dressed just like the spa staff, but when Code Seven is announced, they react very differently.

Nick Grafton is frozen in my doorway as men and women wearing grey silk kimono jackets and very little else race by.

I can hear shouting now, and some banging. Just like everyone else who works here, I have attended training sessions for this exact set of circumstances. I have the certificate to prove it.

And damned if I can remember one single thing that I am supposed to be doing.

Standing lopsided at my desk with one heeled sandal on and one off, staring like a deer in the headlights, is probably not what I was taught, though.

The shouting is getting louder, and dear god, is that *my* name I hear? Like some horror movie where the demon is closing in on the innocent victim? Nick Grafton and I look at each other.

Rushing toward the source of danger is probably wrong also? I hobble to the door as fast as possible. Three feet away, I trip, pitching forward. Nick catches me by reflex, one hand under my arm and one squarely on my breast as he inserts himself ahead of me, protectively.

I should be totally embarrassed. He's a business associate and a complete stranger, but damn, that feels good. I need to fall more often. I need to practice klutziness. I never realized before what an important skill it is.

At that exact moment, my ex-boyfriend Joe heaves into view, dragging three security guards and screaming, "Chloe! Goddammit, let go of me! *Chloe!*" Joe's tie is loose and his shirt is pulled out. His face is bright red and dripping sweat.

As Aaron Sorkin would say, *this is not happening.*

O's corporate office is not huge. We all know each other, and everyone here knows Joe, at least by sight. The looks of fear on staff members' faces shift to curiosity, and maybe a little embarrassment. But like a traffic accident, they can't look away. They are Relationship Rubberneckers, and I'm a two-car pile-up on the Mass Pike. WBZ should cover this on the threes.

No one moves.

Just then, Joe looks up and sees me in Nick's arms. Or hands. Or both.

He wrenches himself free from the security guards and lunges at Nick, who lets go of me.

"STOP!" I scream.

"She's MINE!" Joe roars, a wave of hot breath expelling from him. Drunk, alcohol-soaked breath.

Nick makes two quick moves, so powerful and authoritative that he seems choreographed. Instinct makes me step back. I'm being protected, even if I didn't ask for Nick's help. His fluid grace takes Joe's clumsy charge and turns his weight against him, overpowering my ex-boyfriend. I choke back a laugh driven by pure shock.

In seconds, Nick's forearm is around Joe's throat and one of Joe's arms is pinned behind his back.

That was unexpected.

And if I weren't mortified beyond belief, I'd have to admit it was kind of hot, too.

The security guards catch up. Nick says something to them that I can't hear, and one of them handcuffs Joe. I can smell alcohol, and French cologne.

"Chloe, I have to talk to you, it's all a mistake, I can explain, I'm so sorry, you know I love you, no one else matters to me, *please.*" Joe's talking fast and low.

Henry comes sprinting in, dressed in a g-string, cowboy boots and a big belt buckle that says *Everything's Bigger in Texas*. "Chloe, what the hell . . . ? *Joe?*"

I'm undone. Without thinking, I take three unbalanced steps toward Henry and throw my arms around his mostly naked torso.

Nick looks at us for a long moment, then walks out behind the guards and Joe, who is still talking.

"Get your hands off of me! Don't you know who I am? Chloe, call them off. Damn it, call them off! Please? C'mon, Chloe, you know I—"

Then—wait? Yep. The unmistakable sound of vomiting.

Some of those roses will need to go to the cleaning crew.

This is not my beautiful life.

♥ ♥ ♥

HENRY DRIVES ME home in his 1996 Audi. A fitting end to a day of uncertainty, discomfort, and some danger. Henry grew up in California, where he learned to drive. He is courteous. He observes the posted speed limit. He yields to the right-of-way.

In Boston traffic, this kind of thing will get you killed. No one expects it and no one knows how to react. Lacking a better idea, they usually respond with their middle fingers.

Surprisingly, we arrive safely at my condo. Climbing out of his car, I pause.

"So . . . you don't mind if Jemma hangs out here tonight? I need some girl time. You come, too."

"I'm going to pretend you didn't say that, Chloe. Anyway, I'm working tonight, so it's perfect. If I get out early, I can do research on my thesis until Jem gets home."

"Thank you, Henry. For everything."

He winks at me. "You're our girl."

I tear up, and wave. He signals, looks over his shoulder, and eases out into the street. Miraculously, no one hits him.

Godspeed.

Inside, a shower. Hot water and ginger-scented soap to wash

everything off my skin. As if Joe never touched me. A clean slate.

By the time Jemma walks in the door, I have assembled the following out of the refrigerator: a container of olives (cocktail mix, the kind with tiny onions and dried cranberries), a small block of Parmesan cheese, a dish of honey, a Granny Smith apple, and three slices of smoked ham. Also some crackers of questionable freshness.

She looks it over.

"Maybe if we boiled a pound of pasta and mixed it all together, we could make a dinner out of this?" She sounds doubtful.

"I have an entire case of Prisoner, Jem," I offer. The Prisoner is our favorite Napa red. Food just became irrelevant. Dinner will be served in a glass tonight. Possibly tomorrow night as well.

She settles on a counter stool as I pour.

"Okay. What's been going on?"

"In the last twelve hours?" I smile wearily. "This morning I gave a kickass presentation to senior management, during which I exposed myself in a black corset. At least they know I don't pierce my nipples. Andrew McCormick green lighted my gO Spa project. I also met an incredible man, who turns out to be the brother of my high school boyfriend. I went back to my office after the presentation and there were dozens of white roses from Joe. I gave them away. He called about sixty times, but I didn't answer, so he showed up at O. Drunk. And tried to fight with Nick, who is the incredible man I met. Then he puked all over the hallway in shades that do not match the color palette."

Jemma blinks. "That's it?"

"And I have a meeting with Nick next week."

"Want to hear about *my* last twenty-four hours?" Jem asks.

I nod.

"Yesterday I had a meeting with my editor, then I went home. Henry made salmon for dinner, after which I exposed myself in a lace bra. This morning I walked three miles. I wrote half of an article on nutrition for pregnant women in displaced populations. I took a nap. Henry called four times and I answered four times.

Then I showed up here. Might get a little bit drunk."

I look at her lovely, serene face.

"I would trade with you in a heartbeat," I say sincerely.

"So Joe Blow earned his nickname," she muses. "I am so sorry, Chloe. That must have been awful."

I know she means the confrontation at work today, but my mind goes back a month.

"Don't call him that. It *was* awful, Jem. I will never get that picture out of my mind." I press my hands to my eyes. "And Blowjob Barbie was wearing a bra printed with Red Sox logos! How *could* he?"

Jemma shudders.

"The only thing worse would have been a Yankees logo."

I throw an olive at her. She catches it neatly in her palm and eats it.

"He tried to fight with some guy at your office?"

"Yes! In front of the whole staff! I tripped and fell, and Nick caught me and somehow he had one hand on my boob, and Joe saw that and went crazy—well, he already was crazy—and took a swing at him. And Nick just went like this," I stand up and do my best to demonstrate how he overpowered Joe, "and that was it. Security took over."

She is just staring at me. I sit down again.

"Oh, and then Joe threw up all over my lovely New Zealand wool carpet. I chose that carpet when we remodeled the building."

She starts to giggle. I see her point and join in, until a horrible thought stops me cold, and my eyes fill up with tears.

"Jemma," I whisper, "What if the adoption people find out about this?"

"Do you think they could?"

"O keeps pretty tight control over information. All the employees know that any leak would cost them their job. But still . . . there's always a chance . . . and it would look so bad. It was a violent outburst. The timing could not be worse."

"Actually, it could. Suppose you hadn't found out he had this in him? Suppose he acted this way around the baby? You know Henry and I were never big fans of Joe's, but I would not have predicted any of this. Did you see it coming?"

I think for a minute. "Not really, no. Maybe I should have. Looking back, I guess a lot of things didn't really add up. But he loved me so much!" I frown. "I mean, I think he really loved me . . . right? He said he did, all the time."

Jemma looks at me sadly.

"He didn't love me, did he?" I ask, but I don't really expect an answer.

"He wasn't really getting a divorce for three years," she says. It clearly pains her. "So . . ."

I make an animal noise in the back of my throat that can only be cured by wine.

"Chloe." Jem takes a deep breath. "Chloe, you are our best friend. You are the best person. You're lovely and kind and smart and funny. You work so hard, and you love so hard. You're true blue. And you deserve so, so much better than Joe Blow. You deserve a guy who will love you every day. *Only* you. A guy who will show you how much he loves you, and not just say the words."

"I look at what you and Henry have, and that's how I know it's possible. It exists."

Jemma sighs. It's the sound a friend makes when she wants to say something she shouldn't, but has to anyway. "Chloe, you know how people ask you sometimes why you decided to adopt?"

"Yes."

"And how you choose not to give a reason?"

"Yes." Where's she going with this?

"I think part of the reason is that you knew you didn't have a future with Joe, so you decided to make your own future."

Ouch.

"Please don't be mad." Her fingers land on my forearm, pressing compassion into me.

"Not mad," I choke out, trying not to cry. "Just blindsided a little. You're right." I look at her with a starkness I wish I could share with a life partner. "Joe was never, ever going to give me what I want." I squeeze her hand.

We share a sad smile.

"Now tell me about this incredible man you met."

"Not much to tell, really." I let out a cleansing breath. "Pretty high up at Anterdec. He's handsome. I think he liked me—he might have been flirting—but I'm not sure."

"Well, he liked you enough to grab your boob," she smiles.

"That was an accident!"

"Ah. He can put another guy in a choke hold with one James Bond move, but he is so klutzy, he can't hold you up without *feeling* you up?"

She raises one eyebrow.

I've always wanted to be able to do that.

"He's my high school boyfriend's older brother. There's something about him, Jem, I can't describe it. I want his arms around me. It's a funny feeling. Safe sexy."

"That *does* sound like my Henry," she says, almost to herself.

"I never felt safe with Joe. Why did I stay with him for so long? How could I not see this coming?"

She just looks at me, and I can see she is really fighting her desire to say *We told you so*.

She struggles. She loses.

"We told you so! About a hundred times! Look, Chloe, I'm not going to say Joe didn't love you at all. I'm sure he did, in a way. But it was just all about him! *His* convenience. *His* rules. *His* fun. And you bent over backwards for years to please him! What the hell was he doing in that conference room?" Her hands are in the air, flailing and gesticulating like she's conducting the Boston Pops with her pent-up emotions.

I stare into my glass.

"He was doing the same thing to me that he's been doing to

Marcy, his wife. Cheating."

I guess it really is that simple.

"All these years, he said he was on the verge of a divorce. God, Jemma. I have to rethink three years of my life," I gasp.

"Oh, honey." Jemma shifts from outrage to compassion.

"He wasn't ever going to get a divorce, was he?" I ask, although I know the answer.

"Of course not. Give up Marcy's money? Lose the country club membership? Never going to happen." I regret telling her those little details about Joe. I feel so stupid.

We sit in silence, sipping our wine.

"What about this new guy?" she asks. "Not married?"

"No idea, but he wasn't wearing a ring."

"Let's Google him—where's your computer?"

I pull it out and flip it open.

Nick Grafton, I type.

Page after page of entries come up:

Nick Grafton, Funeral Director.

Nick Grafton, Marathon Runner.

Nick Grafton, Hollywood Stunt Man.

"Not an unusual name, I guess. It would take hours to sort through this—days, even. But look, here's his picture."

"Wow." Jemma's impressed, her voice drops low. "Look for a wife, keep scrolling."

There are several group shots, obviously taken at public events, but nothing conclusive. Never the same woman twice.

And he's not smiling in a single photo.

I refill our glasses.

"The only thing that really matters now is the baby. Li is due in eight weeks." We're in the safety zone. Crossing thirty weeks, according to the doctor, means that even with a preterm birth, the baby should be fine.

"Think it might be time to buy a few baby things?" Jem asks gently. "Just some basics? A bassinet, maybe? Some clothes? Some little t-shirts or whatever babies wear?"

"It seems too much like tempting fate. What if something goes wrong? So much could still go wrong. Li is just a teenager. She's homeless. Who knows what that first trimester was like. She didn't get medical care until the fourth month. And she can still change her mind. I'm not going to have a peaceful moment until the final papers are signed. And it's going to be an open adoption. Now I have to worry about this fiasco with Joe becoming public knowledge."

"It'll be fine," she says.

"And last week I was supposed to meet her for an ultrasound. Went to the clinic. Waited for two hours. She no-showed, then texted a bunch of apologies that night." I frown into my drink. "I hope she's safe. I hope they're both safe."

"It won't go wrong," she reassures me. "In two months or so you are going to have a tiny new person here to take care of and love every day. Everything's going to change, forever. You won't even remember that you ever knew a guy named Joe Blow."

"Don't call him . . ." I start, but give up. The name fits.

Joe Blow.

CHAPTER SEVEN

Nick

MAMAN SAYS SHE *is coming for my fall concert.*

The text arrives like any other text, resting in my phone, and only now have I seen it. Something in my chest snaps, like a toothpick pressed too hard on the ends, breaking unevenly.

Leaving the possibility for splinters.

Great, I lie, texting back to my daughter Amelie. A dual major in music and computer science, Amelie managed to thrill both her parents by juggling the impossible. This is her senior year, and she has a solo concert. My ex-wife and the mother of my children, Simone, has missed every single other concert in this child's life.

The fact that Amelie has a chance for a spot at Juilliard and Eastman has piqued Simone's interest. Status is like a bat signal for her. To fly all the way from Paris and force herself to spend time in the U.S. is all about bragging rights.

She is coming without Rolf, a second text reads.

I nearly drop the phone.

Great, I text again, this time telling the truth.

He's such an ass, Amelie adds.

"He *is* such an ass," I grumble aloud, surprising myself with my own voice. With my youngest, Jean-Marc, off to NYU for his early start this summer for his freshman year, and twin daughters here in Boston at their respective colleges working on campus before their senior year, the kitchen is quiet.

Too quiet.

My index finger goes numb and I look down, finding purple fingertips and bulging forearm veins. I'm gripping the granite countertop edge so hard, I might snap it in two.

Daddy? Are you there? Are you okay? Don't make me resort to calling, Amelie types.

I chuckle. God forbid they use their phones for actual calls.

Fine. Just beat up a guy at work today. Typical day at the office.

I press Send and start to make a shot of espresso.

"One," I count aloud. "Two. Three. Four."

Ring!

Huh. I should beat people up more often.

"Daddy!" It's Amelie, breathless and intense. "You beat someone up? Was it over a woman?"

Kind of.

"No. Just a drunk jerk who came into a meeting and tried to harass a woman at a presentation."

"You're a hero!"

I haven't heard that tone of admiration in her voice since I scored tickets to a One Direction concert a few years ago, before she declared Harry Stiles "so yesterday."

"If you say so," I reply, laughing.

"Tell me everything. Elodie is going to be so jealous that I got the story first!"

Twins. Life with twins means that everything is a competition.

"Nothing special. Chloe's ex-boyfriend sent her flowers and was drunk when he insisted on seeing her, and—"

"Chloe? I love her name! What's she like?"

Hold on. This conversation just shifted from Daddy the Hero to Chloe in three seconds.

"She's fine. Smart. Sophisticated. One hell of a presenter."

"I don't mean that! I mean—is she your type?"

"Amelie!"

"What?"

"She's a work colleague."

"Oh." She sighs. "That means she's old and ugly."

"Hardly," I mutter, then wince. Oops.

"Oooo, you like her!"

"Honey, that's not how this works."

"Actually, it *is* how this works. You like someone. You say something. You kiss them. You spend time with them. And then Daddy, when a man and a woman lust after each other very much, he goes to the drugstore and buys condoms, and—"

"Cut it out, kiddo." I let the edge in my voice stay.

She goes silent. "Fine. Topic change. Maman left Rolf."

I stop breathing.

"What?"

"She's divorcing him. Says he's boring."

Where have I heard that before?

Beep.

"Hang on, Amelie. Someone's on the other line."

Click.

"I heard my dad is a hero!" Elodie crows into the phone.

"Two children speaking to me at the same time on an actual phone. Has the zombie apocalypse begun?"

She sighs. "I wish it would. Then I wouldn't need to finish this political cartooning paper that's due tomorrow."

"Political cartooning? That's an actual course?" Summer school offers strange choices.

"Yes. I thought it would be a blow-off, but the professor actually expects us to take it seriously and talk about imagery and know political history!"

Her outrage makes me laugh. "How dare he expect you to analyze? And learn! Oh, the humanity!"

"Daddy," she growls. "Who's Chloe?"

"How do you know about Chloe?"

"So she *is* your new crush!" Elodie squeals. "Now I owe Amelie five dollars."

"You two are betting on . . . me?"

"Just your sex life."

"Uh . . ."

"Blame Jean-Marc. He started it. Said as soon as he moved out you'd turn the condo into a shag pad."

"A what?"

"A sex den."

I am not having this conversation.

"I can't wait to tell him you're beating up your competitors for women at work!"

"That's me. Nick Grafton, cage fighter."

Beep.

"Hang on. Your sister's on the other line."

Click.

"Did you drop me for Elodie? Not fair. I had the scoop first. And Maman wants to stay with us."

Us means here, in my townhouse, which means spending days with my ex-wife who left me when the twins were five and Jean-Marc was barely three.

Because I was *boring*.

I would sympathize with Rolf if he hadn't been the person she left me *for*.

"Why does she want to stay here? She's never stayed with us before." Ever. Once a year, by legal agreement, she had the kids for three weeks in the summer. I always flew them there, spent two days in a hotel, and flew back, gutted, hoping they would adjust.

They always did.

Me, on the other hand . . .

"I don't know!" she chirps. "But it'll be nice to have both of my parents at an event for once."

And gutted again.

"Right," I say faintly, swallowing a suddenly dry mouth. "We'll figure it all out."

"I'm so happy to hear you're dating, Daddy!"

"I'm not dating!"

"If you say so . . . Love you! Gotta get on the T!"

Click.

I switch back to Elodie. Gone.

And then I look at my texts.

Three requests for money.

One from each kid.

I set my phone down, shake my head, and pick out tonight's date.

Pinot Noir, or a nice Flemish red sour ale?

Black Sails or *The Wire*?

Twenty minutes later, a sandwich and a beer in front of me, I pick my poison and settle in for a night of binge watching.

By the second sex scene in Black Sails, I'm twitching, unable to stop thinking about Chloe, the piles of roses outside her office, the horrified look on her face when that sonofabitch came barreling down the hallway, screaming her name.

How instinct kicked in.

And I kicked his ass.

"Not bad for an old man, as the kids would say," I mutter with a sigh, going into the kitchen for another beer. I grab my phone off the counter and flip through my contacts. I added Chloe in there on a lark, right after her presentation, a number I'd planned to give my admin to set up a next meeting.

It's not an Anterdec corporate number that Chloe gave me. Looks like her personal cell phone.

Huh.

Chloe

WHEN MY ALARM goes off at six a.m., I know it's time to get up. My meeting with Nick Grafton is today. I've been awake since four, when I woke to find Mink covering my face, fur tickling my nose.

Mink. My living, purring fur coat. My cat.

I tried so hard to hold on to sleep, blissful unconsciousness. General anesthesia.

My brain, however, wanted to watch a slideshow:

The mystery shop report. *Who highlighted all those pages?*

Me, at the market, shopping for treats for Joe.

Me, in the ladies' room, primping a treat for Joe.

Joe, getting treated. By someone else.

I have read that it's essentially impossible to think of nothing, but I tried. I visualized grey. The O shade.

Quite right. Impossible. I started running through the alphabet backwards.

Z Y X . . . W . . . not as easy as you would think, right?

. . . P O . . .

N . . . Nick Grafton in my office doorway, somehow familiar. Starched white shirt. The scent of Bay Rhum when he caught me. If *masculine* has a scent, it's Bay Rhum.

. . . M L K . . .

J . . . Joe, red-faced and drunk, Nick's arm around his neck. Pathetic. I wish I could un-see this.

. . . D C . . .

B . . . Baby. Baby coming soon. Life will change, forever. Am I ready? I think so. But is anyone ever ready? Maybe I'm *too* ready— what if Li changes her mind? Should I buy diapers, baby clothes, a crib? Would I be tempting fate? So far I just have an infant car seat. If this doesn't happen, I can just put it in the closet. *Way* far back in the closet where I can't see it.

Li is so young. Old enough to get pregnant but far too young to be a mother. In so many ways, she's really still a baby herself. She's been forced into a situation with no possible happy ending—at least not for her. Her tragedy will make my dream come true. Can I help make some of her dreams come true in return? She wants to be an esthetician, told me the day I met her on the gO Spa. Can I find a scholarship for her? Create one?

A . . . Anterdec. Meeting today with Nick Grafton. Okay. This is better. This I can handle. What to wear?

I am representing O. I visualize grey again. Dove grey suit of raw silk, seamed to fit my body perfectly, never too tight or too loose. High heels, but not too spiky. And most importantly, a necklace of glass Os, linked together with silver.

And for today's secret power, rose silk cheeky panties that lace up the back. Matching bustier. Grey thigh highs in fine mesh.

On the outside, chic and understated. Underneath, intimate pleasure.

I am O.

♥ ♥ ♥

NICK'S ADMIN SHOWS me into his office. At least, I guess that's where I am, but I'm not sure, because this room is all about the view. Who needs artwork when you have a wall of glass above Boston Harbor, bright blue water glittering in the sun? Sailboats are gliding along, and planes are taking off and landing from Logan Airport.

"How do you get anything done?" I ask, walking straight to the window. "I would just stare outside all day."

"I try to focus on what's right in front of me," he answers quietly. I turn around.

He's looking at me with a small smile. Behind him, on the wall, is a huge silver-leaf painting by Raphael Jaimes-Branger. It must be six feet high.

"Gorgeous!" I breathe.

Nick doesn't take his eyes off me. "Oh, yes."

Then he turns to the painting. "I've been collecting Raphael for years. I love the way he blends traditional and modern art into something of its own. And he works here in Boston."

"The silver-leaf catches the light," I add.

"Beauty all around me," Nick says, and gestures toward a small table. "Let's see what beautiful ideas you've brought for O's brand."

Opening my portfolio cases, I display packaging mock-ups for a limited line of O cosmetics. I describe a line of private-label scents for women, men, and the home—the First Space. I present sketches and samples of French cotton T shirts and embossed Italian leather tote bags, all bearing visually related and recognizable designs based on our simple and elegant O.

But best of all is the jewelry. The necklace I am wearing, the glass chain of Os, is the centerpiece.

"This is where we break through our wall, and take O out to the retail world. Each special piece of this high-end jewelry collection is designed to represent our brand subtly but clearly. Club members will want to wear the jewelry, and chic shoppers will want to belong to the club. Here's how a full-page print ad in *Vogue* might look."

I hand Nick an ad layout, featuring a photograph of my necklace on the curve of a woman's neck and shoulders, the glass reflecting light and shadow on beautiful matte skin. Our fingers brush against each other, the electricity palpable. He studies the ad, his eyes moving to my neck, then back to the ad again.

My design team has been working on this presentation nonstop for ten days, including nights and weekends.

"Chloe, this is much more than I expected. I'm going to see if I can pull Amanda Warrick in to take a look at all this. She's about to become Anterdec's assistant marketing director. Our departments work together closely. If she thinks this has merit, we'll take it to the finance team and see what we're looking at for start-up costs."

He gets up and goes out, leaving the slightest whiff of Bay Rhum behind him. I look around the office for the first time.

This small, round meeting table and four chairs, two upholstered chairs in front of his desk, your typical big mahogany partners' desk. All very nice, but other than the paintings on the walls, everything looks pretty standard-issue. A long, low cabinet behind his desk, covered with framed photographs.

I really, *really* want to get up and study those photos. From here, across the room, they all appear to be photos of teenagers.

Someday I'll have a teenager. Will we share shoes and secrets? Or will she stay out too late and not text me and not answer her phone and frighten me to death and . . . ?

Stop, Chloe, just stop.

Nick seems to have a boy and a girl. Or two girls? Twins? A number of mountaintop skiing group shots, action photos of lacrosse players. One of those professionally-posed beach portraits in black and white, all three kids in white polo shirts and khaki shorts.

If there's a wife in his life, she's not on display.

Please let there be no wife.

Nick comes back in, with Amanda, and we shake hands. That little bell goes off in my head again. The day I gave the O tour to Amanda and the older blonde woman who was with her, the one who was so *enthusiastic* about some of the entertainment . . .

Amanda's about to say something, her eyes warm and pleasant, but I speak first.

"How did your friend's bachelorette party turn out?" I ask. "Now I remember. You were at O a while ago, weren't you? I don't think you booked the party with us?"

Amanda's cheeks turn slightly pink. "It got a little out of hand," she laughs. "Too many people for O. We ended up at a piano bar in Back Bay."

Plausible. After all, why would Anterdec send a marketing exec to mystery shop their own property? And the report was from a firm called Consolidated Evalu-Shop. Hmm. But still, she asked some unusual questions. I make a note to have Carrie research the issue.

Thankfully, Amanda says nothing about Joe's outburst last time we met.

I run swiftly through today's presentation, truncating it. Amanda and Nick are quick studies. I'm relieved; there's nothing quite as fine as realizing you're in a room with people whose minds can pattern-match and analyze so that you can speak in shorthand.

Amanda picks up the jewelry ad and studies it. "Is this you?"

she asks curiously.

"Well, yes," I answer. "We just needed someone for the mock-up shot."

"Chloe, you would be perfect to represent O's image," Amanda says, looking at me closely now.

I laugh. "Oh no, no, thank you, but I don't think so."

"I agree with Amanda. You *are* perfect," Nick says. "I want to go ahead with this, and I want you to be O."

"Really, I'm flattered, but I couldn't," I stammer. "We need a professional model for this. And even if I thought it would work, I couldn't. I'm going to be gone for a while, soon. I'm taking, well, some . . . personal time."

"I'm sending this all to finance," Nick says. "I want you reassigned to the branding project as soon as you can hand off your retail design responsibilities. Amanda too. Chloe, you'll report to me."

"But I just said no to being the face of O." I'm calm and clear. No.

"Then if you won't be the face of O, you'll be the brains behind the operation," Nick says in a voice as firm as mine. His face is blank, those sapphire eyes piercing me.

"I already am."

The placidity cracks, the corner of his mouth twitching. "Touché. You and I will work on the branding. I want you driving the train."

He stands up, and Amanda and I follow. She begins gathering up all the materials on the table.

"Thanks, Chloe. This is going to be so much fun. I'll call you." And she's out the door.

I'm left looking at Nick.

And he's looking back at me.

"How long do you think it will take to clear your schedule?" he asks.

"Nick, you can't just pull me out of daily operations of O like this! I have projects there, and there's no one who can just take over—and I love my job!" I pause. "Plus, I'm cutting back my hours starting in the next few months."

He looks at his watch. "Let's go to lunch and we can talk about it."

That *does* seem like a good idea.

I lift my white leather bag off the back of the chair, and as I am slinging it over my shoulder, the bamboo handle comes unhooked. The bag drops, bouncing off the chair and hitting the floor, and of course it lands sideways. Most of what's inside it spills out, makeup and pens and perfume, aspirin, keys. And—oh please no—my lipstick vibrator rolls under the chair.

Nick is on one knee, gathering coins. I kneel down too, and reach for the little vibrator but he gets it first.

"That's a big lipstick," he comments, holding it up.

"Economy size," I smile brightly, reaching for it.

"Is this one of the mock-ups of O cosmetic packaging?" he asks, pulling the hot pink cap off.

"No!" I say, but too late.

Nick looks down at the USB charger he has just uncapped. Then he looks at me, puzzled.

"Yes!" I backtrack. "Yes, that's a mock-up, yes it is. Part of my *next* presentation. Phase Two." I hold up my hands like a TV game show announcer. "'The Power of O' is what we are calling it."

I'm babbling.

I hold out my hand.

He smiles.

"I'll keep it with the other package ideas," he says, and drops it in his pocket. "You can tell me your plan for it at lunch."

My plan for it was to reduce stress while caught in rush-hour traffic tonight. But maybe it *would* make a good new product line. Driving accessories! Is that dangerous?

'O'verdrive.

I love my job.

♥ ♥ ♥

THIS NEW LITTLE restaurant in The Fort shopping complex looks completely full, but somehow they find a table for Nick, tucked into a corner.

"It's the Anterdec table," he explains. "As long as James McCormick's not in town, I can always get in here."

"Tell me about Charlie," I say. "What's he doing now?"

He looks at his plate of grilled fish. "Charlie's trying to figure out what he wants to do when he grows up. He's on his third career and his second divorce. He's actually been living with me for a few months, though he's out of town right now. I have a lot of extra room with my kids all away at college."

"I can't believe that . . . even as a kid, he always knew he wanted to be a lawyer. He was going to be a public defender, help people who had nowhere else to turn. What happened?"

"He got into Yale Law School, but the pressure was too much. He took a leave of absence and never went back. Then it was culinary school, and now it's some website selling surfing equipment for kids."

"From Yale to surfer dude," I say with a smile. "Only Charlie could pull that off. How's it going?"

"Not well. Kids don't have credit cards." He sighs. "At least culinary school has come in handy. He makes dinner every night. He's pretty good, too."

"And your kids are all in college?" I know I should turn the conversation back to work now, but I'm just so *curious*. "You don't look old enough to have—"

Shut up, Chloe! I scream inside my babbling mind.

My face must betray my thoughts, because Nick just laughs. "I'm flattered." He won't look away. I'm trapped, that electricity between us from earlier arcing, rising up. "My son went to NYU for summer session to get a jumpstart on his freshman year. Couldn't wait to flee to New York. My daughters both work on campus at their colleges here in Boston. It's quiet at home."

"What's it like to have an empty nest?" I blurt, back to safer territory, because a quiet home means an empty bed and. . . .

He thinks for a second, as if dazed. Does he feel it, too?

"I'm at Anterdec because they acquired my company. I had a branding consultancy called FireBrand. Built it from the ground up. We did about $25 million annually, 37 employees. The McCormicks agreed to keep my whole staff."

This is not the answer to my question.

"It was a great opportunity for everyone," he continues. "Some of my people have really moved up fast, working for Anterdec subsidiaries all over the world. They learned the business from me, at FireBrand, and now they're succeeding on a global level. I'm so proud of them."

Still waiting to see where this is going.

"But I used to see everyone every day, and now I don't. They're launched. I just get the occasional email when they have a problem, or want to share some good news."

I get it. "Two empty nests?"

"Exactly."

"Ouch."

He laughs, looking up from the rim of his wine glass to meet my eyes. "More like freedom. So close . . ."

Funny, though. He doesn't look very free.

There's a little bustle at the door. I look up to see Jessica Coffin headed toward our table, with three apparent clones behind her. It's like the Neiman Marcus display window mannequins woke up and went to lunch. They are followed by the maître d'. Aren't *they* supposed to be following *him*?

"Chloe!" Jessica says, looking at Nick. "How are *you*?" It's unclear who she is asking.

He stands and offers his hand. I introduce them, and then hesitate. Jessica helped to make O the success that it's been. In business, you tap into the thought leaders to get your idea to go viral.

In the spa business, you find the equivalent, which means Jessica Coffin and her always-for-rent social media accounts.

Except she deleted her Twitter account a while ago and has been suspiciously silent. Hmm.

"You work for Andrew McCormick," she says to Nick, her mouth twisting oddly as she says Andrew's name. "I met you here, at some charity event."

Right. I don't know why I thought I had to explain the identity of a handsome, successful Boston man to Jessica Coffin. It's her business to know. Might even be in her DNA.

She turns back to me, a tiny smile on her lips. "Chloe, didn't I hear you're about to be a mommy? That's just so exciting. I guess we won't be seeing you at restaurants like this anymore. From now on, you'll only be eating—what are they called?—Happy Meals."

She leans forward to kiss my cheek, then moves off, brushing against Nick as she goes, although there is plenty of space between tables.

He doesn't seem to notice her. He is staring at my stomach.

CHAPTER EIGHT

Nick

A GIANT, OVERSTUFFED blue nylon bag masquerading as one of my daughters appears at the door on this fine Saturday morning. Morning-ish. I look at the clock. Noon. Although for her, that's the crack of dawn.

"Are you selling dirty laundry? If so, that is a terrible business idea."

"Dad!" Elodie whines, the tip of her nose and one wide eye appearing around the large lump. Her long, glossy brown hair is pulled into a ragged top knot and she's wearing flannel pajama pants that are entirely too long, covering feet in flip flops.

Very familiar flannel pajama pants.

"Are those mine?" I grunt, as she thrusts her clothes at me.

I take the load from her arms and she gives me a quick kiss on the cheek, smelling like the T and cotton candy.

She also ignores my question.

"Where's Uncle Charlie? Is he here?"

"No. He's meeting with his business partner. They're trying to trademark the phrase 'Surf the Internet.'"

That gets an eye roll.

"But how wonderful you've come home to visit your dear old dad. What's on the agenda for our relaxing hours together?"

"Is the washer empty? I have literally nothing left to wear and it's '80s karaoke night at school and Brandon is the emcee." She's standing in my doorway, phone in her hands, both thumbs flying. She is not even looking at the screen. How do they do that?

"'80s karaoke. So you're Googling the lyrics to 'With or Without You'? 'Every Breath You Take'? 'Born in the USA'?"

She's nonplussed. "What are those?"

Let's move on.

"How about a game of chess? Or we could play Candyland. You always loved that when you were little."

I get a head toss and a sigh, as she drags her clothes into the laundry room off the kitchen. I accept my role as utilities provider and start up the espresso machine. Having my own washer and dryer has turned out to be a young adult insurance policy. At least once a week, I get their undivided attention for a few hours.

Especially when they know they can raid my pantry, too.

Elodie comes into the kitchen and snipes the shot of espresso I've just finished making. "Almond milk?" she asks, rummaging in the fridge.

"I don't know how to milk an almond. Do they have udders? Besides, last month you drank nothing but coconut milk." I point to the half-gallon I bought for her this week.

"Daddy! That was last month. Now I need the manganese."

"Manganese?"

"It's a mineral."

"I know what manganese is, Elodie, but why do you need to drink it?"

She waves her hand in the air with an air of sophistication that reminds me so much of her mother, Simone, that I freeze, blinking into dead air.

"The college cafeteria refuses to stock almond milk now because of protests." She settles for cinnamon and downs the espresso shot like tequila.

"Protests?"

"Almonds use too much water and some agricultural climate change group thinks we need to stop drinking almond milk because of a moral imperative."

"Almonds have morals?"

"Daddy, *stahp.*" She draws out the word like a Minnesotan, then hoots.

Followed by the evil eye.

"You look different today," she announces, peering at me. Of all my kids, she's the one who looks and acts the most like Simone.

"Different?"

"Happier."

I scowl.

"Ha! That's what you normally look like. You have Resting Jerkface."

I quirk an eyebrow. "What?"

"It's like Resting Bitchface, but for men."

I just peer at her. Sometimes I think I've produced progeny from another planet. Where do they come up with this stuff?

"You frown all the time, Dad! All the time. You never, ever smile."

I give her the fakest grin I can muster.

"Now you'll give me nightmares." She grabs a reusable Trader Joe's bag and starts stealing . . . er, liberally sampling from my pantry. "Where's the good peanut butter?"

"Why don't they make peanut milk?" I ponder, making myself an espresso and sprinkling cinnamon on top.

"Ewwwwww."

"And almond milk is any better?"

She just sighs. Most of her tenth grade year involved nothing but sighs. I am fluent in Sigh. This one means, *Shut Up.*

Now that I think about it, they pretty much all mean *Shut Up.*

"How's Brandon?" I ask.

Elodie has been half-chasing, half-ignoring Brandon for the past six months. I pretend to rifle through my day's mail, giving her covert glances. If you look a young adult straight on while asking a question designed to elicit more than a Shut Up sigh, you will never get actual information out of them. You have to be an information ninja. Eye contact shuts down the speech center.

Better to act distracted, because then they actually try to get your attention. Make them work for it.

"He's great! We hooked up last week and—"

"You went out on a date?"

"Went out, hooked up . . . you know." She blushes.

Oh, no.

Sometimes, my covert information tactics work too well.

Danger, Will Robinson. We've ventured into sex revelation territory. Where's the shotgun when I need it? I take a deep breath and let it out.

Sounding a little too close to Sigh.

"Dad, *stahp!*"

"What?"

"I know you don't like Brandon."

"How can I not like him? I've never met him!"

"What was that sigh?"

"It was an old man deflating. Sometimes we need to let some air out."

"EWWWW!"

"That's not what I meant!"

"Says the man whose favorite bedtime book was *Walter the Farting Dog*."

I start laughing at the memory. That really is one of the best children's books ever.

She peers at me again. "Who is she?"

I choke on my coffee. From farts to women. Elodie can change a topic like no one's business.

"Aha!"

"Aha, what?"

"That was a shot in the dark. So there's a *she*? Finally?"

My front door opens. We peer around the breakfast bar to find another enormous bundle of laundry invading my home. It's an infestation.

"What are you doing here?" Amelie yells, clearly offended by Elodie's presence.

"Talking with Dad about his sex life."

"I do not have a sex life!"

That came out wrong.

True, but wrong.

"That's the problem!" Elodie fumes.

"The problem is that you are hogging the washer and dryer, El," Amelie says, frowning at the tornado of clothing poured out on the floor in the hallway outside the small laundry room. She gives me a pouty face and says, "Make her take turns."

"You are not five any more. You are both twenty-one. If you need your dear old dad to mediate when it comes to laundry, how are you going to get anywhere in the business world?"

Her green eyes flash behind old-fashioned fifties-style glasses, big and rectangular with dark rims. Like her sister, she's wearing flannel pajama bottoms, but her feet are stuffed into unlaced Doc Martens,.

"It's that woman you saved!" Elodie shouts, triumphant. She and her twin share one of the thousands of twin-looks that I can never decipher.

"Who?" Amelie looks as confused as I feel, which is small comfort.

"Dad is dating. He has a girlfriend!" Elodie is majoring in Folklore and the Spoken Tradition at her progressive college. It's a self-crafted major. Highly employable.

"I do not have a girlfriend."

Amelie turns her full attention to me. Elodie's plan is clear to me: distract her sister so she can hog the washing machine.

"You do look different," Amelie says with caution. "More relaxed. Happier."

"Regular sex will do that," Elodie announces.

I close my eyes and—yep.

Sigh.

"I am not—" I was about to say having regular sex, but that crosses a line. "I am not dating."

"You should be." Amelie scowls at me. She and Elodie are fraternal twins, and everyone in our lives has said she's the feminine version of me. I wonder if I look that fierce when I'm studying a project at work.

"You need to ask her out." Elodie has found the good peanut butter, a jar of Nutella, and a batch of Mint Milanos I thought I'd hidden carefully in the pantry, behind the black beans. Guess not carefully enough.

Amelie grabs the cookies and dips one in the peanut butter, then the Nutella, and stuffs her face. I turn away and make myself another espresso. Whatever happened to post-softball-game ice cream cones and fevered discussions about Justin Bieber?

This has veered into dangerous territory. When you become nostalgic for Justin Bieber, it's bad.

"I'm not talking about this."

"We worry about you." They share another one of those looks. Something in my chest tightens and loosens at the same time.

"Why would you worry about me?"

"Because we love you."

I clear my throat, which has suddenly become thick with confusion.

"And because you really need to get laid."

"Elodie." I say her name low and slow. That used to be enough to get her to stop doing whatever she was doing that broke the rules.

"What? It's true," chimes in Amelie.

"Chloe!" Elodie exclaims, snapping her fingers, giving Amelie a conspirator's look. "That was her name. The woman Dad saved from her drunk, half-crazed boyfriend."

"Ex-boyfriend."

Four evaluative eyes land on me.

"See? You totally like her," Elodie declares.

"She's a work colleague. I don't date women at work."

"You don't date women at all," Elodie shoots back.

They share another look.

"Does that mean you date men?" Amelie asks, her voice soft with compassion. "Because if you've been afraid to tell us, we're fine with—"

"As relieved as I am to know you're open-minded, no—I don't date men."

"Maybe he's asexual," Elodie says at the exact moment that the washing machine buzzes. Cycle over. Has this conversation really lasted that long?

No. Those were my clothes.

"Go!" I hiss to Amelie, who sprints down the hall while I step in Elodie's way.

"Daddy! Now I'll only get one load in!"

"Payback."

"For telling the truth?" Her eyes turn into deep brown triangles, challenging and calculating. Before I can give her a wise response, the storm passes and she is aloof. Untouched.

Chloe. Now that her name has been invoked, I find myself completely overwhelmed by the image of that smile. Her poise. The ramrod-straight posture and the confidence that she holds, as if the world is hers to open. I've spent so many years pushing aside opportunities that I knew would just lead down blind alleys, dead ends, and into relationships that would cause more pain than they alleviated. The kids came first.

Always.

Amelie comes back, the distinct sound of the washer filling in the background a taunt aimed at her twin. "Who are you texting?" she asks Elodie.

Who is holding *my* phone.

I snatch it back to find the text function open to Chloe's name.

"You started to write a text to her?" I choke out. Sure enough, there are the words *Would u like 2*

"We have to make sure someone takes care of you in your old age," Elodie huffs.

"First of all, forty-two isn't exactly *old*. Second, I would never abbreviate words like *you* and *to*." I'm not sure which offends me more: being called old, or the grammar hack.

"I would never actually text her," Elodie says with an impish smile. "I just wanted to get you to think about it. You already set up the perfect meet-cute."

"Meet-cute?"

"You rescued her from her creepy stalker drunk ex, Dad!" Amelie exclaims. Now she's fishing through my pantry, taking cans of my favorite soup and stuffing them in her backpack. Don't universities feed their students any more? How much am I paying for room and board so my kids can come home and pilfer?

"That's, like, you're like Bruce Wayne."

"What?" I ask Elodie.

"You know. Nick Grafton by day, superhero by night."

"Right." A memory from work hits me. "They call me Focus Man!"

Withering looks radiate from both of them.

"That is *so* not a sexy superhero name, Dad," Amelie says, shaking her head sadly.

"That's the best he can come up with," Elodie adds, giving Amelie a sigh. "He really needs our help."

"Do not!" I protest.

"Do too!"

They're in stereo.

"Text her! Ask her out for a work dinner. Do it. Do *something*," Amelie urges.

I am not taking dating advice from my daughters.

I am not.

But I am smart enough to realize they're on to something.

I type, *I think we should have another meeting.*

And hit Send to the sound of twin squeals.

Chloe

JEMMA GETS UP from the counter and opens my refrigerator. She refills both our wine glasses. To the brim. And these are balloon glasses.

I raise one eyebrow.

"Saves a trip," she says. "We're going to drink it anyway, why get up twice?"

Right. I am comfortable now. Soft grey leggings with tiny ruffles on the hem, and my black cashmere hoodie. I stretch my legs out and admire my pedicure: *Over the Taupe,* my favorite polish. Goes with everything. Just like the rosé wine.

"You never went back to work after that lunch meeting with Nick?" she asks.

"We just walked around the city all afternoon, talking. About everything. He cancelled his afternoon appointment, said he was in meetings about a new branding initiative for an Anterdec property."

"You walked *all afternoon* in four-inch heels?" Jemma asks skeptically.

"We stopped a lot. Benches. Cafés. A wine bar."

"And talked about the O brand?" She is still skeptical.

"Well, not exactly. We talked about what happened with Joe. And we talked about Nick's job, and his kids. And his ex-wife. She abandoned them all and went back to France. Can you believe that? But it sounds like she still shows up for the kids. Sometimes. When it suits her."

"Did you tell him?" I know what she's really asking.

"Yes, I told him about the baby. A little bit."

"*And?*"

"He didn't say much, just listened. He asked if I had family nearby, or close friends." I look at Jem and my eyes fill up. "I said yes to friends."

The front door opens and Henry comes in.

"*Damn*, it smells good in here," he announces.

Since nothing is cooking, he either means perfume or the faint scent of alcohol.

His arms are full of brown bags. I get up and help him unload. Take-out sushi and three bottles of wine. Red, white, and prosecco. I love bubbles.

I love Henry.

"Jessica Coffin says I will only eat Happy Meals for the rest of my life," I inform them.

"That's ridiculous," Henry says, handing out soy sauce. "What does *she* know? There's Chuck E. Cheese, and pizza, and in about twelve years, you can try a real restaurant if you go at five o'clock."

I try to stab him with a chopstick but he's too fast.

I hate Henry.

"So where were *you* all day yesterday?" he asks me. "Explaining massagasms to the board of directors?"

"Kinda," Jemma answers for me. "One at a time. Starting with Nick Grafton."

"The guy who put Joe Blow in a chokehold?" Henry's confused.

"Don't call him Joe Blow," I say automatically.

Henry puts a spicy tuna roll in his mouth and smiles.

Jem and I exchange a look. "See that box over there, honey?" she asks him. "It's a car seat. Could you finish your sushi and go install it in Chloe's backseat? Or you could just take your container of sushi with you and go now?"

My text pings.

I think we should have another meeting.

I don't recognize the number, but this can only be one person. Henry and Jem are staring at me.

"I think it's Nick," I whisper.

"He can't hear you," Henry whispers back.

Another text bubble appears on the screen.

Does Friday work?

"It's just a work question," I say. Why do I feel a little disappointed? Of course it's just a work question. I report to him now. What else could it be?

Sure, I type back.

Three dots tell me something's coming soon. I wish *I* were coming soon.

Great. Pick you up at 7.

Wordlessly, I hand the phone to Jemma. She reads it and whispers, "Oh my god, Chloe! A Friday night dinner? That's not business!"

"Why are we whispering?" Henry whispers. We ignore him.

Three more dots.

Do you like Mexican?

Nick

"WHAT'S SHE SAY, Dad?"

"She says *dot dot dot.*"

"DAD!" Elodie grabs the phone out of my hands and watches with the intensity of a Pats fan watching Brady shout "Omaha!"

Which is not a bad analogy, all things considered.

"SEE!" Elodie screams.

"See what?"

She shoves the phone in my face.

Ah. Not "see."

Si.

Chloe said *yes.*

"She said yes!" Elodie and Amelie start screaming and jumping in the air, as if I'd just won something on a game show, or caught a foul ball at Fenway.

My heart is imitating them, silently.

"I am done talking about this," I say, mustering my air of authority.

"It's not like we're going to ask you any details. I mean, EWWWWWW," Elodie declares.

"We'll make sure we don't stop by for food or laundry on Friday night, though," Amelie announces, winking at me.

"But I do have to come and do laundry for my big trip," Elodie says to herself.

A sharp inhale from Elodie makes me turn and look.

"What if you date a woman who wants kids?"

"I have kids." I'm confused by this statement.

"I mean more kids." They share bright-eyed excitement at the thought. Where is their brother? Jean-Marc is the cynic in the family. He's also my only kid who doesn't live in Boston right now, which automatically makes him my favorite. Three in college at the same time.

The job at Anterdec needs to be solid.

And here I am, asking a colleague out for dinner, and possibly jeopardizing it. Someone who is adopting a baby in the next few months.

"I have plenty of kids. Don't need more."

"Be upfront, Dad. Don't string her along."

"It's a business dinner," I growl.

"Let's go pick out what he's going to wear on his date!" Elodie shouts, as she sprints down the hall. Amelie darts into my bedroom as I watch her sister double back, turn off the washer, take out the sopping clothes and load her own in.

That one is going to be a lawyer some day, folklore major be damned.

CHAPTER NINE

Chloe

FRIDAY NIGHT. AFTER a week packed with three bachelorette parties, two divorce celebrations, one widow party (yes, we were surprised, but freedom comes in many forms) and a state elevator inspection that took more of my time than it should have, here I am, ready for Nick.

A blue and white pencil skirt in a diamond pattern. White T shirt. Silver hoop earrings, and lots of bracelets. Wedge sandals, which were a good choice because the sidewalks in this neighborhood are uneven brick. Nick holds my arm when I wobble. I love these sidewalks. All sidewalks should be made like these. Wobbling is good.

We decide on an outside table, and order margaritas. It's a beautiful mid-summer night, warm but not humid, and the sun is still out, the July nights still long and festive. Boston's not usually known for its authentic Mexican food, but this place is supposed to be changing that.

"One more good meal before you start your life sentence of chicken nuggets?" Nick smiles.

"Even if Jessica's right about that, it will be worth it," I say seriously. "I want this baby so much, Nick, and I've waited *so* long for her. Anyway, I am never feeding my child a Happy Meal. Ever. She is only going to eat organic food, and I am going to make everything myself, so I will know exactly what she's getting."

"Well, that's admirable, Chloe." He looks . . . amused? "Any other plans?"

"No big plastic toys," I answer. "Just natural materials like wood and paper and cloth. And not too many toys. I want her to use her imagination. Be creative. And no princesses."

"No plastic," Nick repeats. "No princesses."

"Right," I say.

"You are really just very beautiful," he says, as if that follows.

I look into his smiling blue-green eyes. "Did you have, um, basic . . . principles for, you know, raising your kids?" I stammer.

He bursts out laughing. "Yes. Absolutely. Life vests on boats. Helmets on bikes and skis. Stay off the roof."

"No, seriously," I say. "You must have had some ideas?"

"Any ideas that we may have had about children went out the window pretty quickly," he says. "We had three babies in twenty-five months, and we were practically kids ourselves. Then, when I became the only parent on the scene, the kids were three and five. I just wanted to keep them busy every minute, so they wouldn't notice their mom was gone." He makes a face. "I actually thought that was possible."

"That must have been torture." I want to hear more, but I don't want to cause him pain.

"Well, it kept me busy, too," he says slowly. "I didn't want to notice she was gone, either."

He signals the server for another round, and points to the empty basket of chips. More, please. More of everything.

I lean forward on my elbows, waiting.

"She went back to France, you know. Simone, my wife. Ex-wife. She said she wanted the man she married. She wanted a lover, not a daddy. And it turned out, she'd found him."

"What does that mean?"

"She had reconnected with her lover from university days at the Sorbonne. He 'saw her as a woman.' Not a mother."

"Oh Nick."

He shrugs. "It was a long time ago."

"She left her *children*." I can't quite make sense of it. I've devoted years to finding a child to love, and she walked away from hers.

He looks self-conscious. "Let's talk about something happy. Let's talk about you."

Two more rounds of margaritas, one bowl of guacamole, and a very large platter of fajitas later, Nick asks for the check.

We've learned a little more about each other. He loves bluegrass and cowboy songs (go figure). He speaks fluent French (not surprising). He has done an ocean crossing, can explain Fermat's Theorem (it was wasted on me), and has run for town office (he lost). He is deathly afraid of alligators. Somewhere around margarita number three, I discovered that he lost his virginity at age seventeen, to the neighbors' Spanish nanny. This resulted in a lifelong love of olives.

In return, I shared my deep love for the color white in all its many variations, my obsession with Miles Davis, and my entire bucket list, including the part about backpacking in Patagonia. Before margarita number four he stops, begging off to be able to drive, but I keep going. So it's *possible* that I may have told him (oh dear god) about the Power Underwear Theory. My virginity he already knew about. Yep. Charlie.

Do you think I might be just the tiniest bit . . . drunk? Because that would not be good.

Margarita number five was delicious. I had them leave off the salt. Self-control is important.

"So," he starts. "Other than my little brother Charlie and Joe Blow, there must be men in your life. How about that tall, naked guy who was holding you up outside your office? The redhead." His smile fades.

"Henry? Oh my God, no! He and his wife are my best friends." Is it me, or does he look a little bit relieved?

"Have you ever been married?" he asks.

"And don't call him Joe Blow," I add. "No, never been married.

Before Joe, I dated someone for five years, but he got a great job offer and moved to New York, and my job was here. We tried to make it work long distance for about six months, but we both wanted more than that. I want to wake up with someone. I want to come home at night and tell someone about my day, hear about theirs. Go grocery shopping. Have a life." I pause. "Raise a family."

Am I oversharing? Too late to worry about that, I guess.

"I miss that," he says softly. "Even after all this time."

"Why haven't you remarried?" I ask.

He's quiet.

"After Simone left, I was in survival mode. I had all I could do to manage breakfast, lunch, and dinner, never mind soccer games and piano lessons. Although," he smiles ruefully, "I had plenty of offers of help from female friends. All kinds of help."

"I'll bet you did," I smile back. "Did you accept any?"

"No," he shakes his head. "I wasn't going to let any woman near us again. And when the girls got older, they were pretty protective of their turf." He starts to laugh. "Once I had a weekend guest, an old friend who lives in Chicago. The girls went into the guest room on a reconnaissance mission. They were about ten at the time. Just as my friend and I were sitting down to a candlelit dinner, Elodie and Amelie came down the stairs."

"This doesn't sound good," I say, but I'm smiling.

"It wasn't good. But it was pretty funny. They were each wearing one of her silk nightgowns. And high heels. Lipstick. They must have sprayed an entire bottle of her perfume on each other. They were giggling so hard they could barely stand up."

"Oh no—what happened?"

"Let's just say my friend didn't see the humor. And those nightgowns just didn't seem very sexy anymore."

"Hard to be a dad and a date at the same time?" I ask.

"Very. But they're off at college now. All of them. It's a whole new world."

"A new world for me, too, but I'm just at the beginning."

Nick looks at me thoughtfully.

And signals for the check.

♥ ♥ ♥

THERE IS CONSIDERABLY more wobbling on the way back to his car, but I think the walk does me good. By the time the black Range Rover comes into view, most of the margaritas have worn off. Anticipation has not. My breath quickens, all my senses suddenly acute. The press of his fingers against my spine as he guides me. The brush of his hip against mine as we turn. How his hair curls at the collar, like it's cozying up. The light whiff of Bay Rhum that makes me want to nuzzle his neck.

Nick clicks the locks off and opens my door. He's standing so close, one hand on the door handle, leaning in toward me like he's ready to breach the space between us, about to take that penultimate movement before a kiss. I glance up at his face and he's looking at me. Slowly he leans forward and I take Sheryl Sandberg's advice.

I lean in.

Slowly, softly, his lips touch mine, a burst of flavor and heat quenching the anticipation but making me thirst for more. Seconds pass, eternity in the form of intimate touch, the deepening passion turning into a free fall. I'm loose and spinning, falling into nothing and everything at the same time, his hands holding me in place, his hard body locking me into the only location in the world where I need to be.

Not want.

Need.

Then he straightens and smiles into my eyes, questions pooling there, barely held back, lips twitching with intensity. I turn and slide into my seat. Neither of us says a word.

The briefest kiss—a taste, a tease, a promise—and I am undone.

This is a revelation to me.

The Massachusetts Avenue Bridge takes us back to Cambridge. At night, this is my favorite view—suspended over the Charles

River, Boston glittering on one side and Cambridge on the other. Two beautiful cities reflected in the same water. I turn in my seat. On one side of Boston, the gold leaf State House dome is illuminated; on the other side, above Kenmore Square, is the famous neon CITGO sign. The panorama is magical, like being in a snow globe, except it's summer.

I sit back and look up through the open sunroof as the stars slide by slowly.

What's going to happen when we get to my apartment?

Will we sleep together? I want him to sleep with me.

I report to him. He can't.

I look over at him, serene and purposeful, his hand leaving the steering wheel and finding mine, resting our clasped fingers on my thigh.

A promise, all right.

An invitation.

He damn well better kiss me again.

And more.

On the other hand, we work for Anterdec. There is plenty of precedent for inter-office romance. The entire world knows that Declan McCormick just married one of his direct reports. And I still want to know more about what's going on with Andrew and Amanda.

Of course there's no 'Visitor' parking space available on my street. Or on the cross street.

On the next street over, we round the corner just in time to watch a Volvo sliding back into an open spot.

So unfair. So *frustrating*. So Cambridge.

Please can we just fast-forward? Teleport, maybe?

Four blocks away, we finally see a spot at the far end of the street. We look at each other and smile. We pull up alongside the space.

It is the size of a Smartcar. There's no way.

I smack the dashboard. Nick smiles.

I have an idea. "Just go to my parking spot and pull in behind my car," I say. "No one can have a problem with that."

Ten minutes later, we are inside my back door.

"Would you like coffee?" I ask, turning the lock.

His mouth is on mine.

I breathe him in, taste him, move my body along with his. My back is against the door. His hands are pulling my skirt up. His palm runs along my thigh, my hip, pulling me against him. I feel his hardness, and I reach for his belt buckle, frantic for more of him. The clasp opens.

My god, he's gorgeous. I start to bend down and he stops me with a kiss.

"Not here. Not yet. You first," he rasps.

Nick pulls me to my feet and kisses my mouth again. We stumble through my open door. He kicks the door closed and I'm on my back on the couch, my skirt riding up, his face between my legs. There is no pretense here. No quiet flirt, no mixed drink, no spiked coffee and coquettish glances. This is pure, raw energy in sexual form, and we're drawn to each other's hot skin like a magnet to iron.

"You're just as beautiful here as everywhere else," he says softly, and covers me with his warm mouth, his tongue circling slowly, then faster, fingers pulling my thong to the side, his hot breath nearly enough to send me over the edge, and oh, God, this feels divine. I push my hips forward, abandoning myself to the feeling, familiar and yet completely new, as I feel him smile against me, his attentions both masterful and uninhibited.

Now I know how to make him smile.

I am moaning now, in a language even I don't understand. The sensation builds, and builds, my fingers tightening in his hair, until it crests and the intense shimmering heat spreads all through me.

And all I want is more of him.

"You're delicious," he tells me, continuing his gentle sucking as I shudder, half my mind blown away by the sudden intimacy and craving for ten thousand layers more of this man, the other half shattered into ten thousand pieces of confetti that whirl around like a cyclone of arousal.

"I want *you*," I tell him, sitting up, legs weak and thighs wet as I strip out of my t-shirt and he pulls his polo shirt off, our hands frantic, breathing labored.

He steps out of his jeans and, bending down, picks me up in his arms.

"Where is your bed?" he asks.

I point and whisper, "In there."

Then he's laying me down and he's over me, his strong arms on either side, pulling the rest of my clothes off until we're both gloriously naked, the need to touch like a fever that won't break.

I open myself to him, then wrap my legs around his waist. He pauses. I reach for my nightstand drawer and open it. He pulls out a condom and takes care of the niceties, then enters me slowly, his eyes locked on mine, and he gasps. I can barely hear his words, but I think I hear him say, "My Chloe."

Our eyes meet.

"You," he says as he begins to move, then dips his head down to suck one tight nipple into his mouth.

And then he starts to move. We move together, faster and more urgent, until his breathing changes to something more ragged. He makes his final thrust. With a kind of quiet roar, he explodes into me, and his hot pulsing pushes me into my own climax, matching his.

I am his.

♥ ♥ ♥

I WAKE UP slowly, but don't open my eyes. There are strong arms around my waist and slow, steady, warm breath on my neck.

That is not Minky's breath.

Oh my god oh my god, it's Nick!

Lie perfectly still, Chloe, don't wake him up. Try to breathe like a sleeping person. Sloooowly. I just want this moment to last, like forever, and if he wakes up he will grab his clothes and run out the door and I'll be left here making one cup of coffee and trying to smell his scent on the bed pillows. Again.

Or—wait—that was Joe.

But dammit, I have to pee.

And brush my teeth. My mouth tastes like cat box. I can't stand it.

But if I move, he'll wake up and this moment will be over.

My leg is asleep. I can only feel vaguely uncomfortable pinpricks. I need to shift, but if I move . . .

Concentrate on how wonderful his skin smells. Concentrate on the feeling of being held. Relax and concentrate on his breathing.

I can't. I really have to pee.

Maybe if I slowly inch my way out of bed, not moving the mattress at all, and silently slip to the bathroom, and gently close the door so the latch doesn't click, and . . .

This is ridiculous.

I am an adult.

A slightly hungover adult.

Tequila.

Sigh.

I stand up. And almost fall down from my tingling leg.

Nick stirs, and stretches. He opens one eye and smiles sleepily.

"Hurry back," is all he says.

Oh, I hurry. Yes I do. Dash to bathroom, pee, brush teeth, wipe off last night's lipstick, brush hair, little spritz of perfume on all the places that count. All of them.

Takes me thirty seconds, tops.

Sliding back into warm, sex-smelling sheets and feeling your lover's skin welcoming yours, with nowhere else to be and time to spare, is the greatest luxury known to a woman. This is exactly the experience that O tries to approximate for every client. And we can't even come close to the real thing.

His breathing evens out as he slips back into sleep and I curl in his arms, relaxing in a way that is new. No man has spent the night in my bed in a very long time. Joe never did. His wife would wonder. Even when I suggested he pretend he was on a business trip, he always had an excuse.

The slimy ones always do, right?

It's daylight, and I'm entirely sober now. I can really look at Nick, see the muscles in his shoulders and his ass, see where the hair on his chest begins and ends, see how he responds to every touch. His face is relaxed in sleep, light brown hair mixed with dark blond and a little silver, with that slight coloring at the temples that makes him look distinguished. His beard stubble has more grey than brown, and I want to lick his lips. He tasted so good last night.

He *was* so good last night.

I sigh, his arms tightening around me, and I find my mind sinking into a soft place I never go, a place where I just am. I'm not a design director, not a mother-to-be, not a mistress, not a daughter.

I get to be *me*.

And as I fall back asleep, I wonder if Nick feels what I feel, too.

I HAVEN'T WOKEN up with a woman's ass curled against my front in a long, long time.

I've forgotten how good it feels.

Chloe is soft in slumber, her skin golden and relaxed, fine bones angular and artistic in the morning light. She's breathing deeply, slowly, her body loose. I sit up just enough to look over her shoulder and see the sheet is my friend, her breasts peeking out, uncovered. She smells like her verbena perfume, the scent so strong that I wonder if she sprayed herself earlier, when she got up for a moment.

I slept over. In a woman's bed. She's beside me.

I'm beside myself.

A woman hasn't slept all night with me since Simone.

Chloe shifts, as if she senses I'm watching her, and I brush my fingertips along the fine bones of her hip, resting my palm there with a territoriality that feels a little too caveman-like for my own comfort.

Can't help it, though.

We're spooning, which was comfortable a few seconds ago, but as I look at her closed eyes, the lashes resting gently on her creamy skin, the broad planes and high cheekbones of her face a work of art, I feel myself harden.

Last night was amazing.

How about we make the morning even better?

"Mmm," she says, the sound a mix of slow awakening and an offer as she turns over, her body warm, her arm reaching for me, eyes still closed. "Nick?"

"Morning."

She smiles, still not looking at me, and my palm squeezes her, the air freezing in my lungs. What's she thinking?

I take the lead and lean in for a kiss. She wiggles closer, her legs entwining with mine, mouth cute and tentative until the kiss deepens. Within seconds it's clear what we both want.

"Last night was amazing," I say, putting words to what I've been thinking.

"I don't usually do this," she says with an open smile, those dark brown eyes alert yet sultry, aware but still relaxed.

"Do what?"

"Have a sleep over."

"Me neither."

"We're breaking all our rules," she says, her arms reaching up around my neck, her torso pressed against me, hips finding my erection, grinding just enough to make it more than clear what she wants next.

That's how exceptions work, I think, but before I can say it, I'm over her, hands taking in the smooth fullness of her breasts, pert and small but more than enough, one nipple tasting like sweet musk and sunshine.

Blood pounds through me, sending energy to places long dormant, and all I want is to be in her again. The easy intimacy is so foreign. Pure.

Perfect.

And then her head disappears under the covers. No giggles, no hesitation, no awkwardness. Chloe knows what she wants and goes for it.

I'm dreaming, right?

The slick warmth that envelops me and makes my abs tighten isn't part of any dream I've ever had before, though. Miles Davis plays in the background, a tune that morphs into a rhythm that becomes damn near feral.

"Chloe," I choke out, overcome by the hot surprise of this morning gift. I look down to see the covers tenting her, her mouth working magic on me, one hand on my inner thigh, the other cupping my ass.

No woman has ever been so uninhibited in bed.

And then she does something with one hand and her tongue that makes me forget anything exists but her, this bed and—

RING!

I sit up sharply, pulling back, shocked by the sound of my phone's ringtone.

"Nick?" Chloe's muffled voice comes from under the covers, then her face peeks out like a turtle in a shell.

"Damn it. That's my phone. Someone's actually *calling* me."

"Ignore it." Her head disappears under the covers again and oh, God. . . .

I sigh. "I can't." Regret infuses every syllable as I twist and reach for the phone. Where is it? I climb out of bed and search the floor for my pants. "My kids. You know . . ."

"Oh." Her voice holds a tone of surprise. "Right. Of course."

I don't want to blow this. I don't. And if this is some stupid work issue, I'll kill the caller. But if something happened to Elodie or Amelie or Jean-Marc and I didn't answer the phone . . .

I grab my phone and climb back in bed.

Elodie.

Chloe snuggles up as I answer.

"Hello?"

"DADDY! OH MY GOD, YOU'RE ALIVE!" Elodie screams, the sound so loud I flinch and pull the phone back from my ear, dropping it on my knee.

Chloe's eyes pop open and she gives me a questioning look.

A deeply amused, questioning look.

"Of course I'm alive. Has someone told you otherwise?"

"I came home to do laundry and no one is here!"

I look at the time. Seven fourteen a.m. The one time that child is awake before noon. Damn. Long night. Early rise.

Chloe starts playing with the hair on my chest, then gently teases one nipple with the end of a perfectly-manicured fingernail.

I clear my throat with meaning.

Her eyes go impish.

Oh, no.

"Yeah, well. . . ." I can't really speak. I need to get off the damn phone. My erection deflates like a blow-up kid's slide at closing time at a New England town carnival.

"Where are you? On business?"

"You could say that. What are you doing at the house so early?"

"Getting down to business," Chloe mutters, reaching up to bite my earlobe.

Electricity shoots through me.

"Daddy! Amelie said she couldn't find you, either! Remember I'm here early because we need to do all our laundry at once? I'm going on that trip to D.C. for one of my classes tomorrow night. Is something wrong? Have you been kidnapped? The security alarm says you haven't been home since 5:42 p.m. yesterday."

Damn safety system. Installed it to manage escaping kids when they were younger and now they're using it to track me.

"I'm fine."

"He's fine," Chloe says, just loud enough for Elodie to hear. And I let her.

"DADDY! IS THAT A WOMAN?"

I wince. Honesty is the best approach.

"Yes."

"Where are you? Having coffee with someone?"

"Mmm, coffee," Chloe purrs. "Want some in bed?"

"ARE YOU IN BED WITH A WOMAN?" Elodie screeches.

I do what any red-blooded man with a naked woman in bed beside him and his barely-adult daughter screaming on the phone about his sex life would do.

I end the call and turn off my phone.

Before Chloe can get out the room, I grab her from behind and gently throw her on the bed, laughing with her.

"You enjoyed that, didn't you?" I growl, half embarrassed, half amused.

"Do your grown daughters always track you down when you've slept with a woman?" Her tone is light, but I can see the mild horror in her eyes. If the roles were reversed, I'd hesitate, too.

I go serious, brushing a stray lock of hair from her forehead, taking my time to answer. Her body is trim and smooth beneath mine, our exposed skin hot and needy, my elbows supporting my weight as Chloe's pensive look makes me feel everything.

And want more.

"This is the first time."

"The first time you've slept with a woman?" she jokes. "I'm honored."

"The first time I've slept over."

"Ever?" Her eyes are intense, asking questions she can't ask with words.

"Since their mother and I divorced, yes."

Chloe blinks, just enough times for me to tell she's processing the detail, trying to glean meaning. There's plenty to find.

I kiss her, our mouths soft and urgent, and she opens her legs, wrapping them around me, her intent clear. I feel like I'm wearing new skin, trying it out for the first time, finding it's a better fit than the old one.

And feeling every sensation with an acuity that is like being reborn.

Last night was the frenzied rush to taste and tease, to conquer new territory, to try a sample to see what we liked. This morning is slower, more sensual, like a wine tasting where the goal isn't to get drunk.

It's to swirl the glass, inhale deeply, find exactly which bouquet is most appealing.

And oh, the mouthfeel.

I'm not going to miss a single drop.

Sex with Chloe was hot and quick the first time, the frantic rush that comes from wanting to try each other out, from the anticipation that fires the blood and makes everything urgent.

This time, we're more deliberate, and as I kiss my way down her torso, I find myself tasting her sweetness for breakfast, the small sounds of pleasure she makes helping to clear my mind, pushing my body to the limit. Chloe is a delight in bed, her body mine to explore, yet she surprises me now, pulling me up.

"I want you," she gasps, hands wrapping around my ribs as I glide up her body, our kiss twinned with my entering her, her legs wrapping around me as if we planned this all long ago and are executing it in perfect synchrony.

Which is what happens minutes later when we come together, my face buried in her neck, her long legs impossibly twisted around my back, her warm and melting center encasing me, my breath unsteady and my body more at ease touching hers than I've felt in years.

"Nice," she murmurs, "now I understand why they call you Focus Man at work."

As I chuckle, she reaches up to cradle my jaw in both hands, giving me a smoldering kiss that tells me we're not done yet.

Thank God.

The ringtone for the song *It's Raining Men* jingles from the floor.

"I know that's not *my* phone," I mutter, my mouth now full of sweet nipple.

"Henry likes to change my ringtone," she groans. "But no one actually dials my phone unless the spa's on fire," Chloe says, twisting out from under me, leaving me throbbing and slightly chilled as cold air replaces warm woman.

She picks up the phone. "Private number."

"Telemarketer?" I say hopefully.

She shrugs and answers. "Hello? Yes, this is Chloe. Excuse me?" Her eyes look like she's wearing coke-bottle glasses as Chloe turns to me, gloriously nude, one hip jutting out as her arm extends to me, phone in hand, holding it like it's a live, poisonous snake.

"What are you doing?"

"It's . . . your . . . daughter." Chloe gently places the phone in my hand and steps back, turning away, snickering.

"What? My *what*?"

"DADDY!" Elodie screeches from Chloe's phone. "You really *are* there with her!"

This is not happening.

Red rage pumps through me, replacing desire, a poor substitute for passion, but it will have to do for now.

"You did *not* call me on Chloe's cell phone," I grind out, trying not to explode with expletives the kids have only heard from my mouth when I banged something.

Other than a woman.

"I logged in to the family cell plan and found her number on your line, because I had to make sure you're safe, Daddy!"

Chloe is now wheezing with laughter, hugging a pillow. Our eyes meet and she sobers up suddenly, her face slack with surprise.

"I'll go make coffee," she whispers, leaving the room, her ass the gift that keeps on giving.

"YOU!" I bellow into the phone.

"Daddy?" Elodie replies in a small, soft voice.

"I cannot believe you did this, Elodie Laurence Grafton! My private life is mine. MINE!" I can feel the bed shake as I shout, a cat jumping off a chair in the corner and shooting out of the room, my own voice gaining volume as my ire pours out of me.

"But—"

"I am speechless! My private life is off limits. Period. Do not ever do this to me again. Are we clear." It's not a question.

"If you were speechless, you wouldn't be yelling at me," she whispers.

"And I *am* yelling at you, so what does that tell you?"

"But Daddy, I thought you were—" She's crying, her voice hitched.

Good.

She *should* cry.

"Don't even try it. Once I hung up on you the first time, that was it. Done. End of discussion, and now I'm ending *this* discussion."

Click.

I felt passion when I woke up.

Then rage, followed by boiling misery.

Trying on a suit of guilt for size now.

A suit that would fit the Incredible Hulk.

"That sounded intense," Chloe says from the other room. "Coffee's brewing. I'll bring some back in on a tray."

And embarrassment joins the soup of emotions.

I am naked in Chloe's bedroom. My co-worker's bed. My child just tracked me down via my bedmate's cell phone to chew me out for not coming home last night.

I am pretty sure that's a Dan Savage, Dear Abby and Maury Povich event rolled into one.

"Damn!" I shout into a pillow, pitching it across the room, knocking over a towel rack. It clatters to the floor with an anemic series of clicks.

Futile.

"I never liked that accessory anyhow. It falls over every time the cat sneezes," Chloe says with an overly-bright smile, watching me like one would watch a staggering raccoon in the alley. I don't blame her.

I'm feeling pretty damn rabid.

Flashing her a grateful, but tight, smile, I take the coffee from her extended hand, forcing myself to sip the scalding liquid just to buy some time.

Men's Health magazine never has articles on how to handle this kind of mess.

My burnt tongue feels like a rebuke, insult added to injury, and I finally explode.

"This is what happens when you have kids! They rule your life and take all the oxygen in the room. You breathe for them when they're little and when they're older, they think they're entitled to all the air." I huff, trying to drain off the anger, wishing I could stop my tirade, unable to control it. "I'm so damn close. They're all in college now and I can breathe again. Freedom tastes good."

Freedom tastes like you, I nearly say.

And then our eyes meet.

Chloe looks stricken.

What the hell did I say that's so wrong?

Chloe

OKAY.

Okay.

There aren't that many times in my life anymore when I just don't know what I think.

But this is one of those times.

A kid falls into a gorilla habitat at the Cincinnati Zoo, and suddenly everyone in the country has an opinion on the parenting skills in that family. Sure, it looks bad, but what do I know? I've never been responsible for a bunch of active kids at a zoo. Am I entitled to judge?

So when Nick's daughter calls looking for him, frantic with worry, and he yells at her, is that bad? He's her only real parent, her only security, right?

But what he's saying about kids ruling your life, and having no freedom—well, that's maybe my biggest fear right now. The fear I can't admit to anyone. I think and pray that the best part of my life will begin when the baby comes, but what if it's too much? I've never had to be utterly responsible for another human being before.

A single parent.

What if I am overwhelmed?

Even Nick appears to be overwhelmed right now, and he's been doing it—being a single parent—for more than fifteen years.

What if, someday when my child is at college, I am having the most romantic night of my *entire life*, and my cell phone starts ringing and ringing? Will I feel needed and loved, or will I feel harassed beyond enduring?

Moot point. I just had the most romantic night of my life. Nothing will ever top last night.

Except this morning, of course.

Usually the first time is a little bit awkward, right? Exciting, sure, and new, and fun (usually). But neither of you knows where to touch, or when, or how, or for how long. There's no choreography.

That's not how it felt with Nick.

It just felt right.

And that's terrifying.

I need to talk to Jemma.

You see? I just don't know what I think.

"Chloe. Come here," Nick says. He puts down his coffee and opens his arms. "Looks like second runner-up for Father of the Year again. Third if Amelie gets to vote too. Damn."

"Maybe you should call her back?" I offer tentatively.

"And what does she take away from that? That there are no boundaries? The house was not burning down, no one was hurt or missing or even upset. Once she reached me the first time, she knew I was fine. For her to call your phone was WAY out of line. She was playing a game."

"You told me the girls are used to being first in your life. That story about dressing up in your date's lingerie?"

"Yes, but they were ten. It's not okay anymore. And if they start thinking they rank above you, we will have a big problem. Not unlike pack animals." He smiles, his cheek against my hair. "Or toddlers."

"In less than two years, I'll have one of those," I whisper.

"And then you will begin to understand."

He sits on the bed, pulling me down with him. We settle into spoons and he pulls the sheet over us.

"Getting this baby feels like when you go on a trip to a country you've always wanted to visit, but you've never been there before." I try to explain this. "It's a completely different culture, and you don't speak the language. So it's exciting and fun, but when you get off the airplane, you don't even know how to get to your hotel. And reading all the guidebooks really doesn't help at all."

He laughs. "Fair enough. But you only have to learn one neighborhood at a time."

"But I'm moving there for twenty years!" I sit up, and turn to face him.

He laughs harder. "Just when I am moving back to my country of origin."

And then he stops laughing.

CHAPTER TEN

Nick

"**W**AIT A MINUTE," my brother, Charlie, chokes out in between deep, uncontrollable bouts of laughter. "You're telling me your kid called your lover while you were in the middle of hot sex?"

"We'd just *finished* having hot sex," I correct him, draining my Sea Belt Scotch Ale. The soundtrack to *Brother, Where Art Thou?* strums away in the background. Charlie and I are eating pizza out of the box. Feels like twenty years ago. His half has banana peppers, anchovies, and pineapple on it.

My half is trying desperately to escape his half, the pepperoni offended by his taste buds.

I haven't told Charlie exactly who my lover is. I also hate the word lover. *Lover* is what Simone called Rolf.

I preferred the term *schweinhund*. Google it.

Charlie shakes his head. "Elodie. Remember when she was four and she insisted on dressing like Coco Chanel and refused to speak English at school that day?"

"How could I forget? My kid was almost expelled from Montessori for perpetuating cultural stereotypes."

As Charlie picks up his final piece of pizza, an anchovy breaks in half and lands on the cardboard.

"Hey!"

"What?" he says, his dismissive look one I've seen since he was little. Charlie looks like our mother, with dark brown hair and pale brown eyes the color of cafe au lait. No one ever thinks we're brothers. Aside from the same body type, we're nothing alike.

"Your piece of salty fish nearly ruined my dinner."

"Maybe removing the stick up your ass will improve your appetite. The sex was that bad?"

"Shut up," I growl. I'm not talking about sex with Chloe. After one of her many margaritas, Chloe whispered the fact that Charlie had been her first. Knowing we've both slept with her is bad enough. Having to tell Charlie is worse. If I can hold off a little longer, maybe it'll be easier.

"Is that why Elodie's not here? She's staying scarce?"

"So far, yeah. Amelie brought an extra bag of laundry with her yesterday, though."

"Those two are each other's best friends and worst enemies. Frenemies. They fight over who gets the washing machine, but give them a common enemy and they're tight."

I shoot Charlie a look. "And we're any different?"

His grin is filled with pizza.

"Jesus, Charlie. Swallow before you smile."

"That's what I always say, too." He leers.

I groan. "For that, I pick the movie."

"Not another foreign film," he groans, then perks up. "Unless it's French. Love the French films."

"That's because they all have threesomes in them. At least, the ones *you* watch."

"YouPorn has an excellent selection of high-quality foreign films." He pops open another beer and shrugs.

"Please tell me your laptop has a screen protector on it."

He nods. "Keyboard, too. You really have to, with the USB attachments they make now." His eyes go blank, and he begins to talk in a businesslike, clipped tone. "If you don't, the keyboard gets sticky, and no one wants to go to the Apple Genius Bar with the equivalent of an artificial insemination sample."

"Charlie!"

"I'm not kidding. You know that company that makes the surfing equipment we sell? They've been bought out by the same mega-corporation that's making dildo drones."

"Did you say dildo *drones?*" I look at my beer with suspicion. Two empties are next to me, so unless he spiked this with a hallucinogen, I'm not the crazy one here.

"Sure. It's like Google Glass, or Virtual Reality. Next great invention."

"No, the next great invention would be a vaccine that cures the Zika virus. Or cold fusion. Dildo drones rank somewhere above dog bongs and below remote-controlled zippers."

"Already exist."

"Remote-controlled zippers?"

"Dog bongs."

"Someone invented a marijuana bong for canines?"

"Sure. Even doggies need to chill once in a while. Plus, the endocannabinoid system can be very powerful when it comes to inflammatory diseases, and in veterinary medicine—"

"Dog bongs, Charlie. Can dogs even inhale?" My brother's a Yale Law dropout who couldn't manage past his first year, but he clearly just picked the wrong grad school program. Biochemistry would have been a better fit. Only Charlie could struggle to maintain a permanent address and a steady job, but know the inner workings of the canine neurotransmitter system.

Then again, he might have become Walter White. Don't let the man anywhere near an RV.

"I guess so. No one would have invented the dog bongs if they couldn't."

"Charlie, who do you think would create such a device?"

Silence.

"Stoners. People who are baked out of their minds. People who go through the Taco Bell drive-thru and buy a ten-pack of soft tacos and who think God talks to them through the microphone while their fingers turn into antennae."

He shoots me a dirty look.

"Those same people are the ones who look at their mother's bichon frise in the basement apartment where they live and think, 'Poor Peanut needs a bong.'" I'm pretty sure they invented most of the television shows my kids watched as toddlers. Whoever came up with *The Big Comfy Couch* and the French show *Téléchat* must have been huffing on some very human bongs.

"I happen to be friends with the guy who is waiting for his patent for dog bongs to clear." Charlie runs a hand through his hair and starts peeling the beer label on his bottle. "And it was a yorkie poo named Fluffy," he says under his breath.

"I work eighty hour weeks as a corporate drone in the Financial District and there are guys making money getting the family pet *high*."

"It's a growing field."

"So is Alzheimer's research."

"Got to follow your bliss," Charlie says softly. "When did you turn into a grumpy old man? All you need to do is start wearing socks with sandals, get some Sansabelt slacks, start using Viagra and yell at kids on your lawn. You're becoming Grandpa Louie."

"I don't have a lawn. I live in a townhouse." I give him the hairy eyeball. "And I don't need Viagra."

"*We* live in a townhouse."

"You're only here for a visit."

"And don't knock Viagra. It's great as a recreational drug."

"I do not want to hear about your twelve-hour erection."

"That's *not* what she said."

"That's it. We're watching *The Revenant*."

"What? No, Nick, c'mon. Don't make me watch Leo DiCaprio having sex with a bear."

I do a double take. "There's no bestiality in the movie."

"I heard it sucked."

"No. What sucks is listening to you right now." Dog bongs.

What's next? Edibles for hermit crabs?

The front door slowly opens, the sound making us both tense by instinct. We share a look of primal danger. Then I realize Charlie's more worried about his beer as he scrambles to catch it.

"You expecting anyone?" Charlie whispers.

"No."

"Daddy?" It's Elodie, looking shame-faced, the crease between her eyes making her resemble Simone. It's been a week since she called Chloe's phone. I haven't seen her since. Not a single text other than *I'm sorry.*

This has been the longest I've ever gone without contact. Even when the kids were in France for their annual visits with their mother, we had daily phone calls and texts.

"Hi, honey," I say, studying her. Whatever she feels she needs to say, I don't plan to make it easy. Not hard, either. But this is a life lesson, and I don't have many more to impart to my kids.

"Uncle Charlie!" she chirps as she spots him, running into his arms with a sweet abandon so different from her cultivated worry. I see her face over Charlie's shoulder as he bear hugs her, lifting her off the ground, her pony tail stuck under his arm as he laughs.

"I can't believe you cockblocked your dad, Coco," he says as she's midair.

Elodie scrambles out of his arms and gives him a look designed to make her uncle spontaneously combust.

"Technically," I correct him again, "she didn't—"

"*Non!*" Elodie shrieks, fingers in her ears. "I do not want to know more! *Merde!* This is bad enough. It's been so bad I called Maman for advice!"

When my kids mix French with their English, I know they're upset.

When Elodie tells me she called my ex-wife to talk about my sex life, I know *I'm* upset.

"You what?"

"I didn't tell her *why* you hate me, Daddy!" Elodie says with great drama, including wide, sweeping hand gestures that remind me of Joan Crawford's overacting.

Charlie gives me a look that says, *This is your kid.*

Yeah. It is.

And Chloe wants one of these?

"Please tell Chloe I am so sorry," Elodie begs.

Charlie eyes freeze on me.

"Chloe? Your lover's name is Chloe?"

"Ewww, Uncle Charlie! Don't call Chloe Daddy's lover. She's just a one-night stand." She gives me a hopeful look. "Right? Because if you're seriously dating her I am going to curl into a tiny ball of horror and just die right here on the couch, because it would be soooooo embarrassing to ever have to face her."

"Chloe what?" Charlie asks, his eyes slanting with a slow, taunting grin.

"Just Chloe," I answer.

"What's her last name, Nick? You know I dated a Chloe in high school. There aren't that many in Boston." His smile broadens and my fingers curl into my palms. Can't hit my own brother.

Not okay.

"She was fine. Better than fine. A little wild and crazy, and she had this thing she did with her tongue that—"

"STOP!"

Being six years older than Charlie has its perks, chief among them that my angry voice has been programmed in him since birth.

"It's the same Chloe."

Elodie's eyes widen. She looks just enough like Zooey Deschanel that I do a double take.

"Wow. You look just like Katy Perry when you stare at your dad with that look of extreme shock," Charlie tells Elodie. He gives her a weird grin before looking at me. "Chloe Browne?"

"Right."

"You're sleeping with my ex."

"I'm sleeping with an extraordinary thirty-five-year-old

professional woman who likes my company as well."

We stare at each other.

"This isn't awkward at all," Elodie says.

In French.

"C'mon. Not fair. I regret picking Spanish in high school," Charlie whines. "If I'd have known you'd marry a Parisian, I'd have picked French."

"If I'd have known how wonderful Chloe was, I'd have dated her in high school before you could."

"She was fifteen. You were twenty-one and about to have the twins. That's kind of sick, Nick."

"Daddy!" Elodie gasps.

I fold my arms across my shoulders, puffing out my chest. "You know what I mean."

Charlie digests this information by drinking an entire beer in one long ribbon of swallows, then holding up a finger.

Elodie starts clapping in anticipation.

And Charlie burps like a dog with indigestion.

And not a dog who has access to a bong.

"I can see how that was funny when you were little, El, but come on. Charlie was a teenager then. Now he's just a thirty-something man with a Peter Pan complex."

Charlie grins. "Thank you."

"That wasn't a compliment."

"Depends on your point of view," he says with a nonchalant shrug that triggers unexpected fury in me. Must be nice to slack your way through life.

I'm about to say as much when I'm interrupted.

"I'msorryDaddyIshouldneverhavecalledChloe'sphoneand caughtyouhavingsexandthatwaswrongpleasedon'thateme," Elodie says in one long, unfurling ribbon of panicky blabber.

Charlie's eyes narrow. He ignores the firehose of contrition pouring our of his niece. "You and Chloe. No way. She's *way* too carefree for you."

"I don't hate you," I say to Elodie.

The relief on her face is palpable.

"And what the hell do you mean by that?" I ask Charlie, going into full-on older brother domineering mode.

"Daddy, I think he means you—"

Charlie holds up a palm, aimed at her. "I can speak for myself. What I mean is . . ." He falters, frowning. "I mean that the Chloe I slept with—"

"Ew!" Elodie squeals. "You *shared* Chloe?"

We've gone from dangerous territory right into full-blown toxic soup. The is the Chernobyl of family conversations.

"Not at the same time," Charlie helpfully clarifies. "Twenty years apart."

"I don't understand," Elodie gasps. "What does he mean, Daddy?"

"I need an interpreter too, honey."

Charlie takes a deep, irritated breath. "Chloe needs a guy who's passionate and impulsive. Romantic and wild. She needs a guy who—"

"—who likes to use a strap-on," Elodie elaborates.

I drop my empty beer bottle. It crashes to the floor, cracking unevenly, pieces skittering along the kitchen floor like they're desperately trying to escape.

Charlie's face twists with horror. "Elodie! How do you know what a—what that—what?"

"STOP!" I shout, closing my eyes. "WE ARE NOT DOING THIS AGAIN."

"Again?' Charlie's voice shoots up an octave. "You've had previous conversations with your daughter about strap—" He can't look at her. "About—that? Those?"

"No."

"Then I am very confused."

"Now you know what it's like to have a conversation with *you*, Charlie."

"Hey, man. I talk about dog bongs. Not—"

Elodie bends at the same time I drop down, both of us carefully picking up the larger pieces of green glass among the broken bits.

"Dog bongs? That's a thing?" Elodie asks.

I groan. "Please stop. Stop now. For the sake of the remaining brain cells I have left that aren't waving a white flag of surrender, let's reboot this entire conversation."

"L'ex de Chloé vend le strap-on qu'elle lui avait mis, Papa," Elodie blurts out.

My hand jerks so badly I cut myself, the red bloom along the line of my palm filling in the pale skin. "She *what?*" I say in English, followed by a string of profanity in French.

My daughter did not just say, *Chloe's ex-lover is selling the strap-on she used on him, Daddy.*

"That's why I came to see you."

Charlie appears with the broom and dust pan. Elodie waves my hands away, urging me to go to the sink. The two continue cleaning. I run my wound under cold water and close my eyes, wincing.

"It hurts that bad?" Elodie asks.

"This conversation does, yes."

"I meant your hand."

"The hand is a welcome distraction from talking about Chloe, strap-ons, dog bongs, and my sex life." Never thought I'd utter the words *dog bongs* and *my sex life* in the same sentence.

Charlie eyes us with suspicion. "What did you say in French? I heard strap-on again." He looks away.

Neither Elodie nor I answer, instead focusing on cleaning the mess. The cut's so superficial it stops bleeding almost instantly, leaving a sting from the beer. I rummage through the kitchen junk drawer and find a Band-aid, absentmindedly applying it.

A Disney Princess looks back at me. Jasmine. She was always my favorite. It's the hair.

How long has it been since I've cleaned the junk drawer?

Elodie makes a great show of taking out her phone, tapping on the screen, and showing us an auction.

"eBay? What does eBay have to do with Chloe?" I ask.

"It's not eBay, Daddy. It's an auction site where you sell all the things your ex gave you that remind you of them."

Can you sell your children on this site?

"Like eBay for relationship revenge?" Charlie asks, perking up. "Smart concept. I'll bet they got great venture capital funding." Charlie has worked for nine different start-ups since dropping out of Yale.

All nine have failed.

"Right. Most of the sales are for engagement rings, wedding dresses, books and mementos. That kind of stuff. Sometimes it's furniture or books. But, um, this one came up and it's going viral."

She turned the glass screen toward me. I squint.

A strap-on.

"How did you find this?"

"Buzzfeed and TMZ are covering it."

Oh, hell.

"It's getting that much coverage already?"

"Is that her, Daddy? I came as soon as I saw it. I know you're not serious with her or anything, but I thought you should know. She should know. It's so embarrassing and—"

I hold up one finger, buying time.

Chloe's batshit-crazy drunk ex-boyfriend has gone on this website for people who want to sell their gifts from exes and has started one hell of a smear campaign.

The ad for the strap-on reads:

Khloe Brown was the love of my life.

She dumped me for no reason. Three years down the drain.

We had a love that was so rare. So accepting. So nonconformist. We created our own world and lived in it, inhabiting a space no one else ever had the right to enter.

And now she's gone, screwing a coworker who looks like every corn-fed Midwestern basketball player lead actor combined with the intellectual curiosity of George W. Bush.

I start choking. Is he talking about *me*? Stretching up to full height, I look down. No belly. Flat abs. My arms are long, and I can still do a slam dunk on the court. Knees hurt like a sonofabitch the next day, but I can do it.

I ignore the GWB comment.

"Daddy? Why are you, uh . . . examining yourself?"

I quickly return to the description on the phone. There are worse insults than being called "corn-fed Midwestern basketball player lead actor."

I went to see her at work. Sent her eight dozen roses. Pleaded with her, and her new fuckbuddy got me in a headlock and beat me until I bled.

"What?" I shout. If that were true, I'd be charged with assault. Idiot.

"Keep reading, Daddy." Elodie shakes her head and offers me another beer. "Keep reading."

Nothing bled as much as my heart, though. I shared a love with Khloe and a sensuality that is without parallel. Do you see that dildo in the picture? It represents her.

Beer really hurts when you inhale it.

Charlie has his own phone in hand. He picks up where I leave off as I hack up a lung and some intellectual curiosity.

"*She was a stunning Amazon warrior princess in bed, riding me like the stallion that I am. For dumping me the way she did, refusing my calls and texts and visits—*"

"VISITS!" I say with a gag. "Visits! The asshole's been *stalking* her."

"*—for throwing away my love and support, all the nights we spent together, all the years I devoted to her, I sell this lot of items she gave me with one purpose in mind: that the money should go to a group with purpose and honor. I will donate all proceeds and match the amount.*"

"Who's he donating the money to?" I ask, not wanting to know.

"A men's rights organization led by a pick-up artist," Elodie says with obvious acrimony.

"Of course."

"And!" Charlie continues, trying to read as he laughs. "*Should my heartfelt words touch the cold iceberg of my beloved's heart, I will withdraw this auction in full so we can live out the destiny that we were meant to have.*"

"Pegging is a destiny?" Elodie mutters.

I do not want to know how *she* knows that term.

"What else is for sale?" I ask, cringing.

"A Coldplay t-shirt," Charlie says.

"He's a *monster!*" Elodie shrieks, as if that's somehow more offensive than the strap-on.

"What's wrong with Coldplay?" I ask, genuinely confused. "I like their music."

Charlie and Elodie share a look of camaraderie in their shared disgust.

"*That's* what's wrong with Coldplay," she mutters, adding a shiver.

"And a bunch of very nice cashmere sweaters, size M," Charlie continues. "An original vinyl print from a Dave Brubaker album he says was a gift from her."

She has good taste.

"And a Rush album."

Maybe not.

"A very nice Rolex and some Montblanc fountain pens."

"Chloe must be horrified," I say, slumping into a barstool at the kitchen counter. I feel my pulse in my hand where I cut it. "You said it's all over social media now?" I ask Elodie, who nods.

"Wait!" Charlie shouts. "The last sentence says: *May someone else put this strap-on to good use, so you can get screwed just like Khloe screwed me over.*"

I read over the same words. "Bastard was with her for three years and still doesn't know how to spell her name right? Khloe with a K is a Kardashian," I grumble.

"The auction is riddled with typos," Charlie explains with a shrug.

"Guy must have been drunk," I muse. Poor Chloe. The strap-on issue is intriguing. I cringe.

"Daddy, how can you like Coldplay and know who the Kardashians are? You're a pop culture contradiction."

"I'm young enough to pay attention but old enough not to care, honey."

"What's the name of the guy? The asshole ex?" Charlie asks, eyes gleaming.

"Joe."

"Joe what? You know his last name?"

"Joe Blow."

Even Charlie rolls his eyes.

"Why?" My voice goes low. Charlie is scheming. This can lead to no good.

"Because I have an idea."

"All of your ideas suck, Charlie."

"Only the ones involving other people's money."

Fair enough. "I can call Anterdec and find out from security."

"You're going to rescue Chloe again, aren't you, Daddy?" Elodie is breathless with the excitement of a young woman who sees potential in every situation but has not yet experienced the full consequences that potential can bring.

"Again?" Charlie's eyebrow goes up.

"Daddy tackled him in the hallway at work when Joe came after Chloe! He was like a Navy SEAL!"

"A Navy SEAL, huh?" Charlie can't help but laugh. "They teach you that at RISD?"

"Yes. I took a course on 'Evasive Maneuvers When Choosing Fabrics for Branding.' It was useful when I finally got to business school at Harvard."

"What's your idea?"

"Find the guy. Contact his wife. Blow the lid on the affair."

"How'd you know it was an affair?"

Charlie shrugs. "No guy *that* desperate isn't married."

Good point. "And then what? I don't want this to come back and bite Chloe."

Charlie taps on his screen and grins. "I don't think you have to worry. I just Googled Khloe Brown, the way he spelled it—look."

The top news story shouted in all caps:

PORN STAR KHLOE BROWN PEGGED AS ONLINE AUCTION MYSTERY WOMAN

"Chloe spells her first name with a C and there's an E at the end of Browne," I say slowly.

"He misspelled it. On purpose?" Charlie asks.

"Definitely drunk."

"Gotcha. Good thing. Looks like Perkie Workie's getting a nice PR boost."

"Perkie—what?"

"That's Khloe Brown's character. You know . . . in her series."

"Series?"

"Her porn series. She's this milkmaid who—""

"Got it. Done. No need to elaborate."

"I only know this because at my last job, our developer team had just worked on an integrated USB device system for the production company for her series, and—"

I ignore him, reaching for my laptop bag, logging in.

"What are you doing?"

"I have an idea." I find the site, Never Liked It Anyway, and search for the strap-on.

"Whoa. Five hundred eighteen bucks for this thing. Eleven hundred for the entire lot," I say, rubbing my hand on my chin, my stubble irritating the cut on my palm.

"*Deadpool* made pegging cool," Elodie elaborates. "Prices are higher for—"

"Would you stop saying that?" I grouse.

"What? *Deadpool?*"

"No."

She smirks at Charlie, who stifles a laugh.

I put in a bid.

"You're going to buy Chloe's strap-on?" Charlie asks, agog.

That's right. I can be carefree. Just watch me.

Carefree with my Visa, that is.

"Just curious how this works," I say with a meaningful throat clearing.

"You're hardcore, Daddy."

"I don't think this is a particularly strong example of *anything,* my dear."

"You're saving Chloe."

I don't know what I'm doing, frankly, but I won't admit that to my kid. I just know that shutting down Joe's antics is priority number one. The longer this stays online, the sooner it'll get back to Chloe, and possibly hurt her personally or professionally.

Five minutes after a call with Anterdec security, I have Joe's last name.

And Charlie gets to work.

CHAPTER ELEVEN

Chloe

YOUR AVERAGE SUNDAY. Read the papers, drink coffee, do laundry, look at Facebook. Wish Nick would call. Go for walk, take shower, wish Nick would call. Scoop catbox, wish Nick would . . .

You get the idea.

At six p.m., I decide on an early dinner for one. I am putting the chicken breast in the baking dish, closely supervised by Minky, when the back door bursts open and there's Henry, with Jemma just behind him.

"Hey!" I greet them. "There's only one chicken breast but we can make chicken chili. I have tomatoes and . . ."

"Chloe, what the hell? Why aren't you answering your phone?" Henry interrupts.

"It hasn't rung. .?"

Now that I think of it, it hasn't rung all day. Which is odd.

"The social worker called," Jemma says urgently. "Yvonne called us because she couldn't reach you, and we're your emergency contacts. Li had the baby. A baby girl, just like in the ultrasound."

There is silence. I just look at them.

"Chloe, honey?" Jem puts her hand on my arm. "There's more. She had the baby, and then she disappeared. She checked herself out of the hospital. No one knows where she is."

I'm still staring. This is not in the birth plan.

"No one knows. .? Where. . but where. .?" I stammer.

"The baby is at the hospital. Li signed all the papers with Yvonne before she left. The baby is yours, but the hospital social worker and Yvonne have been calling all day and you didn't answer. Why haven't you answered?"

"It didn't *ring!*"

"Well, we've got to call them right now. And get over there. We'll drive you." Henry hands me my jacket. Jemma's turning off the oven and putting the chicken back in the refrigerator.

I grab my bag and shuffle through it, looking for my cell. The phone case is bright orange, chosen for this exact reason: so I can find it in a bag full of other things, which are all bigger than the phone.

Here it is. I press the button.

Twice.

Dead.

"Never mind," Henry says, "You can use ours. Let's go."

They've parked behind me in my spot.

"No," I finally find my voice. "We have to take mine, it has the baby seat in it."

"We'll take both," Henry says. "You come with me. Jemma can drive yours."

At this point, for the first time in my life, I will do exactly as I am told. I hand Jem my keys and get in their car.

To get my daughter.

♥ ♥ ♥

HAVE YOU EVER seen race-walkers? It's that sport where the athletes look like they're just walking, but they're actually moving at five times normal speed? That's what we look like headed down the hospital hallway toward the maternity ward.

Unsurprisingly, Henry gets there first.

"We just had a baby," he says urgently to the woman seated behind the reception desk. "We need to find her right away."

The woman gives her co-worker the side-eye, the kind that says, *I may need you to call security very soon.* She arranges her face into an expression of calm concern.

"Can you give me a little more information?" she asks. "Are you the father? Can you tell me your name?"

"Henry Holliday. This is my wife. And this—" he pulls me forward "—is the mother."

She looks at me nervously. "And you just gave birth, dear?"

"Yes! No!" That should clear things up. "My baby is here. I'm Chloe Browne, you called me, my phone was dead, I don't know how that happened, I'm so sorry, but here I am! Where is she?"

Before the receptionist can answer, an office door behind her swings open and a tiny, curly-haired woman with an ID badge around her neck comes rushing out.

"Ms. Browne? I'm Kate Moss. We've been waiting for you."

Conversation stops as we all stare at her. She sighs.

"Not *that* Kate Moss. I'm the social worker on duty. Yvonne will come back tomorrow to go over specifics. I need you to fill out some forms, and then we can go to the nursery. This is a bit of an unusual situation."

A bit.

"Go ahead. We'll wait right here." Jemma gives me a quick hug.

In Kate's office, I sink into a chair. She picks up a folder from her desk and hands me a pen.

"What about Li?" I ask her. "The birth mother. Do you know where she is?"

"I'm sorry," Kate answers. "I know you have a personal relationship with her, but I can't tell you anything. You could try calling the Boston police."

Police? Why would I need to call the police? What the hell happened to Li?

"Is she alive?" I ask, hearing the hysteria in my voice, knowing I need to tone it down. They won't hand a precious newborn off to a woman who's falling apart in front of them.

The social worker frowns, then sighs. "All I can say is that we're pretty sure she is."

"Pretty sure? She wasn't the victim of—has Li been—oh, God, she's almost a child herself!"

"Ms. Browne," Kate the social worker says, her eyes going kind. "The police are working on the case with the birth mother. Let's help you focus on the baby."

There is too much happening right now to process. I just need my baby. I need to take her home. Then I can think about everything else.

I sign the papers, I fill in the information, I produce my identifying documents. Kate makes copies.

And then.

Then we go to the nursery.

It's climate-controlled in here. There are rows of plastic bins, each with a tiny occupant sporting a knitted cap with a pink or blue ribbon, each swaddled in a pastel-striped cotton blanket. A few are protesting, as best they know how, but it doesn't sound very serious. White-painted rocking chairs are positioned here and there, and seated in one of them is a new mom in a bathrobe and slippers, intently nursing her newborn.

Nurses move silently between the bins, going about their routines. Kate talks to one of them briefly, showing her paperwork and nodding toward me with a smile. She catches my eye and points to one of the rocking chairs.

I sit, and a moment later the nurse appears at my side. She is holding a small bundle with a pink hat, and she leans down and places it in my arms. It's surprisingly light.

Here she is, at last.

Oh, *hello.*

I'm almost afraid to look at her. Can this be happening? Can she really be mine? This was supposed to happen in the future. Months from now.

Her baby skin. Her tightly closed eyes, her impossibly small pink lips. With a shaking hand, I slide her cap off, uncovering a head of silky black hair. I didn't know they came with long hair? I stroke it with one fingertip. Someday I will braid this little girl's hair, tie a bow in it, pin it up with flowers for her prom. Someday in our future.

Forever starts right now.

I want to see all of her, her hands and fingers and knees and toes, but she's wrapped so tightly, a little baby package. Tentatively, I pull on the edge of the blanket, and it loosens enough for me to find one of her perfect, miniature hands. She's only hours old. This brand-new hand has never been held before. I'll never let it go.

She breathes in and out, all by herself. Miraculous.

Mine. She is mine.

"I'm yours," I whisper.

I'm her mother. She's my daughter. Every yearning, every fear, every fight, everything that led to this moment, all worth it.

I don't know how to change her diaper.

Panic bubbles up in my chest. What does she *eat*? When does she eat it? What if I have to take a shower—who will watch her? I can't just leave her alone in her crib! What if *she* has to have a bath—how is *that* supposed to happen? Can I hire someone? Oh dear god, I am unqualified for this assignment!

I used to have a recurring nightmare in which I was standing in a board room, about to give an important presentation, and couldn't think of a thing to say. Everyone was staring at me, waiting. I was exposed as knowing nothing about my job. This feels horribly similar.

Only worse. In the dream, no one's life depended on me.

The nurse—her ID tag says Keisha—touches my shoulder. "Everything all right?" she asks quietly, wide brown eyes peering at me with an expression that says she's figured out I have no idea what I'm doing. .

"I don't—I can't—I don't . . ." My eyes fill up with tears. "She's so early! Li wasn't due for eight weeks!"

Keisha looks at the baby's chart, then gives me a sad smile. "I see the due date is far in the future, but the doctors assured us she's full term. Sometimes due dates are wrong, especially when prenatal care is—" She pauses, clearly searching for a tactful way to say what she needs to say.

"Uncertain."

Her face floods with relief. I've rescued her. "Yes."

"But she's healthy? The baby?"

"Great APGAR scores. 10/10," Keisha says proudly, like my daughter nailed the SATs.

"Thank God." I'm staring at this baby with eyes that don't know the world. Everything is new. Everything is shiny and heavy with responsibility and gravitas. She's seven pounds but as heavy as the universe.

"No sign of drug withdrawal either. We'll have blood work results soon."

I tense. Oh, Li. Oh, baby. "The, um, birth mother said she didn't do drugs."

Keisha nods slowly. "That's good." I can tell she wants to say more, but is measuring her words.

"I'll show you how to change her and feed her, and we have booklets on other basic skills," she says. "Don't worry, you'll figure it out. Just remind yourself that every parent has to figure it out the first time. Did you bring an outfit for her to wear home?"

"Oh, yes." I reach into my bag and pull out a doll-size suit with embroidered ducks. And a matching hat with yellow fluff on top. My mother sent them from Italy last week. The child doesn't yet have a crib, doesn't even own a teddy bear, but by god, she can make a chic appearance on the streets of Rome. That's my mother for you.

"Bring her over here and you can change her," Keisha says.

"Bring her . . . ? Me?"

She laughs. "Yes, you, Mom. Stand up. You won't drop her."

Mom.

I scoot forward in the chair and successfully rise to my feet, both arms securely around my bundle. Not too hard. Then I look down at my bag on the floor. My eyes fill up again.

Keisha takes pity on me and picks up the bag. She leads the way back to our bin.

"Okay. I'm going to show you how to change her diaper, then you can dress her." She pulls the blanket open and unsnaps the hospital undershirt. I watch her every move as if it were surgery. I see how she supports the baby's head and guides her little arms. Then she opens the tabs on the ridiculously small diaper.

I look down and gasp.

"Oh my god, what is that? What's wrong? It's horrible! Will she live?"

For a moment, Keisha is nonplussed. Then she starts to laugh. "That's the umbilical cord stump, honey. Everyone's born with one. It will fall off in a week or so."

"*Fall off?* Are you sure that's normal?"

Keisha tries hard not to roll her eyes, and she almost succeeds. She finishes the diaper demonstration. "I'll get you a full set of booklets," she says. "And some handouts. And an emergency-number sheet. Now you get her dressed." She walks away. I almost call her back.

My daughter's eyes are still closed. I am becoming suspicious. Is she really sleeping, or is she afraid to look?

I regard the yellow and white suit in my hand. Two arms, two legs, and a long zipper. This simple garment suddenly seems extremely complicated.

Come on, Chloe. You can figure this out. Think of it as a very, very small slipcover.

I take a deep breath. Then another.

I unzip the suit, spread it open, and carefully edge the baby onto it. Her eyes are still closed. So far, so good.

Fifteen minutes later, I have coaxed all four tiny limbs into the correct openings. She is properly dressed and looks, if I may say so, adorable. Maybe I'll be okay after all. A drop of sweat rolls down my nose. I look around proudly for Keisha.

At that moment, I hear a sound like the tiniest cough and look down. Without ever opening her eyes, my baby scrunches up her face and begins to squall. It must be my fault, but what did I do?

"Keisha! Keisha!"

She's right there at my elbow. "Everyone okay here?"

"No, it's not okay! She's crying! Something is wrong! What's wrong?"

"Babies cry," she says imperturbably. "Get used to it. It's time for her feeding. I'll show you how we do that and you can feed her. Then we just have to wait for the discharge nurse to come through and you can take her home."

Home? By myself? I mean, I knew this was the plan, but everything's happening so quickly.

"Tonight?"

"Of course." She looks at me questioningly, and I realize it's time to pull it together.

"Right. Just checking." I focus my attention on what she's doing with the baby formula. I am intelligent and competent. A take-charge kind of person. Calm under pressure. Resourceful. I am a mother. I hold back my tears.

Back in the rocker, I touch the bottle's nipple to my baby's bottom lip, as instructed. She opens her mouth. I make a mental note to research—what's it called?—'gifted and talented.' The child is clearly advanced for her age. I hold this miracle baby close, watch her drink the bottle that I am holding.

She needs me. I need her.

And that's when it happens. I fall in love.

Nick

"NO TEXT?"

I wake up and shuffle into the kitchen to find Charlie in front of the fridge wearing only underwear, the quart of milk nearly vertical and upside down as he drinks straight from the container, his Adam's apple bobbing as he swallows. He looks like a Got Milk? ad.

"No text." I confirm.

Charlie finishes the milk, crumples the carton, and makes a three-point toss straight into the trash can, without touching the rim.

"I'm sure she's fine. Just busy."

"Guess I'll drink my coffee black," I mutter.

"We have another carton."

"We do?"

"I bought some yesterday."

I come to an abrupt halt, hand in midair with a spoon of coffee grounds in it. "You did? You mean you anticipated a future need and prepared for it?"

"Yes."

"Charlie! I'm impressed! Your frontal lobe is finally developing."

"You're welcome."

A few minutes later, as I pour milk into my coffee, I realize no one other than me has bought milk for the household in nearly twenty years. Even when Simone lived here, she hated American supermarkets, preferring to pay for delivery or going out to eat. Parisian women don't cook, they order in, she always insisted.

"I wonder what Chloe's going to be like as a mother." Charlie's statement takes all the breath out of me.

"Can we wait until after I've had my coffee before we put emotional bamboo under my fingernails?"

"She couldn't even keep a plant alive when we were dating," he adds. "I tried growing a pot plant from some seeds I found in your top dresser drawer when you were away at college, and—"

That wakes me up.

"You *what?*"

"I knew Mom would become suspicious if she saw me growing

something, so I asked Chloe to take care of it for me. Went to her house every day to tend to it. Then her mom took her to the Bahamas for a week of vacation and when she came back it was brown and withered." He sips my coffee. I slap him away.

"On the basis of that touching—and incredibly disturbing on so many levels—story, you've determined that Chloe's unfit for motherhood?"

"No. I'm just still sore about the fact that she killed my one and only successful grow op."

Not enough coffee in the world for this conversation.

"I'll wait for her," I say aloud as I finish my coffee. "When she's ready, she'll text."

"What if she's never ready?"

It's been three days. We've barely dated. How can someone I've barely begun dating make me ache so deeply?

Yeah.

Because she does.

That's all I need to know.

When Simone left, I filled the woman-sized hole inside me with every kid activity and work-related project I could find. As the kids have matured and left the nest, that hole's revealed itself. It's different. A more mature hole, more like a holding space than a blasted-open abyss.

It has purpose.

It has needs.

And right now, it's the exact shape, size, and volume of Chloe.

"Can't hurt to text her again, right?" I say.

He shrugs.

Shit. This is bad. I'm seeking validation from Charlie. His idea of a relationship involves paying for the Über.

I don't need advice. I'm decisive. I'm a take-charge guy.

What's new? I text her.

And wait.

Chloe

ONE HOUR LATER, we are standing in the bassinet aisle at Babies'R'Us, after an emergency stop for dinner. Apparently Jessica Coffin was right about the fine dining in my future. My first meal as a mother? A six-pack of chicken nuggets. And they were delicious, too.

It is 10:30 at night. I don't know why a baby superstore is open at this hour, but I am not questioning their retail logic. And we're not the only shoppers in here.

Jemma is pushing a cart loaded with a case of newborn-size diapers, a six-pack of bottles, packages of cotton receiving blankets, tiny T-shirts, and microscopic socks.

Also in the cart is a bottle of hypo-allergenic, organic baby massage oil. Henry insisted.

He is standing beside me, wiping his eyes with a tissue. He has been weeping since I filled out the birth certificate form, and he saw the baby's name.

Holliday Browne.

"Henry, please don't cry," I say, patting his arm.

"I can't help it," he sniffles. "You named her after us."

"Lucky for her your last name isn't Hooker," I smile. "Now can you reach that box on the top shelf?"

Of course he can. He's seven feet tall. In his stocking feet.

"I think that's all we need for now."

"I'll take it back to your place," Henry suggests. "I can set up the bassinet. Jem can go back to the hospital with you, and I'll come get you all when they say you can leave."

"You're exhausted," I tell them. "You both go home. I'll call you when we're ready."

We're heading for the checkout lane when I am stopped cold by a display of breast pumps.

"No, sweetie, you don't need one of those," Jem says gently.

"Li. Where is she? We have to find her!" I finally got someone to unofficially explain what the hell happened. A kind nurse swore me to secrecy. Li arrived in full labor in the emergency room. Had the baby in less than two hours. Our adoption social worker happened to be on another case in the hospital and stopped by to check on Li, who insisted on signing away all rights on the spot. While Yvonne told her she had time, Li was adamant. Yvonne and Kate produced the papers, and within hours, Li disappeared.

Just walked out into the streets of Boston, less than a day after giving birth. No explanation. No note. No nothing.

No—everything.

She left me *everything*.

"DSS and the police are looking for her," Henry says. "Don't worry."

"She could need a doctor! She's all alone! My God, Henry, she just gave birth! Where would she go? She's only sixteen!" I knew from talks with her that she was homeless, and while she swore she didn't do drugs . . .

Henry puts his hands on my shoulders.

"There is nothing official that you can do," he says slowly. "She's not your child."

"But her child is my child!"

"All we can do is wait. They'll find her."

I'll think of something.

I always do.

My phone buzzes with a text. I grab and look eagerly. It's my mother.

I need pictures! Now! What size would you say she is?

Tears fill my eyes. Pictures. My daughter. Her granddaughter.

And only Charlotte would lead with her dress size.

A baby squawks in the distance. Someone's shopping here with their baby. With their child. Soon I'll go out in public with my baby, the one back at the hospital, the one who's been abandoned by Li and entrusted into my care forever.

And ever.

Through the blur of tears, I see another text, this one from Nick.

Hah. Until a few hours ago, all I could think about was receiving this text. I tap.

What's new? is all it says.

Hysterical laughter pours out of me, right there in the aisle next to the baby gates and the window shades for cars.

"Chloe?" Jem asks softly.

I fold in half, hands on my knees, the phone sliding to the ground. Henry picks it up while Jemma says small, soothing words to me that don't make sense.

Henry looks at my phone and starts to laugh, too, a friendly sound of understanding.

And then my giggles tighten in my throat and turn into a stinging pain that shoots up my nose, into my eyes, and I'm sobbing in their arms, half-collapsed on the floor, a bundle of joy and fear and excitement and most of all—something new.

I am a mother.

"How—" I wail, "—do I answer that?"

Henry closes the screen and tucks the phone in the back pocket of his pants. "You don't. Not now. Nick can wait. Little Holliday Browne can't."

CHAPTER TWELVE

Chloe

FOR ALL THOSE years, in my dreams and daydreams of having a child, I always knew exactly what I was doing. And it was easy. Relaxed. Natural.

I imagined rides on the Swan Boats in the Public Gardens on sunny Saturday afternoons, reading bedtime stories and drinking cocoa in our pajamas, solving for x in algebra homework. (That's algebra, right? Or is it calculus? *Damn.*)

Oh, sure, I knew it wouldn't all be bliss and birthday cake. Tantrums happen in crowded stores, broken arms ruin ski trips. Teenagers make poor choices.

But through it all, I would be calm, capable, and maybe even wise. I would be A Mom.

So is there a certain time when all that maternal wisdom is going to kick in? Because it's two a.m., and I have absolutely no idea what I am supposed to do next.

Henry and Jemma brought us home an hour ago, and got us safely into the apartment. I am now sitting on my bed, watching Holly breathe in her bassinet. Occasionally there is the faint sound of a car passing on the street. Once I hear a siren in the distance.

I can't go to sleep, because who will watch her?

What if she wakes up? What if she doesn't wake up? Am I supposed to wake her up?

I could call my mother for advice, but waking *her* up is never a good idea.

Only one other expert comes to mind. I pick up my cell phone and type *www.whattoexpect*, which informs me that "For a newborn, three hours is about as long as you can expect him to sleep."

Okay. I'll wait.

Carefully, I gather up my sleeping baby. I settle back against the bed pillows, holding her in my arms.

"I'm here with you," I whisper. "I'll always be here with you. No matter what."

Except, when do I sleep?

When did my mother, Charlotte, sleep? My mother adopted me, all by herself, when I was just this small, and it wasn't such a common thing back then. What did she think about on her first night all alone with me? Was she scared, thrilled, awed, exhausted but wide awake? All of the above? Like me?

And my birth mother, who had to let me go so that I could have the blessed and secure life that I've had—was she like Li, young and alone? Does she ever wonder about me?

I've registered (secretly—Charlotte would be devastated if she knew) for every adoption registry out there. I'd love to meet my birth mother. Somewhere out there, people who look like me walk the streets, working at jobs, raising children, living life. I've never looked into the face of a parent or sibling who looks like me.

I wonder what that would be like.

I look at Holly.

If we can't find Li, my daughter will wonder, too.

Impulsively, I pick up my phone and dial Charlotte's number. The worst she can do is hang up on me, right?

"Hello?" It's a man's voice. My mother's boyfriend.

"Howard? It's Chloe." Without meaning to, I start to cry.

"Hi, darling, what's wrong?"

"Nothing, everything's wonderful," I sob. "I have the baby. Could I—is Charlotte there?"

"Of course sweetheart, hold on."

"Chloe? What is it?" My mother's voice is thick with sleep.

"Mom? I have the baby. She's here." Tears are streaming down my face. I haven't called her Mom since I was eight years old.

"Oh, honey. Oh, Chloe. I know. Are you all right?" I can tell she's waking up now.

"Mom, I don't know what I'm supposed to do!"

"All you have to do is feed her and change her. You don't need to worry about anything else right now. You don't need to play Mozart or read Shakespeare aloud. Try to sleep when she sleeps. Keep a little bib on her in case she spits up, because formula stains."

"But what if she cries and I don't wake up?"

"You will. It's instinctual. Don't worry."

"I was wondering . . . is this how you felt when you got me?"

There's a short silence as she thinks.

"I remember you were like a kitten. I remember that I brought you home in a pink snowsuit, and I had a new white coat, and I wore pink gloves. We looked adorable." She sighs with pleasure. "That was a really good day."

"You mean because my adoption finally went through and I was yours?"

"I mean I was having a really good hair day, so the photos were wonderful. I'll send you one. Howard, remind me to get out the pictures tomorrow."

"But were you scared? Did you know how to be a mother?"

"Well, we didn't worry so much about it then, you know. And my family was close by, in Newton. You remember going to Nana's house, and playing with your cousins."

"I do, but you weren't married either. Did you ever think you couldn't do it?"

"Chloe, I knew I could love you, and I knew that was all that really mattered. Just like you. You have all the love that baby needs." My mother is not the sentimental type, and as her voice softens with love, my throat tightens, squeezing out more tears.

I hear myself say, "I was thinking maybe you could come up

and visit? You could bring the pictures with you."

She pauses. I hear her breathing.

Her voice is tight. "Of course, sweetie."

The tightness is from tears. She sniffles.

My own come pouring out with hers. I need her now more than I ever have.

"Let me check my schedule and choose a time that doesn't interfere with golf."

Right.

"And Howard will be devastated if I leave him for too long."

Of course.

"This is your only daughter and granddaughter, Charlotte!" Howard's voice slips through the phone like aromatherapy, soothing and commanding at the same time. "Take all the time you need."

I love Howard.

"It's settled, then," my mother announces. "I shall come and rescue you."

I break out in a cold sweat and smile at the same time.

THE MEETING TO review the goSpa specs would normally make me as excited as talking about the difference between taupe and beige with interior designers, but this one is different. Chloe will be present.

She hasn't answered my texts, and I'm wondering why. Charlie urged me to call, but I'm not going to call when she won't even reply to a text. Dating rituals in the age of instant communication are more complicated than small-town politics, and about as painful, even if the stakes are higher.

The room fills slowly with the major stakeholders, including me, Anterdec's budget director for special projects, Diane Geary from accounting, Amanda Warrick, and my long-time assistant, Marisol. Twice divorced, she's my age, and a modern woman in every way, including keeping her mouth shut at work about her sex life.

In a corporate environment, where buzzwords engender off-site retreats and mission statements can take seven figures and seven months to develop before being kicked back by legal, the sex lives of cubicle dwellers is a treasured diversion for office talk.

Rare is the staff member who remains discreet.

When Mari finally arrives, she gives Diane and me a perplexed look, setting down a box of donuts and a cardboard four-pack of coffees, one marked with my name.

"I'm so sorry, everyone. But Chloe Browne had to cancel."

My gut tightens. "Why?"

"Maternity leave."

Diane's eyebrows shoot up. "Where is she hiding a baby? She's tiny. Does she have hollow legs?"

"Adoption," I mutter. "She's adopting."

"Oh." Diane folds her lips in, over her teeth, as if she's embarrassed. She shouldn't be. She couldn't know.

"But the baby's not due for two months or so," I add.

Diane and Mari give me an appraising look.

"I—we talked about it during a business meeting."

Amusement flashes in both sets of eyes. Mari knows I haven't dated in ages. When I ran my own company, it was a running joke. Brother Nick, the Monk.

Having Anterdec colleagues call me Focus Man is an upgrade.

I force myself into cold mode. "Fine. We'll just postpone the project until she's back."

"Good," Diane says. "It's a bizarre one, anyhow. A spa in an RV?"

"You saw the numbers. Great PR."

She taps a folder in front of her and nods. "I know. Numbers don't lie. I trust them over people." She clearly expects me to smile.

I don't.

Mari is used to it, laughing with Diane. Both have dark hair and dark eyes, with curvy figures, though Mari's personality is vitality in human form, while Diane is the epitome of buttoned-up. Mari's business attire runs toward flowing skirts and bright colors, chunky jewelry and layered hair.

Diane looks like a British nanny, hair pulled back in a tight bun, red lips severe.

I don't generally evaluate the women I work with like this. I'm not an actual monk, so my head does turn on occasion, but not with these women. Not in this environment. Every woman I encounter these days catches my eye as I compare them to Chloe.

Chloe wins.

Every damn time.

"Great. Now we have a dozen donuts and four lattes left over," Mari complains.

"I'm sure someone will scavenge if we put them in the employee lounge," Diane says, taking a Boston Cream donut for herself. She flashes Mari a guilty grin. "Thanks."

"No problem." Mari pats her hip. "If they stay on my desk, they'll just end up here."

I walk out of the room, the conversation a blur, as I wonder why Chloe never answered my last text.

Which was, ironically enough, the question, "What's new?"

What's new.

I make my way to my office, so numb, the hot coffee in my hand feels cold. Closing my door, I start pacing, mind spinning, blood racing suddenly.

Baby. She had the baby.

Or, rather, the birth mother did. Chloe told me a bit about her. Homeless teen on the streets. Met her during a volunteer stint with the gO Spa RV. The story sounded crazy when Chloe told it, and I had my doubts.

I was wrong, apparently.

The coffee burns my throat as I swallow, and I choke, forced to feel something tangible, some specific sensation that cuts through the blurring rush of too many conclusions I'm jumping to, too many emotions pouring through me.

Damn it.

Why didn't she answer my text?

Is this a brush off? As my kids would say, am I being "ghosted"?

It's not like I can go on Reddit and ask someone the modern dating protocol for what to do when the woman you're with suddenly adopts a baby and doesn't return texts.

I'm pretty sure this is a one-off.

Besides, if she ghosts on me, I'm stuck with over a thousand dollars worth of sex toys and crap from her ex-lover.

I'm also pretty sure I'm screwing up this whole dating thing.

"Think," I mutter. "Think, Nick. What does Chloe *want?*" Memories of her body, under me, over me, the way she tastes during that second kiss, the one where lips part and tongues speak with more authenticity, flood my body, becoming a new pulse, telling me the truth between us.

And then I remember the baby.

Chloe is a *mother.*

Dating? I don't understand the language of dating.

But I speak fluent Parenthood.

Those first few days with a baby are like being handed an octopus and a hand grenade without the pin at the same time you're blindfolded on roller blades. And deprived of any sleep.

Poor Chloe.

My laugh echoes through my office as I remember the first few hours of managing twin newborns.

And yet.

And yet . . . she hasn't reached out.

Bzzz.

I grab my phone like it's a life preserver.

It's Jean-Marc, with a text:

Maman says the divorce decree puts you in charge of paying 100% for my study-abroad fees, Dad. The coordinator said you still owe $500 for *next year's Geneva semester. Sorry, dude.*

Right.

Fluent in parenting.

Lately, my fluency involves currency more than anything.

Opening my laptop, I navigate the NYU bursar's office page and take care of Jean-Marc's bill, deeply torn, wondering why Chloe hasn't sent a text.

A simple text.

I know those first few days are hard, but . . . nothing?

Not one word.

CHAPTER THIRTEEN

Chloe

DAY ONE WITH Charlotte. The countdown begins.

The doorbell rings. Jemma goes to answer it.

"Your grandmother is here," I inform the baby. "Don't spit up, poop, cry, or draw too much attention to yourself. I'm just sayin'."

She studies me intently. She poops.

Sigh.

"You are not off to a good start," I tell her, reaching for the baby wipes. One of her eyes is crossed and she doesn't focus. She fusses as if I've inconvenienced her with this diaper change.

I can hear my mother's voice. She is telling Jemma about the flight.

"Air travel is just not what it used to be," Charlotte's saying. "Have you *seen* what people wear on airplanes? Sweat pants! In first class!"

"Shocking," Jem murmurs. "Awful."

"Even the stewardesses are wearing flats!" Charlotte is outraged.

"Um, I don't think they're called stewardesses anymore," Jemma says, but Charlotte doesn't even hear her.

"I need a martini," my mother announces. "Grey Goose. Two olives."

Silence.

"Please," she adds, like a toddler who has been coached, but who uses the word only as a last resort.

There is a slight pause, and I hear the freezer open. Even feisty Jemma knows that Charlotte must be served. It's just easier that way.

"And where is my granddaughter?"

"Right here," I answer.

Holly, once again clean and sweet smelling, is dressed for the occasion in a tiny white Jacadi bubble suit that Charlotte sent last month from Paris. It has pale blue piping and a ruffled collar, and it probably cost about as much as my last new dress. The difference is that Holly will wear hers maybe twice before she grows out of it.

But she looks undeniably adorable.

Charlotte holds out her arms, and I carefully transfer Holly into them. For a long, quiet moment, the two of them inspect each other.

"Miss Holliday Browne," my mother says softly. "I am very pleased to meet you. I am your grandmother. You may call me Mimi."

Jem gives me the side-eye. "How appropriate," she says sweetly.

There are three martini glasses on the counter. I take one. I'm going to need it.

My mother appears to notice me for the first time.

"Chloe, you look tired."

"Well," I smile, perhaps too brightly, "new baby. Not much sleep for the past week. I'm so glad you're here to help, Mom."

"My bags are by the door," she says. "You can put them in my room."

Right. Will do.

"Okay, then," Jemma begins, standing up. "I can see I'm leaving Chloe and Holly in good hands, so I'll just be getting home to Henry. Thank you for the martini. The T is so much more endurable after a cocktail."

"Oh Jem," I say, with some urgency, "Oh Jem. Why don't you

stay a little while longer? Wouldn't you like another drink? After all, it's Friday . . . isn't it? Don't go yet."

She continues gathering her things. I follow her to the door, alternately pleading, bribing, and threatening.

"Jemma, let's call Henry and he can meet us here. We'll get takeout from the tapas place you love. Just stay for dinner, Jem, and I'll come over when Henry's parents visit! I'll take them to a museum for an entire afternoon!"

She looks at me sympathetically, but keeps buttoning her coat.

"Chloe, it will be fine," she says firmly. "Charlotte is here to help. Get some rest. Take a nap."

"Ha," I reply bitterly. "They'll be napping. I'll be doing their laundry. You know how it always goes."

"First thing in the morning, send Charlotte off to shop on Newbury Street," she advises. "You won't see her for the rest of the day. Especially now that she has Holly to shop for, too."

Charlotte calls from the kitchen.

"Chloe? I need to lie down before you make dinner. Come take the baby."

"See?" I hiss at Jemma.

"And I need to unpack," Charlotte continues. "A few of my things are going to need to be ironed. Where shall I put them?"

I hear Holly start to fuss, tentatively.

Jemma waves her fingers and slips out the door.

"Chloe?" my mother calls. "She's crying."

Right.

When I walk back into the kitchen, Holly is quietly sucking on my mother's manicured pinky finger.

Charlotte's martini glass is in front of her on the counter, about two-thirds empty. She looks at me innocently. Way too innocently. I narrow my eyes.

"Mom. You wouldn't," I start. "You wouldn't give vodka to a tiny baby . . . ?"

My mother removes her finger from the baby's mouth, stands,

and hands Holly over to me. The baby looks surprised, then her little face wrinkles up in outrage. She turns bright red. She's too little to make much noise, but she's giving it her all. With my spare hand, I get a bottle of infant formula out of the fridge.

Charlotte, meanwhile, has topped off her glass. She picks it up and heads out of the room, leaving behind a cloud of Chanel No. 5. Her signature scent.

I cough. Quietly, I hope.

She reappears in the door. "The sooner I can unpack, the less ironing there will be," she says, and disappears again. My mother is nothing if not considerate.

It's going to be a very long two weeks.

I reach for my phone and check for texts.

Nothing.

♥ ♥ ♥

DAY TWO WITH Charlotte.

Holly was hungry at 1:00 a.m., 4:00 a.m., and 6:30. At 7:15 a.m., she finally falls peacefully to sleep. I stagger into the kitchen and start the coffee maker. Which I loaded last night in anticipation of this desperate moment. I drag a counter stool over to the machine and sit watching each life-giving drop fall as if it were an IV drip in intensive care.

It is, actually. Except I'm giving the intensive care instead of getting it.

There's a distinct smell of Chanel No. 5. I jump.

"Good morning," Charlotte says. She is wearing a light cotton robe in a lavender animal print. In which jungle, exactly, are there lavender ocelots? Her slippers have tulle pompoms on the toes.

They also have kitten heels. I guess that's appropriate?

She is wearing crystal drop earrings. And lipstick. Her ash-blonde hair is pulled up in a twist.

I am wearing a grey hoodie from college. My hair has not been washed in three days. I could lubricate machinery with it.

"Is the coffee ready?" she continues. "I didn't hear the coffee grinder. You did grind the beans fresh, didn't you, dear? Is there low-fat milk? Organic?"

I don't answer.

"Chloe? Is there low-fat milk? You know I'm not a breakfast eater, but are there any of those hazelnut biscotti from that bakery in the North End? I need a little extra energy this morning. You woke me up three times last night, turning on lights and banging around in the kitchen. Broken sleep makes it very difficult for the human brain to function."

I take deep, cleansing breaths. They don't help. She's still there.

"Really, Mom?" I start. "Lack of sleep causes problems?"

At that moment, the coffee maker hisses and sends up a cloud of steam. I bite my tongue.

Be nice, Chloe.

She came all the way from Florida to help. She is missing the monthly dinner dance at the club. She is sacrificing her Wednesday golf game. She has left her boyfriend, Howard, in Palm Beach.

Howard is 78. Or so he says. He adores my mother. She refuses to marry him, or even move in with him, so he bought the condo next door to hers. He likes to keep an eye on her.

Maybe he'd like to keep a close eye and visit us.

Now.

"Coffee's ready," I announce. "There is milk. There are no biscotti, but there are cinnamon crackers."

"Oh," she says. "Oh. Maybe you could get some today. It would be a nice outing for you and the baby."

It is going to be 95 degrees today, with ninety-eight percent humidity. The word they are using on weather.com is *oppressive*.

A trip on the T with a newborn baby to the North End of Boston to buy Italian cookies for my mother, who is supposed to be easing my exhaustion as I adjust to motherhood, is not a "nice outing." It is a slow, suffocating cattle car to the first circle of hell. And back.

"Well," I answer, gritting my teeth, "maybe." Tomorrow. I can stall until tomorrow. My mother is easily distracted. If I dangle a different shiny idea in front of her, she will give me a twenty-four-hour reprieve.

"And now," she says, in martyred tones, "why don't you just rest? I'll take the baby for you."

The baby has been asleep for half an hour. According to her daily pattern, she will be asleep for another two hours.

"Thanks, Mom."

"Honey?" she adds, as I head to the shower, "In case you're going to do any hand-washing, I left a few fine unmentionables by your sink."

I check my phone for texts. Nothing.

Nothing from anyone.

Nothing from Nick.

Nick

"DUDE, YOU GOT a package," Charlie announced, tossing it lightly in his arms before handing it off to me. "From some place called Never Liked It Anyway?"

I groan. "Damn." Work involved fourteen hours of conference calls and team meetings to debate the intellectual property implications of using a logo with a mark that was just close enough to a major sportswear company's signature logo. Fourteen hours of lawyers and designers and clients going head to head.

I'm about to find out if I own enough beer to make this day go away.

"Is that the strap-on?" Charlie asks.

I huff. "Open it if you want."

"I don't exactly want to open it." Charlie contemplates the seemingly-innocent white box with a broken red heart and piles of money as the logo. "But I gotta admit I'm curious."

"Right. Like watching presidential primary debates."

"Exactly." His face lights up.

I undo my tie, shrug out of my suit jacket, and enjoy the blast of cold that hits me when I open the fridge.

No beer.

"Charlie," I say in a low growl. "Where's the beer?"

He smacks his forehead. "I knew I forgot to do something today!"

"What else were you supposed to do in your incredibly jam-packed schedule?" I'm sure he didn't forget the all-important two o'clock nap.

"I was helping Amelie." One of the most endearing—and annoying as hell—qualities in Charlie is his Teflon-like ability to let other people's anger roll off him. Most people absorb whatever people around them radiate.

Charlie doesn't.

I envy him.

Until *I'm* the person whose anger—justifiably pointed at him—rolls off his back.

"Let's go for a walk. I'll be your pack mule."

"My what?"

"My bad. I forgot. Let's go to the store and get some beer. I'll carry it. You look like you could use a walk, Nick. Your shoulders are around your ears."

"Wait. You were helping Amelie? With what?"

"Her concert."

"Which concert?"

"The one Simone's coming home for."

Coming home and *Simone* don't sit well in the same sentence.

"That's not for a while, Charlie."

"Right. But Amelie wants it to be perfect."

The last thing I need today is more confusion. I grab the house keys and start for the door. "Fine, Pack Mule. Let's go. I'm loading up on Sea Belt and red sour ales."

Charlie flexes his arms, showing off guns. His t-shirt's torn and he's wearing Celtics green basketball shorts. He looks like he hasn't showered in days. "Great. Bring it on."

"And it's your turn to buy."

"No prob."

We're halfway down the block when I reluctantly ask. "What do you mean, 'no prob'? You wouldn't be couch surfing at my place if money were 'no prob.'"

"Bitcoin investment paid off. Some guy—"

"Oh, god, Charlie." If I let him, the next five blocks to the liquor store will be dominated by talks about cryptocurrency and undervalued Second Life Linden dollars, along with some other currency called Ether.

"What? I made a few grand."

"Regained what you lost?"

"Yep. Broke even."

"Congrats. When are you getting a job? A real one."

"I have one!"

"One that involves actual income. Not a business that lives in your MacAir."

"Hey—this is how I want to live. I don't have kids tying me down. Don't care about stuff. Why does it bother you so much, Nick?"

Good question.

"You *choose* to be the corporate slave," he adds.

Here we go. Same old conversation. Charlie the free spirit vs. Nick the drone.

"My kids' college tuition is my form of indentured servitude."

"But that ends soon. You won't need all the board meetings and the endless talk about logos and the secretary who dominates the coffee machine and the asshole above you who specializes in Six Sigma like it's a cult. You can sell everything and live a tetherless life."

"My kids are my tether, Charlie."

"But things don't have to be."

"Is this the point in the conversation where I start sounding like Dad? I can never remember my lines. Got a script?" We're at the liquor store now, the pneumatic door opening before I can bash it with my tense arms, and as we walk down the warehouse-like aisles, Charlie is on my heels.

"Look, Nick, I've watched you sacrifice everything for the kids. And you're a good father. The best damn dad I've ever seen. Even better than ours."

I stop short. That's high praise.

"And he'd have been proud of you."

Damn it. The bridge of my nose tingles. I pinch it, blinking. Haven't changed my contacts since I got up at 5 a.m. Eyes are dry and scratchy. My throat starts to close. Dusk settles in outside. My day has been filled with nothing but tension and conflict, indecision and complaints.

And that's just work.

And then I sigh.

"Where's the Red Poppy Ale?" I am not having an emotional landmine-filled conversation with my shiftless little brother in the lager aisle at the local liquor store.

"Why do you want that crap? Get Jack's Abbey instead."

Now we're on even more familiar territory.

"I like Flemish red sour ales, Charlie."

"You have the taste buds of an eighty-year-old nun, Nick."

"Glad you're buying and that you're the pack mule." I hand him four four-packs. He grins.

And then I pick out two six-packs of Jack's Abbey.

The grin falters.

"Nick, you're not—"

"Pack mules don't argue, Charlie, they just figure out how to carry the burden."

"That's you, man."

That's been me. True. For fifteen years, I've adjusted to

whatever life's thrown my way, as long as it didn't involve emotional involvement.

Chloe's now about as emotionally involved as anyone can be.

Do I want to reset the clock? They're a package deal. Chloe and the baby. I know that.

Oh, how I know that.

Charlie buys my beer without comment and struggles under the weight of the huge cardboard box filled with beer. I enjoy my freedom, stretching as we walk.

"You're right, Charlie." I take mercy and grab two six-packs from the box. He squares his shoulders with relief.

"How'm I right?"

"Freedom. It has a different feel."

"Different good, or different bad?"

That's the question.

Which is it?

Five minutes later, we're back home, beers open, Charlie cutting the tape on the Never Liked It Anyway box.

He pulls out a blue strap-on.

"Aw, man. Nick, you have a First Aid kit somewhere, right? I need latex gloves to touch this."

I take the box out of his hands and reach in.

"Jesus!" I shout. "That dildo has to be twelve inches long!"

"Chloe always was uninhibited in bed."

I throw it at his face. Years of pitching baseball in high school pay off as the end of the wiggly rubber dildo slaps Charlie flat against his nose, like a musketeer's loose glove being used to challenge a man to a duel.

"Nick!" he screams.

"Don't you talk about sex with Chloe."

He looks at the strap on resting at a crooked angle on the ground, then at me, mouth gaping. Charlie points down. "You just threw the strap on she used on her ex-lover at my face. That's the epitome of talking about sex with Chloe. Plus you almost broke my nose!"

"Charlie." I'm being irrational. I know it.

I don't care.

A vision of her using it on—

No.

Nope.

Not going there.

"Technically," I declare, "the auction never said she used it on him."

Charlie just laughs.

I stand abruptly, knocking over the rest of the items in the box, which include a Coldplay t-shirt, some Cashmere sweaters in a size too small for me, the Dave Brubaker vinyl album (which I might keep), the Rush album (which Charlie claims dibs on), a nice Rolex my son could enjoy, and Montblanc pens that are better suited for James McCormick than anyone else in the world.

Joe has also added a tube of warming gel, a non-fiction historical monograph on sodomy and pirates (signed by the author), a mood ring made for a man's ring size, a small polished Zen rock with the word Patience etched into it, some t-shirts, and a set of Buckyballs.

He's random, if nothing else.

"You paid over a grand for this shit," Charlie says with a low whistle, palming the Rush album as I leave the room, marching down the hall into my bedroom, furiously changing into a t-shirt and running shorts.

I ignore him and come out into the living room, finding my running shoes by the door, throwing them on.

"What are you doing?"

"Going for a run."

"Nick, you haven't gone for a run since the kids were toddlers."

"Maybe that's what freedom's all about. Discovering new things."

"The only new thing you want to discover is Chloe, man."

I nearly hit him. I do. I come so close when our eyes meet and he leans away. I walk past him, slam the door, and go for my first run in years.

The only problem is that I'm not sure what I'm running away from.

Or *to*.

CHAPTER FOURTEEN

Chloe

D AY THREE WITH Charlotte.
   "You girls have fun!" Charlotte chirped, as we struggled
   out the door this morning. "Get some of the almond biscotti,
and some of the chocolate dipped. And some anise flavored."

"While we're gone, Mom, do you think you could maybe unload the dishwasher?"

"Well, I would, of course," she said, "but I don't know where
you keep things. It would just make more work for you. I'm going
to call Howard. I forgot my email password. He'll know what it is."

Everyone should have a Howard. I need a Howard.

"Then this afternoon, you can take me to O. I need one of
those stress-reduction treatments—the two-hour full-body massage with herb-infused lotions and ambient sound from a dolphin's
womb. And the rosemary mint martini in the sippy cup." Her eyes
glazed over. "I need a break from all this stress."

"Right. Maybe," I answered.

That was half an hour ago.

And here I am, in the middle of Boston Summer Soup, wearing a baby who is not much more than a tiny octopus tucked into a
diaper.

"Don't talk to strangers," I instruct Holly, who is tucked into a
Baby Bjorn on my chest, tuft of straight jet-black hair tickling my
chin. "Be aware of what's going on around you. Mind the gap."

The T train is pulling up. Please god let the air conditioning be working.

The doors slide open, and *yes!* The temperature inside is at least five degrees below unbearable.

I hoist the folded stroller and hitch the diaper bag up on my shoulder. I stagger onto the train.

On the T now, I spot two empty seats and sink down gratefully, the stroller propped up on the railing next to me. Holly is quiet. I pull out my phone.

Hi Howard, I type. *Hope all is well. I know you must be missing Charlotte.*

Three dots, wiggling.

Hi honey, Howard responds. *Is she getting to you already?*

Oh no, I type back. *It's great. I just think we're stressing her out. Not good for her.*

I'm on it.

That's all he says. I love Howard.

My phone pings. It's Charlotte this time: *Chloe, just so you know, the cat box needs changing.*

I look at Holly, who catches my eye, eyebrows raising as if she's taken aback as well.

Solidarity. My daughter and I are one.

"Let's get out of here," I whisper, grabbing the stroller.

Holly replies with a fist punch into thin air, followed by a spectacular belch that I feel.

I feel it because that's not just a burp. The space between the Baby Bjorn and my only clean T-shirt is now a war zone.

We are home by noon, sweaty and exhausted, with two white paper bags containing three dozen Italian biscotti. Tucked into the diaper bag is a can of ground espresso, a pound of fresh handmade linguine, and a small plastic Madonna that the shopkeeper pressed on me when he saw Holly.

When you work in an office, you have no idea how long a weekday really is. It should be dinner time by now.

My mother sweeps into the kitchen, beaming.

"Wonderful news!" she trills. "Howard is on his way. He said he couldn't be without me one day longer."

I smile. "That *is* wonderful news. I'll make up the other bed."

She smiles back. "Oh, no, dear. We'll need to use your bed. After all, there are two of us and only one of you."

Right.

Although technically, there are now two of me.

Nick

Congratulations, I type. It doesn't convey what I feel, but it will have to do. I'm done with ambiguity.

Screw indecision.

I know what I want.

I hit Send. I start to turn off my phone, but the finality is too much. I set it down, face up.

I stare at the pile of papers on my home office desk. It is noon, and I have a massive proposal due tomorrow, complete with a contract that needs to be pounded out for final negotiations. Legal already went over the portions they need to review. My turn to figure out the rest.

If I bury myself in work, I can give myself hours of hope. Not hope, exactly, but something more than this grinding ambiguity that turns my gut into a barbed wire fence. At best, Chloe will reply sometime today.

Or never.

A black plastic bag with a slim tome in it taunts me. Yesterday, I went to the Harvard Book Store and bought Chloe's baby the best children's book ever.

Walter the Farting Dog.

Simone hated that book.

I smile at the memory.

Movement on my fading phone screen catches my eye. Three dots.

Three beautiful, sophisticated, exceptionally delicious

Chloe-flavored dots.

Thank you, she texts back. *Sorry for not replying sooner.*

The phone is a football in my hands, and I'm fumbling at the goal line. It lands on the carpet. I pounce.

How is the baby? What's its name? I reply.

Her name is Holly. She's perfect.

You're perfect, I almost type back. Sheer force of will stops me.

I'm sure she is, I answer, smiling as I tap out the words. I remember babymoons. *Welcome to the wonderful world of daughters. Start saving now. Justin Bieber obsessions aren't cheap.*

I hit Send and stare at the screen. A physical ache builds between my ribs. The space inside me where Chloe belongs is empty. I wonder if she has holes inside her shaped like me.

I'd like to be in that hole.

I grimace. That's not what I meant.

And yet . . .

Minutes pass. No reply. Shit.

Twenty minutes pass and I realize I am no better than my teenagers, breathlessly waiting for the next Snapchat post from a crush.

With a sigh, I return to work, happy to have some communication with Chloe. At least we "talked." She knows I'm here. She can find me when she's ready.

If she's ever ready.

The words on the first contract in front of me blur. I feel my pulse in my eyes. The first delivery date for five designs is egregiously soon. *Slash.* The terms for failure to deliver are draconian.

Slash.

I need to take out my frustration somewhere.

My red pen's half empty by the time I make it through the twenty-nine pages of this mess.

Bzzzz.

I leap across the desk and read:

sorry. diaper blow out. typing one fingered with baby on arm

God, I want to see her. I take the leap.

I'd love to meet her, I type.

An eternity passes in the form of one minute. Then two. Five. Finally:

Tn8?

I'm reasonably fluent in textspeak, but this is a new one.

Yes, tonight, I reply, assuming.

k

Tn8 and *k* are my new favorite words.

I've got it bad.

CHAPTER FIFTEEN

Nick

"**U**TTERLY INAPPROPRIATE BABY gift?" Charlie asks, as if we are in a countdown.

"Check." I humor him.

"Her ex's strap-on dildo you bought for her on an online auction site where people assume she's a porn star?"

I frown. He's not wrong, technically.

"Check," I say softly, tapping the table next to the box in question for emphasis, jaw tight.

"Condoms?"

"Charlie," I growl.

"What? I was about to ask if you'd choked the chicken in advance so you don't jump the gun when you finally do the two-backed nasty, but I thought that was little too personal."

"Thank you for your exquisite tact." I shoot him a sour look. "And all those mixed metaphors."

He shrugs. "So?"

"So what?"

"Did you?" He makes a *hmph* sound in the back of his throat, the noise suggestive and inquisitive at the same time.

A perfect encapsulation of my brother.

"None of your business."

He grins. "Smart man." He frowns. "Unless being old changes that."

"Changes what?"

He lowers his voice. "Maybe instead of worrying about jumping the gun, you need Viagra?" He gives me a once-over. "You are six and a half years older than me. Plumbing changes." He frowns, looking down at his own pipe.

My response makes me realize where Elodie got her eye roll.

"No." Hell, no. Hell, no on many levels. "I'm going to meet a newborn, Charlie. Not sleep with her mother."

"Babies nap. You could have a little afternoon delight."

"Babies also wake up and scream bloody murder. Trust me. I know this. Simone and I should have named Jean-Marc 'cockblocker.'"

Charlie's in the middle of a swig of ginger ale. He begins choking.

I grin.

"Wait 'til you have kids."

"It'll be a long wait," he gasps.

My front door opens, and in walks a giant black hole whose gravitational pull yanks at my wallet.

"Speak of the devil," Charlie says, as my youngest chucks a hockey-sized bag across my threshold, his face buried in a phone screen.

"Dad?" Jean-Marc doesn't look up. "Can you help me with that?"

Charlie grabs the bag, then gets yanked back to the floor. "Jesus, JM! Or should I call you CB?"

I give Charlie a dirty look.

He winks back. "What's in there? Gold?"

"Close. Textbooks. A bunch of my new friends weren't patient enough for the buy-back at the university bookstore, so I paid them out. Need to list them online at a profit and make bank next semester."

Says the kid who cries poor all the time.

He finally finishes his business online and approaches me for a hug. Jean-Marc is dark like Simone, but with a Grafton male body, which means tall and lean. He's a good two inches taller than me now. Did the kid grow in the last two months?

"How's school?" I ask, realizing my cheek is brushing something on his chin that approximates a beard. He's only been at NYU for a handful of weeks. There are no grades.

He pulls back and laughs, blue eyes like mine practically glowing. "Straight A's so far." He shoots me a defiant look. "I didn't give permission for you to see them, by the way. You know about this law called FERPA?"

"Yes. You're eighteen now. I don't have the legal right to see your grades unless you give permission."

"Cool, huh?"

"Saved my ass when I was an undergrad," Charlie says.

"You got into Yale Law, Charlie." Jean-Marc says with a worshipful tone. Haven't heard that directed toward me since he was eleven.

"Yep. Bor-ing. Who wants to spend their days in classes and research, all cooped up in a . . ." Charlie's voice fades out as he catches my eye. "I mean, great job with the 4.0." He winks at my son.

Jean-Marc laughs, then looks at me. "Who's the present for?"

Before I can answer, Charlie says, "Your dad's girlfriend's new baby."

My son frowns. "Girlfriend? Baby? I go away for a few weeks and everything changes. Do I have a little sister now?"

I cock one eyebrow, gut clenching. I know he's joking, but the teasing puts me on edge in a disarming way. "No need to play dumb. Elodie told you."

"No. Amelie did." He laughs. "Elodie chased you down in bed with a chick. Amelie won't let her live it down."

"Woman. Not chick."

He shrugs.

"And she has a brand-new baby?" His look makes it clear he thinks I've gone off the deep end.

He might be right.

"Adopted. In the last two weeks. The adoption was in the planning stages for a long time before we met. She's a single mother by choice."

"Oh." The corners of his eyes and mouth drop down in a contemplative look. "Makes sense. Is that the baby gift?" He takes the wrapped book out of my hands, then grins, looking like a little boy for a split second. "It isn't . . . ?"

"It is."

"*Walter the Farting Dog*. Spreading the joy of flatulent canines to a new generation." His eyes meet mine, nostalgia and memory reflecting back like sunlight on a prism.

And then: "Anyone using the washing machine?"

The moment has passed.

"Nope. It's all yours," Charlie declares, gesturing like a model on a game show.

"You gone all night, Dad?" Hope blossoms in my chest. He's asking to spend time with me.

"No. I'll be back after dinner."

"Cool. Board game?"

"Cards Against Humanity?" Charlie asks with an eagerness that makes me groan. "I'll make nachos."

"Sure." I'll suffer through my brother's perverted card combinations if it means time with my son.

"See you tonight." His back retreats down the hallway. I hear shuffling sounds, then the water turns on for the laundry.

"Have fun," Charlie says, laughing. "Remember when the height of his day was sitting on the sofa, being read to?"

I look at my kid, whose size-fourteen shoes now litter the shoe rack, longer than mine.

"Like it was yesterday."

Because it was.

♥ ♥ ♥

THE ENTIRE DRIVE over to Chloe's place in Cambridge feels like someone has a radio dial in my head and is hitting the Scan button over and over. So many words. So many thoughts.

Not enough kissing.

I'm not sure what I'm supposed to feel right now. I miss her. More than I have any right to admit.

I admire her. The kind of woman who decides what she wants and doesn't wait for someone else to make it happen is appealing. Simone expected me to make her happy. Demanded that I take charge of her emotional state. Insisted that I was responsible for whether she had a good life or not.

Years later, I know she's wrong. Hell, I knew it back then, too.

Meeting Chloe just confirms it. Sophisticated, genuine, smart, funny, and sensual as hell, she's the whole package.

And now she comes with a ten-day-old newborn attached.

Different package.

A Masshole with a Second Amendment bumper sticker next to a gay pride rainbow cuts me off at Western Avenue, my laughter at the cognitive dissonance a welcome break.

Can two wildly disparate ideas truly co-exist?

Maybe on a car bumper, sure.

But in real life?

Lady Luck is with me as I slide into an easy parking spot down the block from Chloe's place. Maybe it's a message, as Elodie would say. A sign. A manifestation of deep wishes.

Or maybe it's just someone running out for an errand and the timing's right.

I grab my gift, leaving the shoebox filled with Chloe's past with her ex in the backseat, ready to give it to her when the time is right. She's now less than a block away and I can't tolerate the distance. Must close it.

Must smell her. Taste her. Look at her with hungry eyes.

And meet her new life.

My old life is back at my house, doing laundry and playing

Pokemon Go.

The road Chloe lives on is neat, with condos galore, most of the building fronts containing gardens and neatly-manicured yards. Bushes trimmed and outlined, mulch and multi-colored blooming plants, and stars that are painted the right colors all feed into the image of a neighborhood for people who live in Cambridge for all the right reasons.

As I hit the buzzer for Chloe's front door, I hear the unmistakable sound of rushing footsteps, trying to keep the peace. Chloe opens the door and looks at me with a thousand-watt smile. My heart speeds up, my hands tightening on the gift in my hands, and then she's in my arms, pressing against my chest, my hands desperate to find more of her in the embrace.

"You're here! She's sleeping," Chloe whispers, her breath hot on my neck. I kiss her cheek with a gentle *hello* that feels like everything and nothing.

As she lets go, we pull back slightly, catching each other's eyes, her hands on my forearms, brushing against my tight arms, fingertips turning me tense with desire.

I inhale, catching a sweet citrusy smell. And baby powder.

Strange combo.

"I'm so glad you—"

Without thinking, I kiss her, my palm splayed against the base of her spine, covering her sacrum, my hands hot and grateful for the way she melts into the kiss. Her palms press against my shoulders, then ride up my chest, to the nape of my neck. I breathe hard, her intoxicating presence making me forget all my earlier confusion.

The compartment in my mind that allows me to be Nicholas Grafton, director of branding for a Fortune 500 company, boss to more than twenty employees, father to three young adults, good citizen and decent brother, feels hollow, woefully empty and false as my kiss with Chloe turns into a series of touches and breaths, tongues searching, lips warm and minty, her cheek burning against my clean-shaven face, my fingers on the fine bones of her spine as she molds against me.

This isn't just about sexual attraction, of which there is plenty. A sense of completion consumes me as the fire we ignite burns and burns. Her body is mine as my fingertips press into her ass, anchored by her body. Having her in my arms for the first time in weeks, the box inside me designed to be filled with love feels occupied. Full.

Love.

I pause.

Chloe breaks the kiss, panting, looking up at me through long lashes, her lipstick intact though slightly blurred on her upper lip.

"You sure do know how to greet a woman," she says with a saucy smile.

"You make it very easy," I say, pulling her close again, taking the plunge. "I missed you." My breath mingles in her hair, making her shiver, her neck smooth as I press my lips against the hollow beneath her ear. She feels good. Real and raw.

"Me, too," she murmurs, hand on my hip, fingers hooking into my belt loop. The gesture is so casual and deceptively simple.

"Chloe?" A man's voice, older and filled with an elegant gravel sound, comes from Chloe's kitchen.

"That's my mother's boyfriend, Howard. Come in and meet everyone."

I hook my arm around her waist, not wanting to lose contact.

"Here we go," she says under her breath, then puts on a dazzling smile, like she's ready for the red carpet.

Chloe

JUST AS NICK and I enter the kitchen, Charlotte sweeps into the room, a vision in a pink Oscar de la Renta dress and black patent sandals. Her idea of what to wear for a quiet night at home, babysitting.

"I am *exhausted*," she announces. "Just *wiped out*. What a day."

Let's think about this for a second. Let's compare days.

"Well," she says, inspecting me, "Look at you. Is that *lipstick?*"

"Chloe always looks beautiful," Howard says calmly. "She's your daughter."

Howard missed his true calling. He should have been a high-level diplomat. An ambassador between warring nations. Instead he became a manufacturer of high-design kitchen tools. Still a service to humanity, IMHO, but he made millions. He arrived an hour ago, and already my stress level has dropped.

While my mother has failed to acknowledge the man on my arm, Howard's giving him the once-over, like an old lion sizing up the new alpha, his jowls turning down with an impressive, contemplative frown. I pour two glasses of bourbon, start to drink one, and nearly drink the other before giving it to Nick.

"It's a sample from our new private-label cosmetics line," I tell her. "The shade is called 'Go CommandO.' Do you like it?"

She squints. "Nice. A little on the red side for you. Are there any more samples?"

"I'll have Carrie send some over."

Howard hands her a frosted martini glass, with a kiss on the cheek and side-eye at Nick that I can't decipher. Grey Goose, two olives. The olives are Charlotte's idea of hors d'oeuvres. Ten calories each. And green vegetables, sort of.

"You're right. She does always look beautiful," Nick says quietly. My skin suddenly feels hot.

"This is Nick," I say quickly. "Nick, this is my mother, Charlotte."

She gives him a hundred-watt smile, and her manicured hand. Her bracelets jingle as they shake hands.

"And this is Howard." The two men square off, Nick towering over Howard. The strength of their handshake could bend iron girders, Howard's protectiveness obvious, his mouth leveling out into a look that says Nick passed his first test.

Handshake grip acceptable.

"How *lovely* to meet you, Nick." She looks at his glass of bourbon. "I see you have a cocktail. *Why* are we all in the kitchen? Chloe has become such a casual person. This is *not* how she was raised."

"Having a new baby will do that to you. I don't think I've even turned on the lights in the living room since Holly arrived."

"Let's go turn them on now." Charlotte's already headed in that direction, with a bowl of Marcona almonds in one hand and her martini in the other.

Nick clears his throat. "I think Chloe's way is perfect. I always feel comfortable here. And welcome. She's a great hostess."

He's only been here once before, but Charlotte doesn't know that. I smile at him gratefully.

"Bless your heart," she says, "what lovely manners."

She's back before the rest of us have stood up.

"Chloe, there seems to be laundry on every seat in there. What have you been *doing* all day?"

I actually can't think of a good answer to that.

"I just remembered, I brought this for Holly." Nick says quickly. He picks up a wrapped and beribboned package and hands it to me. "Open it."

I smile at him and slide the ribbon off, and at that moment Holly starts to fuss in the bedroom.

"I'll go get her and be right back." I hesitate briefly, because this means leaving Nick exposed to Charlotte, but Howard will run interference.

I love picking Holly up from her naps. I get so excited to see her again, feel the weight and warmth of her little body.

I perform a quick diaper change. Funny to think how panicked I was about diaper skills. Was that only weeks ago?

"Turn on the charm, girlfriend," I advise her, as I snap her leggings. "Make eye contact. Be interested in others."

She ignores me and stares at the ceiling.

Okay then. I see where this is going.

As we head back toward the kitchen, I hear Charlotte saying,

"Charlie is your younger brother? How *is* Charlie? That boy could sell ice to the Eskimos. Terrible influence on Chloe."

"He's currently selling surfboards to the landlocked," Nick replies. "And is a terrible influence on my kids."

"Ah, you have children! And how old are they?"

"My daughters are twenty-one, and my son is nineteen."

"Oh my, they're grown! Your job is done. You're an empty-nester! I remember that wonderful feeling of freedom." She smiles.

Perfect. Thanks, Mom. Well done.

Charlotte frowns. "Did you say daughters? Both twenty-one?"

"Yes. Twins." When he smiles, a dimple appears in his chin.

"That's a bit excessive, don't you think?" Only my mother could make an act of biology into a breach of etiquette.

"And here they are!" Howard says with great cheer, as we enter. Holly looks like a muppet. I realize I have a mental image but don't know the name of the one with red hair that stands up on end. I huff her baby scalp. In a year, I imagine, I'll know the names of every single muppet. I'll probably know their birthdates and social security numbers by memory. I wonder if Elmo dresses left.

Nick looks up and meets my eyes, and the world goes quiet. I realize I am holding my breath.

He stands and walks over to us.

"Well, hello, little girl," he says softly to Holly. And to me, "I'd forgotten how small they are." He's so enchanted. The way Nick looks at Holly takes my breath away. I wish a man would look at me like that.

And then he does.

"*But little girls get bigger every day,*" Howard sings.

"*Gigi,*" Charlotte sighs. "That movie changed my life. Even as a child, I just knew I'd love Paris."

Howard begins murmuring in her ear.

"Would you . . . like to . . . hold her?" I ask Nick. "I need to get her bottle ready. Or I can put her in her basket."

"Of course. Sure. I'd like to." He smiles. "I'd love to."

He takes her in his arms, experienced and assured but maybe a little rusty, and turns back to sit on his stool. I take a bottle from the fridge, put it in a bowl, and run hot water. When I glance up, he's looking at her tiny face, completely absorbed. And she's looking right back at him. He has one of her hands between two big fingers. She looks even smaller than usual.

My heart skitters.

Why?

Howard and Charlotte stand and walk out of the room, his arm around her, their heads together. He catches my eye and winks.

I think I may have lost my babysitters for tonight.

I test Holly's bottle on my wrist. Feels right.

"Thanks," I tell Nick. "Her bottle's ready. I'll take her."

He looks up, surprised. He holds out one hand.

"I'll do it. Let's see if I remember how."

With nothing else to do for the moment, I sink down onto the next stool and watch them.

After a minute, Nick smiles at me. "Like it was yesterday. Muscle memory. I wonder how many bottles I've given?"

There's a clatter in the front hall, and a moment later Howard appears, Charlotte behind him. She is wearing a cashmere wrap and carrying her handbag.

"Chloe," Howard says, "it is always wonderful to see you, and now Holly, too. She's an angel. And I know how much it means to you to have your mother here to help with everything when you're so tired and overwhelmed."

He looks suspiciously like he's trying not to smile.

"Oh, Howard. You just don't know what it means," I contribute. "Really, you don't." Wild hope is rising inside me.

"I think I do, actually. Please try to find it in your heart to forgive me for taking her away," he continues. "She is wearing herself to the bone taking care of you both, and I just feel I must step in before she makes herself ill. I've made a reservation at the Four Seasons for tonight, and tomorrow we fly to France."

"Whatever you think best," I assure him. "Of course. We'll manage somehow."

"I'm sorry, dear." Charlotte steps forward and kisses me on both cheeks. "Howard is right. It was too much." She brightens. "But I'll send you both some dresses from Paris. We'll be back in a few days, and I can help more after I've recovered."

Nick is watching all this like it's an episode of *Arrested Development*. He can't shake hands, but Charlotte kisses him and Howard pats him on the back. And then they're gone, leaving behind just the scent of Chanel No. 5.

I cough.

"Looks like we're not going out for dinner," Nick says. "Pizza?"

I burst out laughing, the kind of hysterical peals you can't quite believe are coming out of your mouth. Holly's eyes widen, darting to look at Nick, and then her mouth does the telltale tightening I've come to know.

"Oh, baby," I whisper, my laugh halting midstream as she turns her head aside, spitting out the bottle nipple, and makes a squeaky newborn cry that says she's just getting started.

I hold out my hands to take her back. No man wants to hold a screaming baby as foreplay on a date. The night just shattered, for good or bad, and this date turned into a threesome.

And not an O party threesome.

"I've got her." He stands, all fluid grace and muscle memory, moving her to his shoulder and patting her back harder than I would.

Scrambling, I get a cloth on his shoulder, fussing with the space between Holly's tiny body and Nick's broad shoulder. I have to stand on tiptoe, even in heels, to make Nick as spit-up proof as possible.

I manage.

He laughs, the rumble making me suddenly aware of the space between *our* bodies. "It's just a little spit up, Chloe. It washes out."

"Charlotte acted like it was napalm. She wore latex gloves and a Tyvek suit while burping Holly. I've seen Ebola researchers wear less."

"Why do you call your mother by her first name?"

"Because it's slightly less painful than using her preferred form of address."

"Which is?"

"Your Majesty."

Nick is in the middle of finishing his bourbon. He chokes, clapping a palm across his mouth to cough discreetly, those bright blue eyes mesmerizing. I could watch them for hours.

Being with him feels so good.

He's bouncing and patting little Holly, who decides the world isn't so scary after all, her little knees tucking up under her, face burrowing into Nick's shoulder.

I think I'm a little jealous.

Jealous of my own daughter.

This is how far I have fallen in a few weeks?

"How's life?" he whispers, his tone clearly implying that life as I know it is over.

"I've had a good life. A great life. Now this is my new life."

Holly's diaper begins making sounds you normally only hear in Lord of the Rings movies featuring the fiery pits of hell. I continue talking, because I'm used to it. It's not unlike working with a construction crew after the local food truck makes a stop.

Nick is so obviously an experienced dad, because he completely ignores Holly Vesuvius. I take her back from him.

"When you have kids," Nick says quietly, "it brings up all your own unprocessed issues."

"What unprocessed issues?" I say, pretending to be offended.

"Like your mother?" His eyebrows shoot up.

"What about my mother?" Even as the words roll off my tongue like a ribbon of error, I regret them.

"She's a little—"

I interrupt him. "Petty?"

"I would use the word 'narcissistic.'"

I shrug. "We all view the world through our personal lenses, right?"

"Chloe."

"She means well."

"She's slowly driving you to the brink of collapse."

"Only the brink. I've lived on the brink for long stretches of my life, Nick. It's not such a bad place to live."

Holly begins to cry.

"Diaper change," I announce.

Nick peels her out of my arms and turns away.

"What are you doing?"

"Changing her."

I gape at him. "Why?"

He frowns. "Because you just said 'diaper change.'"

"That wasn't an order," I say with a laugh that turns onto a yawn. "Just an observation."

He blinks, slowly. I haven't quite gotten used to seeing him in his glasses. They're stylish horn-rim frames and they make him look more distinguished. Not older, just wiser.

And more vulnerable. Messy. Casual.

Holly curls on his shoulder like a turtle that has crawled out of its shell and seeks comfort.

"Maybe I have some unprocessed issues, too, because Simone rarely changed a diaper. She would declare 'diaper change' and that meant I should do it." His eyes go unfocused. He's clearly two decades in the past.

Gently, so gently, I reach over, sliding my fingertips between his pecs and Holly's little body, the back of my hand brushing against his bare, slightly-hairy chest where his shirt is unbuttoned as I find the right grasp to take the baby.

"Chloe, no, I—"

I get her in my arms and give him a firm look. "Some patterns can't be reinforced, even if they're for the right reasons."

"That doesn't mean I'll never change a diaper!"

"Of course. Just not this one, Nick." I'm a pro. Holly's freshened up in under two minutes, and I hand her back to him, triumphant.

"How about we take her for a walk in her stroller?" Nick suggests, using a sing-songy voice, the low timbre of his voice soothing. "If she falls asleep, we can find an outdoor table somewhere for dinner."

"Food that isn't microwaved? Dinner that isn't delivered in a white cardboard carton? What is this planet you live on?"

"Planet Empty Nest," he whispers as, on his own, he finds the stroller and uses Jedi Mind Tricks to get Holly on her back and snuggled up in the little pod, blankets tucked neatly around her.

Ouch. Not sure what to say to that.

I pop the pacifier in her mouth, then look up at him and say what I'm really thinking.

"You are a god," I say, completely sincerely, in awe at his prowess.

With babies.

"I hear that a lot." He shoots me a grin as he reaches for me, warm hands on my waist, the hug delightful even if my face *is* smashed against Holly's burp cloth. "Mostly in bed."

Nick

THE JOKE IS awful. Terrible. I'm not on my game, but I have to say something to cover for the "Planet Empty Nest" comment. The look on Chloe's face feels like a slap.

But I'm not taking it back.

A kiss is a perfect way to delay the chance that I'll say something stupid again, so I go for it. She melts into me, her body different, looser and more casual, even as I feel the effects of stress and sleep deprivation in the way she holds herself. Chloe tastes good. Great.

And then the baby starts to cry.

Chloe breaks away instantly, practically leaping away from me as if I'd burned her, eyes wild. Her reflexes are primed for newborn care, attention swiftly focused on the baby as she fusses over her in the stroller, muttering aloud about whether to pick her up or not.

"Let's get her outside in the fresh air," I say, taking the decision away from her. She looks at me with those big brown eyes, circles under them, the slight slant at the corners somehow deeper, the charm intensified by her vulnerability. With a grateful air, she follows as I steer the stroller out her front door, picking it up and walking down the handful of stairs to the sidewalk.

I turn around to find her gaping at me.

"What?" I ask.

"You did that so effortlessly. I have to turn the stroller around and coax it down, one step at a time, careful to make sure poor Holly doesn't bunch up at the end like a neatly-folded suit in a carryon."

Holly's wiggling under the blanket, trying to decide whether she's upset or not.

"Let's move," I say quietly. Funny how all this baby stuff kicks in after years of not doing it, like riding a bicycle.

Or making love.

Within a minute, the baby has settled down, and Chloe's squinting in the sun. She looks like a hermit who has lived in a cave for a year and is finally seeing daylight.

We pass by my car. I look at Chloe, then at the box on my backseat. Holly begins to snurgle and Chloe's distracted, hovering. I seize the chance and pull the box out of the back seat, tucking it in the carriage bottom.

"What's that?"

I bite back a grin. "You'll see." Might as well get this over with. The damn thing is like a bad penny. I assume she'll throw it away once I give it to her. As we walk, Chloe pushing the stroller now, I begin to have second thoughts.

"Thank you," she says with a sigh, her shoulders releasing, one hand massaging her own neck. "I've been taking her out for walks, but then she cries and I can't calm her down. You ever start crying *with* your baby?"

"Can't say I ever did."

"It's pretty embarrassing. Especially when you cry louder than the infant."

I rest the palm of my hand on her back. She lets out a little sound, so faint I almost don't catch it. The sweetness in it, the unbearable contentment, makes me want to elicit that sound from her every day.

We walk like this, happy and free, Chloe nattering with great pleasure about Holly's daily habits, her birthmarks, the way she pulls her fists into her sleeves and how she already sticks her tongue out in imitation. I watch Chloe, who is the same woman I met a month ago, yet she's different.

She isn't pregnant. Didn't give birth.

But she glows.

"How does it feel?" I ask her as we halt at a stoplight, waiting our turn.

"What? Being a mother?"

"How does it feel to have gone through so much work to get here—and now you're here?"

She blinks, taking in a deep breath, nodding, her mind clearly churning to find the right answer. I like this about her. She doesn't react.

Chloe *processes*.

"Inevitable." She says just one word, then smiles. Her eyes say she's tired, but her mouth says she's thrilled.

"That's one hell of an answer to unpack."

"Is it? Why?"

The light changes. We begin to enter the crosswalk as an older woman walks in tandem with us, peeking in the stroller.

She beams.

"Congratulations, you two! How old is your baby?"

I damn near freeze in the middle of the crosswalk.

"She's almost two weeks old," Chloe answers, smooth as silk. Looking right at me, she smiles, raising one shoulder just enough to say, *Go with it.*

My throat tightens. My pulse races. I put one foot in front of the other and my hand that rests on Chloe's shoulder feels like it's a thousand pounds.

"Beautiful! Is she your first?"

Chloe's eyes widen. The ruse has gone too far.

"No," I say truthfully. "She's not." I don't mention that she's not mine at all.

"Enjoy! They grow up so fast!" The woman pivots to make a left turn. "Mine are in college now. I'd trade the freedom for a day of their babyhood in a heartbeat."

I can't feel my feet. I can't hear traffic. A roar of blood pounds my ears. I'm walking only because of primal programming that warns my rat brain to get out of the way of the big metal predators in the road.

Chloe laughs softly, the sound full of questions.

"That was cute."

That was *something.*

Just as we reach the curb, Holly starts to scream, a high-pitched, frantic newborn cry that requires an instantaneous response. Chloe's arms are under her in seconds, lifting the baby up, the red-faced scream continuing, unabated.

It's like having fingernails raked down an exposed nerve.

The sound triggers a kind of parenting PTSD in me, taking me back twenty years. My body becomes my twenty-two-year-old self, my eyes overly alert and senses on edge.

"What's wrong, honeybee?" Chloe coos. "It's okay." She makes some *shhh shhh shhh* sounds to soothe the baby while I stand there, dumbly, blinking in the sunlight.

"Is Elo—um, Holly okay?" Damn. Almost called her by *my*

daughter's name.

"I don't know! She doesn't scream like this."

And then Holly lets out a frat-boy belch that my brother would approve of.

Spit up pours out of her like a volcano.

Chloe goes into awkward new-parent mode, trying to avoid being a target, while comforting one pissed-off infant.

Breaking out of my trance, I hand her the first thing I find in the carriage bottom.

"Here."

She begins mopping up Holly, then stops. "Joe?"

Shit. She's forgotten my name.

"No. Nick."

Her laugh comes out as a gaspy-wheezy sound, like she's having an asthma attack. "No, I mean—how did Joe's old Coldplay t-shirt get into my daughter's stroller? I thought I got rid of this." She wrinkles her nose. "It smells like his old cologne."

I look in the carriage bottom. The top of the shoebox where I stored the auction items bounced off, the contents of the box spilling out. I happened to grab what turns out to be her ex-lover's t-shirt.

"Um." My brilliant response rings through the air.

Chloe's eyebrows go up.

"Nick?"

"If you're going to mop up baby puke, a Coldplay t-shirt is a great candidate."

She doesn't laugh. Damn.

This is going downhill fast. A glimmer of light on water catches my eye.

"Let's walk to the bridge," I say, my hand on her back as she puts Holly down. The baby's front is wet, but she settles in quietly, bubble thoroughly evacuated.

The look on Chloe's face makes it clear a long explanation is in order.

One more block and we're at the Charles River, coxswains calling out orders and encouragement to their crew teams, kayakers frolicking in the water. The early fall weather draws people out of their tiny boxes in the city, giving Cambridge an air of vitality. Students fill the streets, going for runs, wearing backpacks, and cluttering the side roads.

"How, exactly, did you come to possess my ex's t-shirt?"

"It's a long story."

She points to the now-sleeping Holly, one corner of her mouth twisting up with mirth. "I've got about twenty minutes."

"Not sure that's long enough."

"That's what she said." Chloe speaks through the side of her mouth, tone husky and with great affect. But she's tightly-wound and twitchy.

I groan.

"Spill."

Bending down, I re-collect Joe's auction items, placing them carefully in the box, the strap-on centered on top of the rest of the items. I stand up holding a closed parcel.

"Here." I thrust it at her.

She opens it, nearly choking as she sees what's on top.

Then she looks at me and says dryly, "Most guys wait until the third date to suggest the strap-on."

My butthole clenches involuntarily.

"Oh, god," she groans. "This is, um . . . I know this particular strap-on."

"Intimately, I'd imagine."

She looks up sharply, real anger in her face, and it's clear I've crossed a line.

Damn, she's hot when she's pissed.

"This is Joe's stuff! These are all the items he used to leave at my place while we . . . when we were . . ." A speculative horror fills her face. "Why are you gifting me a sex toy Joe bought after seeing *Deadpool?*" She fishes around the box, horror filling her features.

"And no, I did not use it on him! He begged me, but . . ."

I start to laugh.

"—we never even got to March for International Women's Day!"

I stop laughing.

Chloe grips the stroller and slowly begins to back away from me, a protective air around her. "What is this, Nick? Did you do something to Joe?"

"*Do* something?"

"You had him in a headlock that day at the office. Maybe you've . . . hurt him?"

"Hurt him? Hurt him how?"

"How else would you have these very personal items of his?"

"I bought them. Paid $1,077.51 in an auction."

"Auction? You spent *what*? You're not making any sense."

"Ever heard of a site called Never Liked It Anyway?"

Her hand flies to her mouth. The strap-on drops out of her other hand and plunks softly on the bonnet of Holly's carriage, rolling slightly to settle into a groove. It looks like a space-age dog toy.

That would be one hell of a game of fetch.

"He *didn't*! Joe did not sell my . . . our . . . what?" Her face fills with genuine horror and shock.

"You didn't know?" I'm blown away. "Chloe, the auction was all over social media. One of those three-day phenomenons shared all over Facebook, Tumblr, Snapchat, Twitter—you name it. No one in modern America could have missed it."

"Henry and Jemma said something about a porn star with a name like mine having an ex sell their sex toys online. It was right in the middle of Li giving birth and disappearing, so I put it out of my head and—oh, my god, Nick, how many people know about this?" She points at the strap-on.

"A few million?" I guess.

"I'm ruined."

"Not really. Between buying Joe's auction items and shutting down his account, and having Charlie get a hacker to—"

"*Charlie* knows about this?"

"Sure."

"Who else? And how did you find out about it?"

"Elodie."

"Your *daughter* found out my ex was selling our shared strap-on and sought you out to tell you?"

Progressive parenting at its finest.

"It didn't quite go that way." Although she's damn close.

Chloe begins to pant slightly, the sound a little too close to hyperventilation for comfort. Holly sucks on her pacifier like it's an Olympic sport. I feel like I made a terrible mistake, but I can't take it back.

I glance at the strap-on.

Definitely can't take *that* back.

Seizing the item by the dildo end, Chloe pulls her arm back with impressive form. She must have played softball from a young age, because the pitch has perfect arc and aim, flying rubber tip over belt as she releases the strap-on into the throw.

I resist the urge to hum the theme to *Wonder Woman*.

As the strap-on makes its third mid-air revolution, the bow of a racing shell filled with eight rowers shoots from under the bridge.

Chloe's throw is perfect.

The strap-on beans the coxswain right in the head.

Then plunks into the water, like a very porny orca at a Sea World aquatics show.

"Hey!" The coxswain looks around wildly, focusing on us. We're the only two people by the bridge.

And then Chloe kisses me, her mouth tight and fierce against mine, lips bruised as she bangs into me, teeth aching until one hand settles on my shirt, pressing into my ribs, and she softens, the kiss taking new form.

"What's that for?" I mumble against her mouth, wanting more of it, my hands mimicking hers, one palm on the stroller handle, one on Chloe's ass.

"For being so deeply depraved."

"That deserves a kiss?"

"Here's the problem," she whispers. "You don't look like a weirdo."

"That's a problem?"

"You look like one of those guys who has his shit together. A grownup. A real one. The kind I find intimidating."

"Intimidating."

"Yeah. The kind of guy who would never flash a nipple to a conference room because of a bustier malfunction."

"That will never happen," I agree, looking down at my chest.

"The kind of guy who doesn't make mistakes. Who is guided by certainty."

"I look like that guy?"

"You *are* that guy."

In her eyes, I am.

"Chloe," I say, kissing her ear. "I'm Nick. I'm a father and a man and a director and a guy. I'm imperfect and uncertain sometimes. I make mistakes and I can be gross and I yell and get upset."

"You? Gross? Charlie, sure. But not you."

"Spend enough time with me and you'll see."

She answers that with a kiss.

"I knew you were nuanced, though. Suspected it all along, when you wouldn't smile."

"Wouldn't smile?"

"The day we met. I figured anyone who has that kind facial control has some deep layers."

"I do."

"And a warped side." Chloe takes all the other items out of the box and dumps them, one by one, into the river.

She finds her lipstick vibrator last and holds it up, speechless.

"You kept this!"

"Your special O 'lipstick." I lean in to her ear and whisper "Bzz

bzz."

Laughing, she considers me. "Didn't fool you from the start, did I?" She starts to drop it in the water, reconsiders, and tucks it in her bra.

I raise my eyebrows.

With a shrug, she says, "The Charles can have Joe's strap-on." She looks back at the water, the sex toy long gone, being nibbled by fishes in its watery grave.

"Never liked it anyway," she sighs, one hand on the stroller's handle, the other threading fingers through my own.

Chloe

I CAN'T BELIEVE he's *still* here.

If that sounds snarky, it isn't. I sincerely cannot believe he's still here. With me. With *us*. What man would put up with my mother, a cancelled dinner date, a screaming infant, spit-up, his predecessor's strap-on, possible arrest for assault on an innocent rower, my throwing trash in the Charles River, a long walk on a chilly late afternoon, and a woman who paid absolutely zero attention to him until her child was fed, bathed, and asleep? Not to mention the garbage needed to go out, and as Charlotte announced, there are three loads of unfolded laundry in the living room.

No one else would put up with it, that's who. Joe would have been out the door two minutes after Charlotte left.

At least my hair is clean. And my underwear (thank god I did all that laundry this morning).

Holly's deep, even breathing tells me she has finally fallen asleep. I rise from the rocking chair very slowly and move across the darkened room, where I carefully peel her from my chest and lower her into her crib. Wait to see if she stays asleep. Check the baby monitor. Check the thermostat. Tiptoe out. Exhale.

At least, I hope he's still here?

Heading down the hall, I begin to smell something delicious

and realize I am starving. I pass the living room and do a sort of walking double take, backing up a few steps to look.

The room is now lit by candles and the flicker of the fireplace. The cocktail table is set with plates, napkins, and chopsticks in paper sleeves. Champagne glasses are sparkling in the candlelight. There are two large brown paper bags on the floor next to the table. Sinatra is crooning "Just in Time." There is no laundry in sight.

Nick comes walking in with an open Champagne bottle.

"I figured you like Thai food since I saw the delivery menu in the kitchen drawer," he says. "I had to guess at what to order, though." He chuckles. "I waited at the door because I was afraid the doorbell would ring at exactly the wrong time."

"I can't believe you did this! It's amazing!"

"I dialed the number on the menu," he laughs. "I didn't cook it myself. Any ten-year-old could produce the same meal, if they can pronounce 'tom yam goong.'"

"Ten-year-olds can't pop a Champagne cork, though," I say, accepting a glass, "and Holly is not allowed to light candles until she is twenty. At least."

"All three of my children could open a Champagne bottle properly by age eight. No big pops. Just a tiny puff of air. We just have to teach her to point the cork away from her face."

That "we" hangs there in the air for a moment.

"Let's eat," I suggest. I kneel on the floor and pull open the paper bags. Inside are six appetizers and four main course dishes in plastic containers.

"Are we expecting other people?" I ask, confused.

"I wanted to be sure there was something you liked."

I look in his eyes, and a smile spreads across my face.

"There's definitely something I like."

And the food is good, too.

Eventually I lay down my chopsticks, unable to take another bite. Nick stands and picks up our plates.

"No, no!" I protest, unfolding my legs and trying to get up

from the floor. "I'll clear. You've done everything so far!"

"Sorry," he says. "House rule is that mothers of children under three months do not wait on adults. I'll be right back."

"But it's my house!"

"But it's my rule," he smiles.

"Wish you had explained that rule to Charlotte," is all I can say. But I settle back down and enjoy the luxury of being taken care of, just for one night. I am stuffed. Content. As Nick leaves the room, I let myself fall backwards on the carpet, the food and wine and warmth all washing over me.

▼ ▼ ▼

NICK IS SEATED on my sofa, reading on his iPad. I'm looking up at him from an odd angle. Why?

He notices me. "Hey," he says softly.

"Hey," I answer, sitting up stiffly. "Oh no—I fell asleep? I am so sorry!"

"Nothing to be sorry about. You're exhausted. Come up here." He touches the sofa next to him, shifting to wrap his arms around me as I sit. He rests his chin on top of my head.

"Soon she'll sleep through the night. And then she'll be a teenager, and she'll sleep till one in the afternoon, and you'll be trying to wake her up all the time. Every stage has its challenges. As soon as you figure one stage out, they pass through it, and you have to figure out the next one."

"And you did it alone too. With three of them."

"Yes, and only two hands." He chuckles.

"What was the hardest part?"

"Oh, without a doubt, the times when there was supposed to be a mother on the scene. You know, school events, proms, awards. Milestone things. My parents would come sometimes, but it wasn't the same."

"Your parents?" I realize I don't know much about Nick, but I did date his brother.

"My dad died a few years ago," he explains.

"Oh!" A memory of Charlie's parents flickers through me. Norm was a tall, lean guy with big hands who spent a lot of time doing woodwork in their garage. Their mother, Celia, was a tough-as-nails kindergarten teacher. "I'm so sorry. What about your mom?"

"Retired. Lives in Florida now."

"Sounds like they really helped you when the kids were little." He shrugs.

I turn and look at him, heartbreak on my face.

"Will it be like that for Holly? Will she miss having a dad terribly?"

The contemplative way that he takes his time before answering is endearing, and it makes me listen carefully. "To be honest, I think it was a lot harder on me than on the kids. For them, it was kind of normal. But as a parent, you just can't stand for anyone to hurt your child. And I had a lot of anger towards Simone that I had to keep hidden."

A quiet moment passes, as I think about what he's told me. This exceptional man.

"I think it's going to be a little easier for you and Holly. I think there's more of an understanding now that families look different in many ways, but it's only the love that matters."

He picks something up from the floor beside him.

"You started to open this earlier, but you didn't finish. It's for Holly."

He looks so excited, like it's a gift for him. I separate the tissue paper in the bag and find a flat gift. I pull off the wrapping paper and see that it's a children's book with a bright cover featuring an illustration of a little girl and a big dog. The little girl is holding her nose.

"Walter, the Farting Dog," I read aloud.

I look at Nick.

I am speechless.

"I know I said 'no princesses,'" I begin, "but . . ."

He's shaking with laughter.

"Best. Children's. Book. Ever." he manages. "This book got me through story time for years. I can't wait to read it again."

"But . . ." I begin.

"Listen to this!" he interrupts me. "Backstory—"

"Backstory? A children's book with *backstory*?"

"Yes! That's why this is the greatest children's book known to man. Poor Walter got depressed and ate a twenty-five pound bag of low-fart dog biscuits."

I'm trying to follow this. I really am.

"Low-fart dog biscuits?" I ask, eyebrows hitting the moon. Note to self: time to get threaded.

"And poor Walter tries to hold in his gas, but then burglars arrive. So he lets it go." Nick picks up the book and points to the page, trying to read. The man is shaking so hard from laughing that he can't speak.

"Ah," I say. I am *really* trying to understand.

"Look at this picture!" He points to an illustration of a dog actually farting on a veterinarian, who is peering into the dog's, uh . . . backside. Tears are now running down Nick's cheeks.

I suddenly understand what he meant earlier, when he said he could be gross.

I take the book from him and leaf through the first few pages. Where I see this introduction: "For everyone who is misjudged or misunderstood."

He's right. This is a book we need on our shelves.

And did he say, "I can't wait to read it again"?

"Thank you," I say sincerely. I put the book on the cocktail table. "Thank you," I whisper, and kiss him.

He's not laughing now. He's kissing me back, the kind of kiss that wants more, wants everything.

He's not laughing as I slide to my knees in front of him.

He's not laughing as I unbuckle his belt. Unzip his pants. Gently free him, and just in time. He's rock hard.

"Chloe," he gasps, as I circle him with my tongue, teasing for a moment. I inhale his intimate scent.

My lips are around him now, moving and sucking, enjoying the connection and the power. Then he begins to move too, fingers threading in my hair, his hands guiding me to his perfect rhythm until I hear him moan and he bursts into my mouth, masculine and delicious.

This is as close as I can get to experiencing what he feels, and I love it.

I love that he loves it.

"*That* was worth waiting for," I say, and I smile to myself.

"Incredible," he's saying, his breathing ragged, "unbelievable."

"Come to bed," I tell him. "You can read Walter at three a.m."

He gives me a sad smile. "An hour ago, I'd have had to decline, because I had plans with my son. But he texted me."

"He ditched you?"

"He postponed."

I stand up and reach my hand toward him. "I'm sorry he did, but his loss is my gain. Now you don't have to postpone with me."

Nick stands and grins, following my lead.

And just as we tiptoe past Holly's room, she begins to cry.

CHAPTER SIXTEEN

Nick

"NICK, DARLING," SIMONE says, Jean-Marc carrying her luggage into the guest bedroom. "Guest bedroom" is a stretch—Jean-Marc gave up his bedroom and is crashing on the sofa bed in the living room, home from fall semester for a break in honor of his mother's appearance. Charlie is couch surfing with a friend. He and Simone were never exactly close.

That's like saying Donald Trump is just a tad unpopular in Scotland.

"Simone." I embrace her, kissing both cheeks, polite to a fault. She wears the same perfume, her style unchanged after all these years, body tight and slimly compact, no extra movement wasted. Her dark hair is pulled back into a chic knot at the nape of her neck. She wears bright red lipstick, with tiny wrinkles lining her mouth. Her lower lids bear thick eyeliner, and all those years of narrowed eyes have left her with a cat-like appearance and what would be called "laugh lines" on anyone else etch deeply into her face, like a series of angry scratches.

"You look the same. How long has it been?" Her question is rhetorical. She knows.

"Nearly four years ago. When the twins graduated high school." Rolf was with her. We spent three hours together. Three hours of watching my kids paraded around for pictures and accolades. Simone excluded me from the rest of her visit on the grounds that Rolf was "too jealous and unstable."

She didn't bother to attend Jean-Marc's graduation, instead flying him and a friend of his choice to spend a special week in Paris with her.

"Four years!" Her smile plays at the corners of her mouth like a surgeon's thread and needle, stretching as it tightens with precision. "Time has been good to you."

The leading compliments aren't designed to flatter me. They're designed to trigger a similar response *from* me.

But I'm not Pavlov's dog any longer.

And Simone's bell doesn't work.

"How was your flight?" I ask, gesturing toward the living room, where sofas and Jean-Marc await.

Her lips part, my offensive behavior duly noted as her tongue saves the day, hiding her reaction, tickling the upper line of teeth. One front top tooth slightly overlaps the other, just enough to be endearing. When she smiles, she is symmetrical, her face so aligned she might have been designed rather than born. The curved tooth always added extra charm. Even Simone had a flaw.

"Tedious, as always. Everyone sits with their face in a screen. First class is no different now. And people wear sweatpants." Her nose crinkles in distaste.

"Maman? Espresso with lemon?"

"Now that is a young man who knows how to treat a woman," she says with a wink, her red lips spreading with a smile, chin upturned as she calls out to our son. "Oui! And a small glass of cognac, s'il te plaît."

I say nothing.

"You've kept the place exactly the same," she says in a tone that makes it clear this is not a compliment. "If I look in your closets, I will find the same suits I helped you choose before the children were born." Her eyes crawl up my body as I stretch on the sofa, one arm across the back, the other clinging to my beer like a life raft. She is cataloguing me in a methodical, seductive manner that would be incredibly arousing if it were any other woman.

If it were Chloe, I would be hard by now, shifting in my seat to adjust myself, mind whirring through all the possibilities such a gaze offered.

But that's not happening now.

Because it is Simone.

She's waiting for me to reply. I've been in my head and memory too long.

"You would," I admit. "You had good taste."

"Had?" She gestures to her dress and earrings, primping her hair jokingly. On the surface, it's all in good fun.

But I know the Simone underneath, and this is anything but fun.

It is a game, though.

"Have." I'll be the gentleman. It costs me nothing.

"We bought this place with nothing, didn't we?" she says looking around with sad eyes. "My trust fund, your graduate school stipend."

"And the trust from my accident," I add. When I was in eighth grade, Charlie and I were playing street hockey one day, out in the street where we grew up in Westwood. A drunk hit us. I broke my arm, Charlie broke a leg, and our parents put the insurance settlement money into a trust for us. When we each turned twenty-one, it was ours.

I invested mine in a down payment for this place.

Charlie's money went into his first failed business.

"How timely," she says with a smile. "You received the money from that car accident in your youth just a week before we learned about the twins."

"And you insisted on buying a home."

"It was a good investment."

But I wasn't, I think, struggling to control two people inside my mind, one trying to override the other, the angry half winning.

"You hated this place from the start."

"It was a starter home, Nick." She shakes her head sadly. "Not meant to be a forever home."

"Was I a starter husband, then?" I say lightly, standing and reaching for the espressos Jean-Marc offers us both, his face neutral, eyes on me.

I don't do this.

And he's picking up on it.

He goes back to the kitchen for Simone's brandy.

You raise babies into toddlers, then preschoolers to tweens, and finally teenagers become young adults, all the while fully formed in their humanity, just needing time to mature and grow. Roots and wings, the saying goes. Children need both.

I've given them roots.

Their mother cared more about her own wings than theirs.

"Starter husband? What an American concept," she says disdainfully, drinking her espresso quickly.

"I think you gave it a French twist," I add, going into the kitchen, grabbing another beer.

Jean-Marc's face lights up. "Dad?" He's looking at the bottle in my hand.

"Of course you may," Simone interrupts, waving her hand. "Drink. Another stupid American concept. You can fight in a war but not have a glass of wine."

It's the first time Jean-Marc's asked since he came home from college. He's nineteen now.

"Sure," I concede. I need all the points I can get.

Simone watches me, eyes calculating, taking in the change. "Why don't you drink some Cabernet, Jean-Marc?"

He cracks a beer and stands next to me across the living room.

Solidarity takes on many forms.

"Maman!" The moment is broken by Elodie and Amelie's twin shrieks as they barrel through the front door, glomming onto Simone like barnacles. She gives them double-cheeked kisses and fusses with Amelie's new haircut.

"Trés chic!" Simone declares, holding Amelie's chin between her thumb and index finger, checking the angle over and over. "You look five years older!"

Amelie beams.

I unclench a millimeter. The kids are always happy to see Simone.

"And Elodie, I expect to meet Brandon. You've told me so much about him."

Elodie's eyes instantly grow shiny with unspilled tears. "Oh. Um, we broke up."

"When?" The question comes out like an accusation.

I re-clench.

"Three weeks ago."

"Oh. Well, you are a beautiful, intelligent young woman. He was stupid to leave you."

"I dumped him, Maman."

"Why?"

"Because he hooked up with someone else."

"Hooked up?"

"He screwed someone else," Jean-Marc announces, giving Elodie the side-eye.

"Shut UP!" The two begin squabbling.

Simone and I exchange a rare look of sympathy.

And then we laugh together for the first time in fifteen years.

It doesn't last long, as Jean-Marc, Elodie, and Amelie stop dead in their tracks—both physical and verbal. Simone reaches for my arm, the butterfly touch of her fingertips against my wrist making electricity shoot through me.

Not the kind I like.

The kind that says you're being stalked by a wild game animal.

The laughter dies in my throat as I realize three sets of curious, very wary eyes are on us.

Our children have not seen us in the same room together in years. Once the girls turned sixteen, they insisted on being independent with their flights to France. I no longer accompanied them. Simone came for their high school graduation nearly four years ago. That was the last time the kids saw us together, and the day was interminably fake.

Of course it was.

Rolf was there.

This feels odd. Off. My protective sense goes into high gear, ears perked, arms and legs filling with pumping blood, ready to shift into danger mode. Simone smiles, her face sweet and genuine for a flicker of time, just enough to make me think of how she looked the day we met on campus during my freshman orientation at RISD, her senior year. The age difference never bothered me; she seemed to enjoy it.

She is from a family with money, a long line of famous sculptors to royalty throughout Europe.

She was a rare bird, exotic and alluring.

I was the solid American, dashing and new.

New World met Old World.

She colonized me.

"The concert starts in three hours. I have to be there early!" Amelie says, making me pay attention to her. Dressed in a classic black suit, the jacket high-waisted, the skirt long and flowing, she's elegant, hair perfect, face done with makeup that is understated and nuanced, designed to show off high cheekbones and a stateliness I've never seen in her before.

"We'll be right behind you," I tell her with a smile. Simone watches me.

Not Amelie.

"You have VIP tickets, so you don't have to rush, Daddy."

Simone stiffens at the word *Daddy*. She's always preferred *Papa*.

Which is why I'm Dad and Daddy. She got to name the kids. I chose what they call *me*.

"But we need to park," Jean-Marc adds with a laugh, then a small belch. I notice his beer bottle's empty. "And the nearest garage is a hike."

"I'll drive," I say, raising my eyebrows at his bottle.

"Of course," Simone says, her hand still on my wrist, remaining. "As it always was."

As it always was.

♥ ♥ ♥

MY DAUGHTER—*OUR* daughter—delivers a flawless performance for her concert.

And all Simone can do is critique.

"Your articulation on the reed needs more precision," she says, her voice all business. I've wondered whether Amelie chose to play oboe because she thought it would bring her closer to Simone. Would offer some affinity, or just a sense of approval.

If that was her motivation, it's backfired horribly.

From the look on Amelie's face, it's time to intervene. What is Simone's purpose in coming to this concert? I spent the better part of the performances mulling over her presence. Why now? Why this event?

Just . . . *why*?

Covert glances from her during the concert look like flirting. That touch on my wrist. The laugh. The flattery.

She's not coming on to me.

Impossible.

Sixteen years ago, she decided we were done. And when Simone is done with something, it doesn't exist for her.

Yet here she is, done to the nines and talking to me as if we've been separated all these years by pure happenstance. Circumstance.

Fate.

And not intent.

"Maman!" Elodie comes up from the rear, hooking her arm in Simone's, interrupting the stream of French coming out of her mother, all of it advice on how Amelie could hold the instrument better. "Where are we going for dinner?"

"We?" Simone's gaze flits to me. "Oh, chérie, we can have dinner tomorrow en famille, together. I hoped to spend some time alone with your father this evening."

You would think that Simone had just said she'd found Chloe's ex's strap-on in my bedroom closet and was about to use it on Rolf at the Esplanade during a Boston Pops concert.

"*What?*" All three of our children ask the same question in unison.

And they look at *me* when they ask.

I frown, turning to Simone in amazement.

"What?" I echo.

She laughs, the sound throaty and sensual. "Oh, Nick. You act as if I'm asking for the moon."

A slightly different analogy, but let's go with it.

"A steak and some wine and good conversation to catch up on all these years is what I ask." She smiles at Amelie, who is dissolving under the surface but putting on a good front. "You understand, chérie. Tomorrow is for you. Tonight is for the adults."

Jean-Marc's nostrils flare. He and Elodie exchange a glance without moving a muscle.

"No. Simone, I—"

Amelie interrupts me, blinking hard, chin up and defiant. "It's fine, Daddy." She gives a tinny laugh that makes one of the chambers of my heart stop working. "You have your dinner tonight. We'll get Maman for a whole day instead, tomorrow."

"Yes," Simone says, beaming with approval. Amelie is on board, locked and loaded, in place as expected. That's all that counts for Simone. What might be churning under the surface does not matter. The words Amelie says, the compliance, are enough.

I had forgotten what it felt like to live in a box. Watching my daughter rein in her expectations, right in front of the woman drawing the edges, is too much.

"But—"

An imperceptible head shake from Amelie and wider, blinking

eyes are the only signs I get from my daughter, who is simultaneously fighting an inner battle and learning the art of decorum. "Daddy, it's fine." The vocal fry at the end of her sentence sears me. These are new dynamics. When did my children become complex, emotionally-nuanced social beings?

It is anything but fine. I open my mouth to argue, but shut it abruptly.

My kids can fight their own battles.

And so can I.

"Fine," I say, a bit gruff, turning to Simone. I name an Italian place in the North End that she hates.

She wrinkles her nose.

I don't react. Simone always despised my poker face.

From her reaction, she still does.

Tough shit.

I pull Amelie into a hug and whisper fiercely, "You can tell her no. You can."

"It's easier this way," she whispers back. I can hear the fear in her voice. I know what she's afraid of.

She's not afraid of Simone. Not afraid of disappointing her.

Amelie is afraid of letting go of the pretend mother who lives only in her imagination.

The real one in front of her, the one scowling at me for choosing a restaurant I know she hates, has already disappointed her.

She cannot let go of the imaginary one just yet.

And I cannot help her. The realization hits me hard, the wind knocked out of me as I nearly choke on my own understanding.

Elodie's hugging me, then I get a clap on the back from Jean-Marc, and they're off, walking toward the T, the girls arm in arm and with huddled heads, Jean-Marc's head down as he texts someone.

"They're so mature," Simone says, in a tone that says homeostasis has been achieved.

"They get it from their father."

"If you were mature, you would not torture me with inferior

Italian food."

"Let's not crack open this topic."

"Fine." She pouts. "I'll suffer in silence. For you."

When the world has only one camera lens and it's your eyes, any other perspective feels like an invasion. I've no doubt she'll suffer.

But not in silence.

We walk slowly, her heels an impediment, my ability to engage in small talk long gone.

Bzzz.

A text. From Chloe.

Parenting manuals don't mention the need for a hazmat suit, tongs, and a never-ending ability to sing Mac the Knife until you're hoarse.

I smile.

"Something funny?" Simone doesn't look at me, staring straight ahead, blinking.

"Something poignant."

I become my son as I walk, half-aware of the sidewalk, mostly focused on my glass screen.

Consider a change in tune, I text back.

Suggestions?

Every suggestion that pops into my mind involves sex.

Honesty is the best policy.

I can't think about lullabies when you're texting me. All I can think about is you, I reply.

Simone huffs. "Must you text and walk at the same time?"

"Work," I mutter.

You wouldn't want to see me. I'm wearing eau de formula and I think I have dried pee on the hem of my shirt, Chloe texts back. *From yesterday,* she adds.

No power underwear? I answer, smiling.

We turn a corner and the front door to the restaurant appears. I halt.

"You're not really texting for work, are you?" Simone asks, her voice dripping with suspicion.

"A colleague," I say. Which is technically true.

Power bustier currently doubling as a diaper-changing pad on sofa, Chloe texts back. *Sexy. I know.*

She doesn't know. She really doesn't know.

"Nick!" Simone's angry hiss makes my name sound like a rebuke. "You picked this place. Be a gentleman and deal with the maître d'!"

TTYL, I type slowly, not caring about the sunburn I'm getting from Simone's heated glare.

SOS, Chloe replies, then adds a wink.

I say two sentences to the man in the white coat and black tie, we're seated, two martinis ordered, and then Simone demands, "I've never seen you that happy about a work issue."

"There's a lot you've never seen about me, Simone." The glow from the quick interchange with Chloe is wearing off.

Fast.

Tends to happen when you talk to an ice queen.

"Is it that woman?"

"*That* woman?" I don't like her tone.

"The one the children told me you're dating."

My turn to narrow my eyes and study her.

She doesn't like it.

I say nothing, but I don't break eye contact.

She squirms. Funny. She never squirmed before when confronted.

"Good for you," she finally says, then sips her martini, evaluating the quality. From her expression, she's satisfied. Barely. "I'd assumed you'd been a monk all these years. The children never mentioned any women."

"We're not going to talk about my love life, Simone."

Her eyes widen. "I wasn't talking about your love life, Nick. I was talking about your *sex* life."

"The fact that you don't realize they can be the same thing tells me nothing's changed."

Her face turns ugly. Deeply ugly, with a pent-up anger that a part of me jumps to soothe. I'm able to stop myself. Old habits run deep, but they're not etched in my core any longer.

She shakes it off, clearly working hard within to find that delicate balance that gives her a feeling of control. "I'm glad to hear you've found some joy. Have you been dating her long?"

"I'm not going to talk about her."

"Chloe, is it? You can't stay away from French women," she says with a smile and a wink, moving with feline grace as she crosses her legs, leaning back in the chair, her smile flirtatious and dangerous.

I start to argue that Chloe isn't French. This is a trap, though. The best way not to engage is to withhold.

That's how the last two years of our marriage worked. Simone poked and demanded, and I withdrew.

And then she left.

"I can't stay away from some women," I say with a laugh, pulling out my phone and typing just as the waiter brings a bread basket. I look up from the phone, ignoring Simone, and order for us both. As she stares at me, nonplussed, I type out a text.

I'll save you. Say the word. Can I come over tonight?

But I don't hit Send.

Not yet.

"You're different." Simone's statement makes me look up, placing the phone face down on the table. I dip a piece of bread into the olive oil the waiter just plated and fill my mouth with something other than a retort.

Mouth full as I chew, I just shrug.

"Harder."

I check in below the belt.

Nope.

"More authoritative."

I raise my eyebrows and look at her.

"More commanding. You've come into your own, Nick. And I

deserve some of this."

It takes everything in me not to choke on the focaccia. A piece of rosemary pokes my tonsil. The martini washes all the uncertainty away.

"You deserve what exactly, Simone?"

"I never thought this would be easy."

"*What* would be easy?" A preternatural sense of unease creeps through my skin, making my hands clench, thighs tighten, body priming for battle.

"Testing the waters. Seeing what's left between us."

Instinct is a double-edged sword. I didn't want to believe it. Didn't think the signs she was sending were real. Couldn't fathom that this was happening. Thought I was making it up.

No.

Simone *is* coming on to me.

"What's left between us are three beautiful, kind, good children we produced, Simone. And that's all."

Caprese salad is delivered. I dig into mine. Simone orders a vodka soda with lime.

Guess the martini didn't meet her standards after all.

"That's all?"

Flavor explodes in my mouth as I chew, the fresh basil sweetening my thoughts. She's looking at me with bedroom eyes, and I can't help myself.

I pick up my phone and push the damn Send button, then set it back down.

I smile.

She smiles.

"Thank you," I say.

She leans in, her mouth tight and loose at the same time, her eyes victorious. Simone looks like the cat that ate the canary.

"For what?"

"For clarity."

Bzzzz.

I check my phone.

k, says the text.

I blink. I look at Simone. Amelie's face flashes through my mind, a snapshot of the moment Simone shunted them off, picking dinner with me over the kids yet again.

Deserve. What does Simone deserve? She doesn't deserve whatever she wants from me. A reconciliation? A roll in the hay for old time's sake? Something in between, more likely.

I'll give her a taste of her own medicine.

My body decides before I do, the napkin against my mouth, folded on the table as I stand, shoving my phone in my back pocket.

"I'm so sorry, Simone. I'm having a work crisis. A colleague needs me."

She flinches, her swan's neck graceful, pulse thready and quivering at the hollow of her throat, where the skin is suddenly flushed with anger. "What?"

I pull out my wallet and throw a handful of twenties on the table, a sense of power building in me. Her face is tipped up in shock, eyes tracking my movements, her expression one of disbelief.

"I'm sure you'll be well taken care of by the waiter, Simone. Perhaps you can call the children and invite them to join you. I can't have dinner tonight."

"You're leaving me for *her*."

"No." And this is the truth. "I'm leaving because I have to go save someone."

Not Chloe.

Me.

♥ ♥ ♥

I WAIT AT her door after pressing the bell. Feels like ninth grade, when I asked Mary Elizabeth Manning to the Valentine's Dance, and had to stand in the cold, wearing an ill-fitting suit, wondering what the hell I'd gotten myself into, but unable to undo it.

The door opens.

Chloe's there, hair in a messy topknot, wearing an Ed Sheeran concert t-shirt and brightly-patterned leggings. No make-up, and she's holding Holly on one hip. The baby is playing with Chloe's ear like it's the best toy ever.

"Nick. Hi." She looks down at herself. "As you can tell, I made a big effort."

God, I've missed her.

I kiss her cheek, then Holly's, trying to hide my disappointment that the baby's awake. They both smell like lavender lotion.

"You look fabulous, as always."

She ignores the compliment. "I'm about to put Miss Fussypants down for the night. Come in!" She shivers. I take her up on the offer, crossing into the warmth of her place.

Holly stares at me, bouncing slightly in Chloe's arms.

Her eyes are so wide.

Wide awake, that is.

"Why the sudden visit?"

I haven't been honest with Chloe. Didn't say a word about Amelie's concert and Simone being in town. I regret it. If I mention it now, my sudden appearance will rub her the wrong way.

If I say nothing, chances are good she'll find out one day, assuming . . .

Assuming this isn't just a short-term relationship.

"Just missed you. Missed talking."

"Talking?" That seductive eyebrow arches, curling like a hand around the base of my shaft.

"Everything. I missed everything about you, Chloe."

Holly yanks a piece of Chloe's hair hard enough to make her yelp, tears filling her eyes.

Holly stares at her mother in wonder, then turns to me and grins.

"Sadist," Chloe mutters, bopping Holly on the nose with great affection. "You infant sadist." The casual way Chloe welcomes me into her place, how she chats with her baby, the way I'm just here, out of the blue, and that's fine, makes my edginess that much worse.

It shouldn't.

It does.

The dissonance between my hours with Simone and these two minutes with Chloe and Holly is so extreme, it's like I'm living parallel lives in two different universes. Two different Nicks. Two different paths.

I want slow, languid time with Chloe. Explorative, contemplative time. I want hours at wine tastings and long walks on the beach, rented houses in Wellfleet and red-eye flights to Rome. We can have that.

We could have had that.

Holly nuzzles Chloe's neck.

I could have that.

Chloe's at the beginning of a life lived in quicktime, where every day feels like a race to get to the end, the finish line resetting itself every sleep-deprived morning. Her batteries will hold a charge less and less over time, and just when she thinks she can't take it anymore—the baby will become a child. Sleep will re-enter her life, but a new set of challenges abound.

I'm at the end of the long tunnel of parenting, the arched doorway of light in the near distance.

Which Nick do I choose?

And where would I fit into Chloe and Holly's life?

"Grab a beer," Chloe tells me. "This could take a while. Have to read her *Guess How Much I Love You* before bed, then rub her back until she closes her eyes."

"No *Walter the Farting Dog*?"

She pauses and turns around, giving me a mock angry look. "You've ruined my daughter with that story."

"Then my work is done."

"And she doesn't even understand the words yet."

Chuckling, she heads down the hallway while I make myself at home. Two bottles of my favorite beer are in the refrigerator.

I'll take that as a sign.

Twenty minutes later, Chloe's ass walks into her living room. Just her ass, as she tiptoes backwards in an exaggerated creeping motion.

"What are you doing?" I whisper, loosened by the beer, relieved to be away from Simone.

"Shhhh," she answers, barely audible.

"Did you say the ritual prayer? Sacrifice a goat to the druid god of sleep?"

She smiles and turns to me, arms in the air like an Olympic gold medalist. "Ah! I did it! Baby asleep." She does a silent victory dance. Hmmm.

No bra. Nice.

We both pause, because the sleep gods do not reward hubris.

No cry.

"C'mere," I order, pulling her into my lap. She's on me, straddling, more aggressive than I could have hoped, her tongue tangling with mine, hands everywhere, supercharged.

"I don't know how long we have," she moans against my mouth, hands pulling at the tails of my shirt, yanking the cloth up, palms on my skin in seconds as I strip her shirt off, one rosy nipple in my mouth.

Which means I can't answer her.

She doesn't seem to mind.

Tell her about Simone.

The thought makes me startle, tensing. There's a time and place for everything, and Chloe's unzipping my pants right now, pulling me out and palming me.

Last person I want to mention is my ex-wife.

We stand, quickly undressing, and then she shoves me onto the sofa, rolls on a condom that comes out of thin air, climbs on board, and sweet god, I'm encased in warm, wet perfection.

This night has not gone as planned.

A moment ago, I was worried about where I fit into Chloe and Holly's life.

I know where I fit in Chloe.

"Oh," she gasps, the outbreath of pleasure tickling my ear, her heat maddening. I reach between us and touch her sweet spot, knowing she'll tighten, familiar enough with her body to stroke her in ways that damn near guarantee she'll come, and come hard, in my arms.

"There," she moans, then urges me at her breast. I bite, a little harder than I should, my restraint so thin it's about to snap. We're slick with sweat and I'm wild-eyed with the speed of change, until my orgasm catches me before I can catch it, my body roaring up, hers matching my rhythm, Chloe biting my shoulder as she screams quietly, the pain enhancing our joining.

My thumb stays on her clit, knowing I can give her more, slow and steady as—

"Waaahhhhh!"

Holly shrieks from down the hallway.

Chloe falls backwards off me, like a spider blown by a gale-force wind onto its back, legs and arms flailing.

I catch her, but it takes precision I don't possess to avoid falling completely. We tumble, my hands bracing the impact, our naked, awkward bodies sticky and inelegant.

"WAAAHHHHHHHHH!"

Deprived of instant comfort, Holly's screams ratchet up. Without a word, Chloe disentangles herself from me and lurches down the hallway, calling out nonsense words in advance of her mother's soothing touch.

I'm on the floor, on my naked ass, sitting on my discarded pants.

What the hell am I doing?

Scrambling, I dress quickly and dispose of the condom, assuming that when Chloe reappears, she'll have something on as well. My mind jumps from thought to thought, scattered like dandelion seeds on the wind, all the thoughts in one direction but without any rhyme or reason.

I left Simone, abandoned in a restaurant she hates, to find comfort with Chloe.

And here I am, about as uncomfortable as I can be.

"Hey," Chloe says, re-appearing in a loose bathrobe, a red-faced, tear-streaked Holly in her arms. "Looks like she has a new tooth coming in." Chloe's doe eyes meet mine, her bewildered expression filled with regret and questions.

"Right."

We smile at each other.

"That was, um . . ." Chloe searches for the right word.

"Intense."

"Yes."

"I should—" I point toward the door.

She nods slowly. "Right." Her face falls.

"Chloe—I don't want you to think I run around doing this all the time."

"Doing . . . ?"

"Showing up at women's doors having a quickie."

"Really? You're not the booty call type? Because I hate to break it to you, Nick, but that's what you just did." Her words come with a heavy dose of amusement.

The words *booty call* hit me like an arrow to the crotch.

"Booty call?" That's what my kids call it.

"You know. Call or text a woman. See if you can come over. Netflix and chill . . ."

I groan. "That's not what this is. That's not who I am."

"I know."

"You do? How?" Because I'm not sure who I am right now. *Tell me*, I want to ask. *Tell me who the hell I am.*

She shrugs. Holly grabs a fistful of her hair. "Because we didn't do the Netflix part."

I groan again.

"And because I can just tell. You have integrity. I can trust you."

Tell her about Simone.

"Chloe, I—"

Holly starts to cry, the sound one of pain.

"I have to go," Chloe says sadly. "Time for some ibuprofen and a long night."

I almost offer to stay. It's reflexive, the impulse to provide assistance.

I fight instinct and don't say a word.

Instead, I kiss her on the cheek, offer a peck for Holly, and make my way quietly into the cold, stark night.

The slap of icy air does not provide clarity.

Damn it.

CHAPTER SEVENTEEN

Chloe

MY MOTHER IS back from Paris, recovered, and in need of a massage after a day of "helping" me.

We pull into my parking space at O, Charlotte, Holly, and of course me, the driver. Or at least we try to pull in, but there is another car in my spot. A decrepit Hyundai that looks like it may have once been red.

Great.

"Okay, Plan B," I say. "I will double park at the front entrance, set up the stroller, put Holly in it, and you can take her to my office. I'll find a place to park on the street."

"I'm sorry, Chloe, but I don't have time. My massage appointment is in seven minutes."

I just look at my mother. She shrugs, the innocent victim of circumstance.

I drop her at the front door. She waves cheerily as the doorman opens it for her.

I circle the block four times.

When I finally stagger into the reception area, there's no one at the desk. A few seconds later, Carrie pops around the corner and looks at me. At us.

"May I help you?" she says frostily.

"Actually, yes, you may. Can you take this diaper bag to my

office?"

There's a pause as she studies me.

"Chloe?"

I smile weakly.

"Oh my god! I didn't know you were coming in! I didn't recognize you! Is that the *baby*? I thought you didn't return to work for another week?"

Bite back sarcastic reply.

"I don't. We're here for my mother. It's a muscle emergency."

By now, Carrie's astonishment has drawn attention. Holly's stroller is surrounded by a crowd of women, all cooing in high-pitched voices and all with their backs to me. I am invisible.

Which is a good thing under the circumstances.

In the flurry of getting Holly dressed to impress on her first visit to O, I sort of forgot about myself. She is wearing a tiny sun-dress, something Charlotte picked up in Switzerland. The skirt has a border of hand painted wildflowers, and it came—inexplicably—with a matching handkerchief. To dry my tears of joy when I am overcome by her sweetness, presumably.

I, on the other hand, am perhaps not at my best.

I didn't really have time to change my clothes, what with getting Holly ready and packing her bag and the equipment, and making a salad for lunch. Charlotte wanted a glass of Sancerre, so I opened that, and then I made up my bed with fresh sheets for Howard's arrival tonight.

We were just out the door when I heard a little noise. Everybody back inside for a diaper change.

Anyway, I'm still in the black Athleta dress and espadrilles I wore to the North End this morning on yet another pastry run for my mother. Was it only this morning? Looking down, I see remnants of powdered sugar at the hem. I brush at it but it doesn't improve.

I am holding the crumpled-up Swiss handkerchief, which I have been using to blot the perspiration from my face.

No wonder Carrie didn't recognize me. *I* don't recognize me.

"I'll just be in my office," I offer, but no one hears me. I clear my throat. "Carrie, could you join me?"

I leave the door open so I can listen for crying—Holly's, that is.

"What's going on today?" I ask Carrie. My desk is covered with papers, fabric samples, magazines. I hate that.

"Big private party tonight," she answers, sitting down across from me. "It was a last-minute booking, but we pulled it together. A divorce celebration. In fact, the woman throwing the party will be here in twenty minutes to finalize details. Catering is tearing their hair out."

I nod, flipping through the piles on my desk. "Could you call security for me? There's a junker car parked in my spot. It needs to be towed."

Both hands fly to her mouth. "It's my car! I'm so sorry! I didn't know you were coming in, and your spot is so much closer to the door than mine!"

"All right, no problem, but could you move it before my meter expires?"

"I'll do it right now." She bolts out the door.

This is the first time I've been completely alone in weeks. And right on cue, I hear the faint sounds of an infant working up to fuss. The receptionist appears at the door, wheeling the stroller.

"Um, Chloe?"

"Thanks, Hayley."

"And there's a client here to see Carrie about her party? But Carrie just ran out. What should I tell her?"

"I'll meet with her. You can send her in."

I pick up the now-outraged Holly, and pull a bottle and a burp towel out of the bag. All sorts of interesting and unusual sounds can be heard in the halls of O, but a crying baby is completely new.

As I'm trying to settle in my chair for Holly's feeding, Hayley reappears. Behind her is a slightly heavy woman in a white skirt and a red-and-hot-pink silk halter. She's not tall, but her four-inch fuchsia heels add height. She is wearing so much heavy gold jewelry, I don't know how she stands up under the weight. Her dark brown hair has clearly just been blown out.

"This is Ms. Silverman," Hayley announces. "Ms. Silverman, this is Chloe . . ."

I attempt to stand up, but drop the bottle in my hand, which must not have been closed tightly, because the top pops off and formula makes a thick greyish puddle on the carpet. Holly cries louder.

Ms. Silverman takes an involuntary step back.

"Please come in," I call over the noise. My hair has come loose and is hanging in my face as I try to mop up the mess with the burp towel. "This will just take a second, and then we can talk. Please sit down."

She sits, carefully, looking at the chair seat first. I get out another bottle and sit back down with Holly. Mercifully, silence falls.

"I'm so sorry," I start. "I'm a new mother, and this is the first time I've brought the baby to work. Just need to get into a routine here. Let's talk about your party tonight."

She looks at me doubtfully. "I have twenty-five friends coming," she begins. "Starting at 5:00, for spa services, then drinks, dinner, and entertainment. I want everything to be perfect. You know, the fourth space? Rest, relax, indulge? You can handle this, right?"

At those words, my mind goes blank. Rest. Relax. Indulge.

"I'm getting a divorce," she continues. "We're celebrating my new life, my freedom. From that lying, cheating, egotistical, high-maintenance alcoholic I was married to."

"I know the type," I mutter.

"Seven years! Seven years of waiting for him to come home at night! Finding thongs in his pockets, scratches on his back, lipstick in places it should not be! And lately he always smells of lemon verbena perfume, when I wear Chanel No. 5! Never marry a lawyer, that's my advice. They know how to hide the truth. For a while, anyway." She makes a bitter sound. "But now I'm free."

Lemon verbena perfume? Lawyers? I look at her closely. But I don't know anyone named Silverman.

"So tonight has to be perfect. I don't care what it costs. Now that I don't have to pay for Joe's expenses anymore, my money is my own. Can I see the menu, please?"

I just stare at her. I do not move. I do not breathe. If I had a paper bag, I would put it over my head.

Joe.

"Of course, Ms . . . Silverman? Let me see if Carrie is back at her desk. She's been managing your event."

"Silverman is my maiden name. I'm taking it back. I'm not really used to it yet." She smiles, a bit shyly.

"Carrie?" I say into the phone. "Can you come in here, please, and bring Ms . . . Silverman's . . . information."

Immediately there's a quick knock on my door frame, but it's Henry. Shockingly, he is dressed in street clothes, khaki pants, a button-down shirt, my god, even a belt. Behind him is Ryan. Henry half-pulls, half-pushes Ryan into the room. He is wearing a Captain America outfit.

Minus most of the costume.

Ryan is wearing a mask, a red, white and blue shoelace thong, and he is holding a shield.

Henry is beaming with pride. Ryan looks miserable and murderous at the same time.

"We've got the costumes," Henry announces. "Carrie sent us in to show you. There wasn't a lot of time, but I think we've nailed it."

Our client rises to her feet and circles Ryan with obvious approval.

"This is fantastic!" she breathes.

Ryan perks up slightly. I swear the tattoos on one arm swell of their own accord.

Henry holds out a hand. "Henry Holliday," he says smoothly. "O's master masseur and costume designer."

Oh *please.*

"Wait until you see Iron Man." Henry *winks*.

I hold back my shudder.

So does poor Ryan.

The client puts her manicured hand in his, looking up. Way up. "I'm Marcy Silverman."

And there you have it. Marcy. Confirmed.

On my first visit back to O, I am helping *Joe's wife* arrange her divorce party. While feeding my baby. You can't make this stuff up.

And I haven't had my eyebrows threaded in *weeks*.

Holly has stopped taking her bottle, about halfway through. I raise her to my shoulder and rub her back while watching Henry and Marcy discuss what the servers will wear. Or *not* wear. Henry is sketching something on a pad. He uses an economy of strokes.

Holly, good girl that she is, produces an impressive belch. There's a brief pause. And I feel something warm running down my shoulder and neck. And back.

Where the hell is Carrie?

The office intercom speaks: *Chloe Browne, you have a call on Line Two.*

Without thinking, I reach for the phone, but before I can pick it up Marcy turns around. She blinks, and then her eyes travel from me, to Holly, to the spit-up formula splashed all over my dress.

"You're Chloe Browne?" she asks in obvious disbelief.

"Um," I say definitively. "Well. Um, yes?"

"That is very strange," Marcy says slowly. "Very coincidental."

"Oh? Do you, ah, do you know someone by that name? Not an unusual name, really. Fairly common, in fact. Lots of Chloe Brownes out there." I am babbling. "Someone even told me there's a porn star with that name. Funny, right?"

I laugh. She doesn't join in.

"My former husband's girlfriend was named Chloe Browne."

She takes a step toward me, and I turn in my chair, shielding Holly. But all Marcy does is inhale deeply.

"I thought I smelled lemon in here, but all I smell now is sour milk. It couldn't be you."

Henry has backed up to the wall. I imagine a hostage being held at gunpoint would look more comfortable.

"It was me, Marcy," I hear myself say, my voice trembling. "But I ended it. I'm so sorry. I thought he was divorcing you, and he told me . . ."

"Oh you poor thing," she interrupts. "You believed everything he said, didn't you? That lying dog. He lied to both of us for years. And look at you now, an unwed mother, trying to hold down a paying job! That tiny-pricked, slobbering snake of a festering twatwaffle!"

"No, no no no!" I am horrified. "You have the wrong idea! This is *my* baby!" But I do like her abundantly creative mastery of insults.

"Brave, *brave* girl." Marcy is undeterred. She takes out her phone. "But don't you worry, you're not alone. I'm going to take care of all your expenses, nannies and private school and college. That slimy bastard whoreson of an asshat. My family foundation will take care of everything. Joe and I never had children. You and I will raise his child together. What's your cell number?"

"Ms. Silverman, Marcy," I start. "This is not Joe's baby."

She looks up from her phone. "Really." Her eyes narrow. "There were others? You had a DNA test?"

"I adopted. She's just mine. No paternity test needed."

She processes this. "You really are a brave girl," she says finally. "Come to my party tonight. Get a babysitter. We're both free of him. A new life for both of us."

"Thank you, Marcy," I say with real gratitude. "I can't, but thank you so much."

I stand, still clutching Holly to my shoulder, and move to hug her. She leans in but suddenly pulls back, and I realize that only someone wearing a hazmat suit would hug me now.

Henry grabs Ryan's arm and they sidle out of the room. As they exit, Carrie enters. She has folders in one hand and a small tray of dessert samples in the other. She walks by Ryan, then spins on one heel in a classic double take. She bursts into incredulous laughter, then catches my eye and tries to swallow it.

Ryan raises his shield to hide his face.

"Carrie! Why don't you take Ms. Silverman to the conference room to finish your meeting? I think everything is in really good shape."

I smile at Marcy, and she smiles right back.

O, the fourth space.

♥ ♥ ♥

I'M GOING BACK to work full time in one week. One week. And everyone from our pediatrician to the supermarket checkout clerk says I need to get this baby on a schedule.

Actually, I'm not sure what this means. And I have no clue at all how one would accomplish it. How do you motivate an infant? Threaten to take away her cell phone? Or maybe the reward system is better—if you finish your cereal I'll let you binge-watch *Sesame Street*?

Anyway, in an effort to establish predictable nap times, on this sunny afternoon, I am taking Holly on a snooze cruise of Back Bay while my mother recovers from her massage at my place. Holly is tucked warmly into her stroller with her binky and stuffed bunny. I am able to study the display windows of all the chic Newbury Street shops, heading for the Public Gardens. There I plan to sit on a bench in a warm place and read a novel while she sleeps.

Like a Beacon Hill nanny, but older.

Except she doesn't sleep.

She scowls, she spits out her binky, she wrestles with her blankets. She is dissatisfied. She makes threatening sounds.

Determined, I keep walking. Through the Gardens, past the Skating Pond, over to Charles Street. Past the antiques dealers and the cafes. I'm about to give up and head toward the Red Line stop when I realize I'm about two blocks from Nick's.

Is dropping in cool?

At his house, I could change her diaper, refill my water bottle, warm up for ten minutes.

Okay, let's be honest. I can do all those things in a coffee shop. I just want to see him.

This is *so* high school.

I turn onto his street, which climbs steeply uphill. The sidewalks here are antique brick, charming but so uneven that I can barely push the stroller forward. Holly is being rocked wildly from side to side. Finally I resort to walking backwards and dragging the stroller up after me. Here's a plus: I definitely do not need to work out after this.

Finally the street levels off a bit. I check Holly.

Sound asleep. Go figure.

Well, I'm here now, in front of Nick's townhouse. After the trip up the hill, I don't really need to warm up anymore—in fact, I am sweating profusely—but at least I can see Nick. I pull the elastic out of my ponytail and re-tie it as best I can without a brush. Before Holly, I never would have left the house without lipstick. I feel in my jacket pocket, and *yes!* I find a tube. I pull it out. ChapStick.

And yet, tucked into the pockets of the stroller are diapers, wipes, Balmex, bottles of formula, an extra binky, pajamas, a sweater, sun lotion, and a bottle of baby ibuprofen drops. Enough baby supplies to last a week.

I ring the doorbell, and keep jiggling the stroller. My nose starts to run from the chilly air, and I am wiping it with a tissue when I hear the clicking and scraping of locks being turned from the inside. My heart beats a little faster.

The door swings in, and there stands a woman so perfect in every respect, I wonder if it might be Siri. She is wearing an ivory tweed suit and lots of pearls, and if that sounds boring, trust me, it isn't. Looks like Chanel. Her dark brown hair is pinned up in a smooth twist.

She's not smiling.

"Oui?" French Siri says.

"Uh," I reply.

"Is it the recycle, or the whales?" she asks impatiently. "Where must I sign?"

"Um. Is, um, is Nick here?"

She looks at me closely now. Her glance falls on the stroller and her eyes narrow.

"And you are?"

I hesitate. "Chloe?" Even I'm not sure anymore.

"I will see if my husband can come to the door," she says coldly. Or maybe it's just the French accent. I really can't tell. "He is busy with our children. Un moment."

The door slams shut. As I regard the brass knocker, I hear her muffled voice, *"Nicolas!"* and then an angry flood of French words, from which I can make out only a bit, but did she just ask him if he was properly dressed?

Oh, god. I've been so stupid.

Again.

I turn away from the door, and as I do, my jacket catches on the railing post. There's a tearing sound, but I can't stop. I untangle my jacket, kick off the stroller's brake pedals, and go back in the direction from which I came.

Downhill is easier.

At the bottom of the street, I turn right towards the T station.

Really there's not a thought in my head. There is a huge, heavy pain in my chest, but not a single thought in my head. The sidewalks are crowded with shoppers, all the urbanites who have been cooped up in their apartments and are now out for air. They are slowing me down considerably. Holly sleeps on, oblivious. Every once in a while her binky quivers as she sucks automatically, dreaming of milk and clouds and happy mommies.

There are noises behind me, a disturbance. A fight, or someone hurt? I glance over my shoulder nervously, and try to pick up speed. Everyplace seems more dangerous these days. I just want to get us home now. Where we can be safe.

Suddenly the disturbance is right behind me, and I hear "Chloe!" as someone grabs my arm. I pull away, hard, terrified, but it's Nick yelling "Chloe! Stop!"

Then I pull away harder.

He has no coat on, and he's panting. Wouldn't you think someone, anyone, would ask if I need help? A woman with a baby being accosted by a frantic man? But no, the crowds just step around us. We get one or two looks of annoyance for blocking the way.

"What?"

"I heard what happened. I'm so sorry. Simone is playing some kind of game. You don't understand."

"Oh, I understand all too well, Nick." My voice is an iceberg. "Go back to your wife."

"Ex-wife!" he roars. "Simone is here for Amelie's concert and she wanted to stay with the kids. It's the first time she's ever done this. It's not what you think!"

"That's what you all say," I hiss, with a bitterness I didn't know was in me. "Go home to your wife, Nick. Go home to your family."

I look down at my little angel.

"I've already got mine."

And with that, I walk away.

Nick

"ARE YOU OUT OF YOUR MIND?" I roar as I enter my own home, winded from running back, destroyed by the look on Chloe's face and her final words to me.

That's what you all say.

Jesus. She just lumped me in with that bastard ex of hers. My god.

I do not care that Simone's recoiling, physically terrified, her impassive face now expressing nothing but sheer horror at . . . me.

At who I am right now. Right here.

The man she made me become.

"You told her I'm your husband!" I bellow at Simone, who gives me a look of pleading. "That's a role you kicked me out of years ago. Get out. Get out of my house *now*."

"Nick, you misunderstand."

Funny. I just said that to Chloe. Deep rage makes me feel the need to apologize again. How anemic are those words. I let her go because there was nothing I could do in the moment.

Nothing I could say to make Chloe stay.

But I could come back here and right a wrong.

Simone puts together all the puzzle pieces of her face and suddenly, she's back to being Simone, pulling on a pearl earring with impatience, as if I'm the one who has transgressed. "I told your little lover that—"

"I heard every word. I was right behind you. Don't lie."

"How dare you call me a—"

"Don't dare me to do anything right now, Simone."

Her face goes pale as fresh cream.

"You will leave. Get a hotel. We'll tell the kids you needed some space. They won't question it, because you've always needed space." My temples pound with fury, my breathing still ragged around the edges from sprinting after Chloe, then racing back to get Simone before she could slip out and avoid the confrontation.

I need this.

I've needed this for years.

"You do not get to make this my fault, Nick!"

"I'm not making it your fault, Simone. You did that nicely all on your own."

"Chloe—is that her name?—is worth all this?" She titters. "Good for you. Finally acting like a man." She sniffs. "Nice to see you have it in you."

That's it.

Gloves off.

"You do not get to define my maleness, Simone. Not now, not ever. Damn it, you made me feel like less of a man for wanting to be more of a father!"

She blinks, hard, her elbow covering one breast as she twists her earring, a sure sign of stress in her. She did that exact movement the day she told me she was leaving. Perfect sleeveless dress, perfect lipstick, hair pulled back in a tight knot at the base of her neck, her skin flawless.

Execution, too. Rejection sounds so impersonal spoken in a second language, as if it's just another lesson you need to learn. It's almost pretty.

"We were young. You—you became obsessed with the children. You stopped paying attention to me, Nick. You were just a roommate suddenly. Up all night with the babies, arguing with me that they couldn't be left to cry themselves to sleep, telling me that we didn't need to go out, that the babies needed us more."

"Because they did!"

"And meanwhile, my womanhood withered on the vine. You looked at me like a mother. Not as a desirable woman. Not as a romantic partner."

"Because you *were* a mother! My God, Simone, you gave me the three greatest gifts of my entire life. You gave me my life's purpose! I loved you even more for that."

"*I* wanted to be your life's purpose. Can't you see? I gave you children and you cast me aside as if you were done." Her eyes flash with indignity, as if my words are weapons designed to hurt, rather than explain.

She never gave me a chance fifteen years ago.

This time, I'm *taking* that chance.

"No. No, Simone. You can't re-write history. That is not what happened. I wanted to find deeper love with you by raising those beautiful children. *Our* children. With you. We were supposed to find even more love by creating them. Not less. You don't get less from me because they get my love, too. The only way to make that happen is to leave. And you did. You took your love away from me. From them. You don't get to make me the bad guy here. I didn't cast you aside. You cast *me* aside."

"Nick, I—"

"You chose Rolf."

"Oh, please, this tired argument? It was a fling, and then—"

"But long before you chose Rolf, you chose yourself. You showed your true self to me, and I loved it. Loved *you*. But once you weren't the center of my world—the *only* center—you couldn't handle it. You couldn't share, could you? You'll never, ever know what it's like to have that deeper sense of love, the purity and divine that comes from giving more than you know you can give."

The air crackles as if I'd slapped her.

"How dare you. The children love me."

"They do. They love you more than you'll ever know. They miss you, too, Simone. Miss you deeply. I'm the one who had to make excuses for you for years. Why Maman didn't visit more. Why she didn't call. All the *didn'ts*. Why didn't Maman this. Why didn't Maman that. . . ."

"We talk! I have a good relationship with my children!"

"Of course you do, because they still crave the love they never got! But you might as well be Aunt Simone. You have a surface level relationship with them, and you're damn lucky for that. They extend you a courtesy. You chose Rolf over them."

Over me.

"*Va te faire voire!*"

"You always shouted that whenever I spoke the truth, Simone." A bone-weary tiredness begins to replace rage. She's diminishing before my eyes, all surface, no depth. All shell, no interior. Instead of making herself vulnerable, trying to find a more authentic truth in the past we share, she needs to win.

"We can't all be saints like you, Nick."

And there it is.

"Never pretended to be one, Simone. All I am is one man."

"All you are is a *father*." Her lips curl up in a snarl. A smear of burgundy lipstick mars one cuspid.

"Is that supposed to be an insult?"

"It means you've chosen not to be whole."

"Said by the woman whose sense of self is created by the man she's with."

"Then we're two of a kind, Nick, because your sense of self comes from being a father."

"No. Fatherhood connected me. But it didn't define me. I define me. No one else can do that."

Real fear flickers in her eyes. She drops her hand from her ear, lips tight, nose wide with fury as she snatches her purse off the table by the door.

"You can explain to the children. Explain to them why I cannot be there today."

"Won't be the first time. I'm a pro at it."

Her shocked look quickly turns to utter fury. "You asshole."

I deserve that. Doesn't make my statement untrue.

"I'll have them text you. They're adults. I won't be your go-between any longer."

"You're really going to ruin this?"

"This . . . what?"

"This chance. I came here to try to re-ignite the spark between us."

"I thought you came to support Amelie at her concert."

She laughs through her nose, the sound irritatingly painful, like a paper cut. "You are so singular. I can accomplish both with one task."

"Task?"

"Don't do this, Nick. Don't analyze my words and give them more meaning than they have."

"I'm a task? Your daughter is a task?"

"I won't let you do this, Nick."

"Do what?"

"Make me feel less."

"Maybe we have more in common than I thought."

She blinks, hard, hope filling her face. "Yes?"

"Because I won't let you make me feel like less of person either, Simone."

And with that, I leave her alone in my townhouse, walking away, abandoning her.

Because I know exactly where to find *more*.

Chloe

"IT'S NOT WHAT you think," he said.

That's what they all say.

I shouldn't turn around and look, but I do.

He's gone.

The heavy pain in my chest has radiated out to every cell and nerve in my body. My fingernails hurt. My eyelashes ache. I keep moving forward, because what else can I do?

That's what they all say. But I thought he was different.

As we approach the turnstile at the T entrance, I automatically reach in my pocket for the card case where I keep my Charlie card.

Nothing. The pocket is empty. In fact, my hand goes right through the cloth.

Shit.

That ripping sound on the doorstep.

Now what?

Oh no no no. Please no. Not a walk of shame all the way back to Nick's. Not hunting around the front of the house in full view of anyone who might be looking.

NOT—please NOT—having to knock and borrow cab fare if the card case is not there.

If it were just me, I could suck it up and walk all the way home. But I can't do that with Holly. And it's not just my T pass that's missing, it's my driver's license, my debit card, my O access card. I have to try to find them.

I turn around. I have no choice.

The streets are not as crowded, now that lunchtime is over. We make better time. And Holly, my good girl, stays sound asleep. I don't care if she's up till midnight, just let her stay asleep now. Has anyone considered nominating the inventor of the binky for a Nobel Peace Prize?

At the foot of Nick's street, I pause and pull the hood of my jacket over my head. I'm already wearing sunglasses. This subterfuge will certainly prevent me from being noticed. A panting and disheveled woman hauling an orange Italian baby stroller up a somnolent and otherwise dignified Beacon Hill street is practically invisible, right?

I take a deep breath. Once more unto the breach, dear friends. Once more.

Summiting the peak, I set the stroller's brakes and commence my search. Nothing on the steps or the sidewalk. I inspect the ground closer to the house.

One of the windows above my head is cracked open, just an inch or two. Classic New England style, gotta have fresh air, even in autumn weather. I hear voices inside, but very faintly. That's good—if they're in the back of the house, they won't see me skulking around here. No card case in sight. I'm about to move to the other side of the steps when the voices rapidly get louder.

I freeze.

Nick's voice is cold. "They're adults. I won't be your go-between any longer."

Then a woman's voice that can only belong to Simone. "You're really going to ruin this?"

I've got to get away from here.

They must be standing right by the window. If I move, I'll draw their attention.

If I move, I won't hear what they're saying.

"This . . . what?"

"This chance. I came here to re-ignite the spark between us."

My stomach turns over.

"I thought you came to support Amelie at her concert."

She laughs. "You are so singular. I can accomplish both with one task."

"Task?"

"Don't do this, Nick. Don't analyze my words and give them more meaning than they have."

"I'm a task? Your daughter is a task?"

"I won't let you do this, Nick."

"Do what?"

"Make me feel less."

"Maybe we have more in common than I thought."

"Yes?"

"Because I won't let you make me feel like less of person either, Simone."

I shouldn't care. I shouldn't. But my heart surges in Nick's favor, as if it's cheering for him. His voice is tight, full of anger and regret, emotions he's never shown me, and a tiny piece of me is jealous.

Jealous that his ex can elicit that kind of reaction from him.

Why do I want men I can't have?

Suddenly the wind rustles a small pile of dead leaves in the corner, and I see a silvery sheen underneath the brown. My card case! I bend down, and just as my fingers close on it, the front door opens fast and slams shut. I look up to see Nick come shooting out the door and down the steps, but he isn't expecting a baby stroller to be parked directly in his path, and he runs right into it.

Nick trips, and regains his balance. But the force of his stumbling into the stroller jolted Holly awake. She bellows as he rights the carriage, reflexes kicking in with military precision, the baby never in danger.

He looks around and sees me. He is completely vulnerable, a thousand emotions flashing through his strong face, a rawness to his movements and expressions I've never seen before.

I hold my breath from the intensity.

I was wrong.

I guess I *can* elicit that kind of reaction in him.

"Come on," he says, and takes off down the hill, pushing my daughter with him, holding on to the carriage like it's a lifeline.

What else can I do?

I follow.

Nick

HOLLY STARES UP at me from her stroller with eyes that trust the world.

Chloe looks at me with eyes devoid of trust.

Half-blind with rage, shaking like I'm primed for battle, I navigate the sidewalks, moving the carriage around trash bins and recycling containers, until we're on our way to a park down the street. I need air. Space. Land.

"Nick!" Chloe gasps from behind. "Slow down!"

I'm half a block ahead of her, the baby beneath me in the stroller, her little fists settling on top of her blanket, eyes closed.

I stop and close my eyes. I see my pulse, like a visual bass drum, the colors behind my eyelids a symphony in blood.

"Here." She peels my fingers off the handle, taking my place, one hand on the stroller, the other slipping Holly's exposed hands under the thick blankets. Chloe rights the baby's pacifier and moves forward, eyes straight ahead, not looking at me.

"Can we talk?" I ask, realizing I haven't extended that basic respect to her. The image of Simone's self-satisfied smirk won't leave me.

"What's there to talk about?" she asks, facing me dead on, eyes accusing.

Everything.

"Plenty."

She nods, slowly, blinking hard as if fighting tears. Her cheeks go pink in the cold, or maybe that's from anger. It's hard to tell.

"Yes. But let's be civilized and do it with caffeine and carbs in front of us."

Chloe steers the carriage toward a little coffee shop with a doorway just wide enough to fit the stroller. One step up and we're in. I order two lattes and can't get Chloe's attention, as she soothes a fussing baby. Biscotti and coffee will have to do.

The savagery inside me diminishes as these civilized transactions take place. Pleasantries, directions, the exchange of money and food, and the walk to the table carrying a tray all require parts of my brain that aren't warrior mind to function.

As I sit, my leg taps with nervous energy. Haven't done that since I was a teen. The coffee scalds my throat but the pain feels good. Focused.

And I'm the Focus Man, right?

Chloe's slipping away from me. I feel it, a physical tug, like someone's cutting a rope that ties us to each other. Not Simone, not Joe—some other force, intangible and unnamed. If you can name a demon, you can vanquish it.

Let it remain without definition and it thrives on chaos.

I struggle to say the right words. The right line. The magic phrase that clears up the mist of confusion that clouds Chloe's face.

Instead, I torture my throat with more scalding coffee and tap my leg like an idiot.

Holly cries.

Chloe fumbles.

And we drift further.

I reach for the baby, to offer some help, but Chloe shakes her head, blinking hard, this time to hold back tears that won't stop.

My tapping stops.

"That wasn't supposed to happen."

She looks up sharply. "Are you so sure?"

I jolt. "What's that supposed to mean?"

"Your ex still wants you."

"I had no idea. None."

"Please." Her look cuts me to the bone. "You're a smart guy. You had to know."

I stay silent. Finally, I open up. I have to. It's only fair.

"Simone's been here for two days."

Chloe looks up sharply. "Two days?"

"She came for Amelie's senior concert."

I watch the calculations in Chloe's eyes. I can almost see time-lines that look like a stock ticker, numbers shooting past. "The other night, when you came over. She was here?"

I nod.

"Your booty call—"

"Don't call it that," I snap. "It was anything but."

"You were escaping her?"

One end of my mouth curls up. "I needed to see *you.*"

"It's meet the ex-wife day," she says with a long sigh. Holly's crying, the sound piercing, and Chloe bounces her on one knee, grabbing her coffee with a desperate hand. "Two in one day. I'm not sure what I did in a prior life to deserve this, but it must have been bad."

"Two ex-wives?" The cloud of confusion just thickened.

"Long story," she says, her mouth twisted in pain. Her coffee must be as hot as mine.

Holly's screaming goes up a notch.

I start tapping my leg again.

This is too much.

"I want to hear it."

Chloe's attention is split between me, the baby, her coffee, and the unsuccessful attempt to stop tears from flowing down her cheeks. Ten minutes ago, I was yelling at my past.

Now I'm listening to my present scream.

What sound does the future make?

"I—"

Holly won't stop crying. Chloe's eye dart to mine, then close, twin tears rolling down her face. Like someone is slowly rolling my gut inside out, I tighten, curling inward, turning to granite.

Inaction is unacceptable.

"Let me hold her," I insist.

Chloe clings to the baby. "No." She stands, upsetting the plate of biscotti, one sliding to the ground and cracking in half. "I need to go. Holly needs to be home."

"I'll walk with you."

The look she gives me breaks my heart.

"Please. No. Nick—this day. This—" She looks everywhere but at me. "This is too much."

I want to beg her. I want to make her stay. I want to take the baby and calm her down. I want to kiss Chloe's tears away.

I made her cry.

I can't undo that.

But I can respect her wishes. I can give her what she needs.

I nod, standing, helping maneuver the carriage outside. The cold slap of air makes Holly whoop, the look on her face precious. Even Chloe laughs through her tears.

"Let me walk with you part of the way?"

Chloe shakes her head. "It's been one hell of a day. Let me—let this all sink in."

"Chloe." I hold her elbow, my heart in my throat, my mind ragged around the edges, unraveling. Think, Nick. Say the right words. Find the core element here that fixes this.

Make this whole again.

"Nothing Simone said is true."

"I know."

"I would never lie to you."

Her eyes narrow, the look deepening between us. "I know."

"Do you?"

She gives me a sad smile. "Yes."

I tip her chin up, "Then why does this feel like we're falling apart?"

Chloe grabs the stroller and begins walking. I keep up.

"Nick, I can't. I just can't right now. I went to work today and met Joe's ex-wife. I came here to talk and be with you and instead I get a second dose of ex-wife karma. It's too much."

"Joe's ex?"

"It's a long story."

"You keep saying that."

"Because it is."

"Tell me. Tell me the story." A part of me knows that if she walks away, this is over. There's no reason to think that. None.

But it feels true.

"Let me go home. Settle Holly down. Think."

"Sure." Her eyes have a hunted look, like I'm right on the brink of pushing her over the edge. Focus Man kicks in.

My focus needs to be on doing the right thing.

Not on winning.

"Text or call any time."

"When I'm ready." She says the words with such sadness.

"I'll be there. What we have, Chloe—I don't want to lose you. I feel like I've been looking for you for most of my life. When you're ready, I'll be here. This is worth waiting for. We're so close."

Her eyes fly open and her face flushes, jaw set, nostrils flaring.

And then she marches off without another word.

CHAPTER EIGHTEEN

Chloe

"**R**EMEMBER THAT PARTY game, Twister?" I ask Jemma. Henry is only half-listening, since the Pats game is on, fourth quarter. Harold is with my mother, off at the Four Seasons again. By the time I arrived home with a still-hysterical Holly, there was only time for an air kiss and a promise to visit again.

I escaped to my safe spot.

Even if it involves football.

"Sure," she answers. "There was a big plastic mat with colored circles, and a spinner, and you had to put a certain body part on a certain circle. And everyone was on the mat at the same time. Eventually someone couldn't reach, or couldn't hold their position, and they collapsed. That caused everyone else to collapse with them."

"I loved that game," Henry says fondly.

"Says the seven-foot-tall dude," Jemma notes bitterly. "I hated that game. I was too short to ever reach the outer circles."

"Well, Twister is what dating in your thirties and forties is like." I take a sip from my bottle of Corona Light.

"What?" she laughs.

"*Sshhhh!*" from Henry.

"The circles are all the different parts of your life," I explain. "So you each have a hand for your kids, and a foot for your job. Maybe the other foot is your former relationships, your exes."

I move to the floor to demonstrate. Henry looks up from the TV screen. I'm stretched out and arched like a spider. I wave my spare hand in the air.

"Now I have this one hand left for a new relationship. The spinner points to a red circle, but it's just a little too far to stretch. I try hard, but I just . . . can't . . . reach . . ." I collapse dramatically on the carpet. "I fall down, and Nick falls on top of me. Game over."

"Yes! That's the whole point!" Henry says, astonished. "Did you not understand that?"

We both glare at him.

"It's a *metaphor*," I sigh.

We are sitting in the living room of their loft. Henry needs a lot of room, so the loft is perfect. Super-high ceilings, wide-open space, and it accommodates their large-scale furniture. Holly is sound asleep in the center of their California-king-size bed, blocked all around by pillows.

"The point is, trying to start a new relationship at this point is different from dating in your twenties. Our lives are full of other responsibilities and experiences, and we can't just let go of them. They make us who we are, but they don't leave a lot of room for more."

"I don't think that's true," Jem says thoughtfully. "At least, I hope it's not true. I think we have an infinite capacity to add love to our lives. You had room for Holly. I think you have room for Nick."

"Holly arrived all by herself. She didn't bring a French wife and three kids who call during sex."

"Wait a minute." Henry's paying attention now. "Ex-wife. But that's not the point. You're not exactly free of baggage yourself, girlfriend."

I squint at the ceiling.

"In fact, Nick spent quite a bit of money buying up some of your baggage online, as I recall."

I begin inspecting my pedicure.

"And he seems pretty willing to play Twister with you. He

doesn't mind putting his hand on your red circles." He pauses. "I mean . . . you know what I mean."

"We all have to live our lives, Chloe," Jemma chimes in. "We experiment and take some detours, probably make a few mistakes. That's how we learn and grow and figure out what's right. We can't just sit and wait for some perfect person to come along."

I look up.

"Worth the wait," I whisper.

"What?"

"Nick said this was worth waiting for. He said he would wait."

"Why would you want to make him wait?"

"I don't know," I say miserably. "But Joe said I was worth waiting for, and I believed him, and then he said it to someone else."

"Even a baby can see that Joe and Nick are nothing alike," Henry observes.

"Speaking of babies, I should go check on mine."

Jemma follows me to their bedroom. Holly's still out like a light, lying on her back with her arms flung wide, totally secure.

We stand and watch her for a moment in peaceful silence.

"I have to find someone to take care of her, for when I go back to work," I sigh. "But I can't bear to think about leaving her all day long with a total stranger."

"I know," Jem agrees. "Henry and I were talking about it. She's precious to us, too."

We tiptoe out of the room.

"We had an idea," she says tentatively. "It's just a thought, and it might not work for you, but . . . I already work at home, and I could just as easily write at your house as here . . . and she knows me . . . and I've spent so much time with her already . . ." she pauses. "And I love her so much."

"Jem. You're not serious."

She studies my face. "Of course you probably want a trained professional nanny, I totally understand, no worries. Someone who speaks three languages or has a degree in babies."

"Jemma! Are you *kidding*? Henry! You would seriously do this? I cannot imagine anything more wonderful! It's such a weight off my shoulders—oh how can I ever thank you?"

Without taking his eyes off the television, Henry suggests "A great benefits package?"

"Anything!" I laugh. "A car, your birthday off, Henry's birthday off, a dry cleaning allowance! I'd offer free massages, but you already get those."

I throw my arms around her, then bend down and hug Henry, who struggles away wildly as the stadium crowd begins roaring. "Chloe! I can't see the play!"

Thus he misses the winning touchdown. He's mad, but I don't care. I scored.

We move to the kitchen for chili, which smells fantastic. Jemma starts ladling it into bowls while I plug in the baby monitor and adjust the volume.

"So how did you leave it with Nick?"

"He said to text or call anytime. I will when I'm ready."

"And just when do you think that might be?"

Is that sarcasm I detect?

"Chloe, I don't really understand." She puts down the ladle and turns to face me. "He's doing everything right. He seems to really like you, and you really like him. The sex is good—"

I make an involuntary sound. She rolls her eyes.

"—okay, the sex is *great*. He's unmarried and gainfully employed and has no arrest record that you know of. You make each other laugh. You belong to the same political party. He can change a diaper and sail a boat, and he likes Sofia Coppola movies. None of your ex-boyfriends could say all of those things. Joe couldn't even say the first three. What exactly is the problem here?"

"I'm so scared," comes out of me in a tiny voice.

"Of what?"

"I *do* really like him. I like him too much. He's *too* good. You know that saying, 'If it's too good to be true,' . . ."

She joins in and finishes it with me.

" . . . 'it's too good to be true'!"

"Jem, I like him too much," I repeat slowly. "When I'm with Nick, I am perfectly happy. It's terrifying. I recently had my heart ripped out, and I remember how it felt. I can't do that anymore. I have a baby now. I can't have a man come into our lives and make us happy, and then go out of our lives and make us miserable. We need emotional stability."

She's quiet for a minute.

"I understand that, and I respect it. Part of a mom's responsibilities involves making good choices, and not taking unnecessary risks. But there are other responsibilities, too."

"What do you mean?"

"It's your job to show Holly what life can hold. I think you have a moral responsibility to live your fullest life, full of love and new experiences."

She holds up a bowl of chili. "Look at this—thick and full of good stuff, tomatoes and meat and tons of spices. It's all been simmering together for a long time over a low flame, so it's got intense flavor. Chips on the side for texture, sour cream for contrast. Delicious. Or instead, I could have served chicken broth. Perfectly good, healthy even, but thin and boring. And you'd be just as hungry after you finished."

You can see why she is so successful as a health journalist. She makes unusual connections to illustrate her points.

"If Holly grows up seeing that you are scared of a loving relationship, she will learn that love is something to avoid. None of us want that little girl to ever have a single unhappy moment, but she will. What she needs to know is that she'll get through it. Sadder but wiser, as my grandmother used to say. So you have to be her model. You have to be brave for her. You have to teach her that love is not chicken broth!"

This is not in my parenting books.

Henry comes in, opens three fresh beers, and settles himself at the island. He regards the steaming bowl in front of him.

"Looks great," he says happily. He has no idea it represents his entire life. "You know your Twister idea?"

We both look at him in surprise, our spoons halfway to our mouths. He really was paying attention.

"There should be another version called Married Twister," he continues. "Or maybe just Twisted Together. Because when you're together, the problems are shared. There are four hands instead of just two. If one of you has a hand on the mother-in-law circle, for example, the other person can cover the kids circle. You help each other stay balanced."

Jem hops off her stool and runs around to kiss him on the cheek. She can reach it when he's sitting down.

"In Married Twister," he chuckles, "I always have a free hand." He holds it up, then reaches around and places it on her ass, which he squeezes.

"Chloe's going to call Nick," she informs him. "She's going to play the game. You can't win if you don't play."

So I guess I'm going to call Nick.

Nick

"Is this going to take long? Because you're making us miss part of the Pats game," Jean-Marc grouses. I get all three kids into the living room, bracing myself.

"Your mother's gone," I say to the three of them, taken back fifteen years to a time when those words stuck in my throat.

"Right," Amelie says with a sad smile.

"I'm surprised she lasted a single night," Jean-Marc says dryly.

I jerk with surprise. "What?"

"Me, too," Elodie adds, grimacing. "She only came back to try to hook up with you, Daddy."

"Excuse me?"

"Pretty elaborate for a booty call," Jean-Marc says under his breath.

These kids.

"You're not . . . upset?" I'm ignoring all mention of the rest of this.

"Sure." Amelie's eyes fill with tears. "But she came. Other than our high school graduation, this is the first big event she's bothered to, you know, like . . . attend."

Jean-Marc's face goes tight. His mother has never attended an event of significance for him.

"When she said she left Rolf, I knew what was going on. Funny how she wasn't interested in coming until I told her about Chloe," Elodie adds with a heavy dose of sarcasm.

I look at her. "What?"

"Maman has this way of talking about you like you're so boring. Or like you're a lap dog. I hate it." Elodie's eyes are alight with fire and indignation. "And normally, she doesn't even ask about you. So when she started prying, I couldn't stand it. Plus, she happened to call the day after, um . . . you know."

"You stalked Dad and interrupted him during—"

"Heeeyyyyyyy." Charlie interrupts, slashing a hand across his neck while looking at Elodie. "Ixnay on the ex-say."

The three kids crack up.

"Beer? I need beer if we have to simultaneously talk about Simone *and* Nick's sex life."

How did my serious talk with my kids turn into this?

"We're not talking about my and Simone's sex life."

All three kids start gagging.

Charlie gives me a devilish grin.

"Daddy," Amelie says, her hand on my forearm, clearly troubled. "We know what Maman is like. How she is. We—well, she's not like you. At all. And," she adds, her voice halting, "it hurts."

There you have it.

I close my eyes, battling my own hurt that Simone has caused, and working not to project that onto my kids. When they were little, I thought I could shield them from the worst about her. And to be fair, the worst that she's done is to be absent. To hold on to herself and refuse to share.

But for a child, that burns, a searing brand on identity formation, and there's only so much I could do.

"I'm sorry, Ami."

"I know."

"She ditched Rolf and decided to check you out," Elodie declares. "Like you've been waiting all these years to be picked back up. Like a purse you stop liking and then it comes back into style."

They all have this tone in their voices.

A protective tone.

When did my kids start to feel the need to defend me?

"She wouldn't come to my high school graduation, but she'll come for a chance to get you under her thumb again," Jean-Marc mutters.

There's a gut punch. And I can't argue with him. He's right.

"It didn't work." I look at them, constantly calculating, mind in motion as I try to balance privacy with their maturity.

All three kids look at each other with frowns.

"We know," Jean-Marc finally says. "I was here."

"Here?" I'm puzzled.

"Here when you yelled at Maman."

A stony silence fills the room.

"Oh." I don't know what to say. "I'm sorry you had to hear that."

"I'm not." His jaw is tight, arms clenched in a fighter's stance. "Every word you said is true, Dad. Every word."

Charlie is uncharacteristically quiet, just watching everyone. He opens his mouth. "Your mother thinks Nick is a lap dog?" he asks Elodie.

She nods. "She said a long time ago that if Daddy had been—" She looks at me in distress.

"It's fine. Go ahead," I say in someone else's voice.

"She said that she did what was best at the time, and that any man who does not live his own life is a poor role model for his children."

I stand suddenly, on my feet via instinct, unaware of the insta-rage that shoots through me like a pipe bomb filled with debris.

Steady, I tell myself. I think of Chloe's mouth, the taste of her, how she felt against my thighs, her delicate skin and fine bones all mine. I run through the last few days, my memory a video in 4x time, the sequence of events gaining a different meaning as I put it together in retrospect.

I sought out the sanctuary of Chloe after Simone came on to me. Not because I needed to feel like more of a man. Not because I needed freedom.

Because I needed *Chloe*. The intimacy is emotional and physical, promising and alluring, and I can be myself and be sexual with her. Find connection in the physical and intellectual realm. She's the whole package. Simone is all surface, no depth, living a life marked by projection.

Chloe's just *living*.

"Nick." Charlie's taking charge here. I shake myself, looking around the room.

"She's wrong," Amelie says. She looks at her phone. "Ooo, text from Kieran. Gotta go."

"Who's Kieran?" I ask.

"New guy. Meeting for coffee." She kisses my cheek and flies out the door.

"Merde!" Jean-Marc calls out, racing to the television. "Pats game! We missed part of it." Charlie joins him, the two glued to the screen in seconds.

The moment is lost.

Bzzz.

My phone vibrates in my back pocket, and when I pull it out, the Holy Grail appears.

A text from Chloe.

A relieved smile fills my face.

Can I come over? Jemma will watch Holly for me.

Of course, I type back.

I want to add, *Thank you,* but I don't.

Wouldn't want anyone to mistake me for a lap dog.

♥ ♥ ♥

CHARLIE TAKES JEAN-MARC to a local sports bar, while Elodie finds some folklore thing to visit, leaving me with an empty house. I'm fidgety, checking the wine bottles, setting and re-setting wine glasses on the kitchen counter. Chloe's text is a sign of hope. I've given her space. She needs it. So do I.

Between Simone, the clash with Chloe, and the decidedly surreal conversation with my kids and Charlie a moment ago, space and time are in short supply.

"Breathe," I tell myself, surprised by the case of nerves that hits me.

The doorbell rings.

"Hi." Her shy smile puts me on guard.

"Hi." I hustle her inside, out of the cold, and take her coat. Just the feel of my hands skimming her clothed arms makes me stop breathing. I can fix this. We can decide.

We can choose to make this work.

"Wine?"

She nods. "Just one glass." There are dark circles under her eyes, though she's carefully made up. Somehow, Chloe manages to look utterly exhausted and radiantly happy at the same time.

New motherhood.

We move to the sofa, where she curls up against the stack of pillows, not touching me. I angle myself so I'm facing her.

"How's Holly?"

"Good. Great."

"Getting any sleep?"

She laughs, then yawns as if to prove the point. "No."

"It'll happen soon."

"Define 'soon.'"

"Jean-Marc didn't sleep through the night until he was nearly two."

"I hate you." She laughs. "Holly is sleeping at Jemma and Henry's right now. I don't have long, but I'll take what I can get."

The physical memory of our rushed night of sex at her place while the baby slept for seven minutes hits me like a tidal wave.

"Right," I choke out.

"Look. I'll get to the point." Her eyes meet mine over the wine glass as she takes a sip. "I will never, ever date a man again who's committed to someone else."

Good thing I'm not drinking. "What?"

"You heard me." Her eyes are hard and cold, like brown rocks. Yet somehow, I feel her pleading with me underneath.

"I'm not with anyone else. I'm *not*," I add, a hard edge to my voice. The stakes are high here, but there's more. If she can't trust me, we can't continue. I won't grovel.

"I know." She tips her head down. "I know I'm projecting some of this. After the choice I made—the stupid choice—to stay with Joe for so long, I find myself unable to find true North."

"North?"

"My compass is a little bit broken. The piece inside you that guides you. Except with Holly." She beams.

I set down my wine glass and take her hand. She lets me. It's cold, and I envelop it in both of mine. "I'll get to the point, too. I don't play games. That's not my style. For fifteen years I've stayed out of entanglements. My kids came first. I came second. I didn't want to be with someone who would complicate my life. That was before I met you."

She's listening. It's a start.

"You walked into the damn conference room so poised and self-assured, smart and funny—damn it, Chloe, you're the whole package. And then the baby . . ."

"The baby." The words come out of her like bubbles, floating on the wind.

I stand, realizing some music would help. I'm all drumbeat in-side, wanting to say the right words, but trying to make sure I don't lose too much of myself in this. I'm done compromising to the point of loss. I put on some Miles Davis, *Kind of Blue*, and she closes her eyes, leaning her head against the back of the couch.

She is breathtaking.

I continue, standing behind her, watching.

"Holly is everything to me, Nick," she says, her voice dreamy."I had no idea you could find so much of yourself in raising a child."

My chest loosens.

"It's not like you lose yourself in them. It's like you find your-self in new ways. I know she'll be grown one day." Chloe yawns. "And I'm excited to know my job will fade out as a parent. Our job is to raise them to be independent souls, right? I don't want an adult child who needs me. I want to have one who *wants* to spend time with me."

She chuckles softly. "But right now, I'd settle for three hours of uninterrupted sleep."

I smooth a strand of hair behind her ear. She sighs into the touch. She finishes her wine and sets the empty glass on the end table next to her, eyes still closed. Her breathing evens out.

"I sacrificed," I tell her. "Put my kids' needs first. Lost my mar-riage and a fair number of friends along the way who couldn't un-derstand that. Made plenty of new friends who did."

"Umm hmm."

"But I never met a woman who got it. Who would enter my world and let me enter hers and share the kind of love you only find through family."

"And I'm that woman?"

Time stops. Seconds tick by. Then a full minute, as I close my own eyes and listen to the voice inside me that wants to say what's true.

Yes, my heart beats.
I open my mouth to say it, and—
She's fallen asleep.

CHAPTER NINETEEN

Chloe

WE ALL KNEW this day was coming, right? The official First Day Back to Work. I stretched my maternity leave as far as I could, stacking accrued vacation and sick leave into a longer break than most moms receive in the United States. Leaving home for ten consecutive hours feels like preparing for a space mission. Five o'clock tonight might as well be ten years away. I can't even foresee returning.

I read that something like seventy percent of mothers in the US work outside the home. Know how many women that is? Thirty-one million. A few lines below that statistic, this caught my eye: "Eighty-six percent of working mothers say they 'sometimes/ frequently' feel stressed."

So it's not just me.

On the other hand, the percentage of working mothers who report being 'very happy'? Eighty-five percent.

Deep breath. I can do this.

News flash, Chloe: you *have* to do this.

My original idea was to reappear in my office today looking pretty much the way I imagine Victoria Beckham looks when she turns up at her office to design her next collection. Cool and calm, fully accessorized, immaculate. She has four kids, right? (I know, probably eight nannies, too, but still.)

Well, that was the concept.

I laid out an outfit last night after Holly went to sleep, but it involved a silk tunic, and I quickly realized that would result in a trip to the dry cleaner. I have no time for another errand. So I rearranged, based around a little cashmere cardigan, but if she spits up, cardigan ruined, so no.

Okay, Round Three. Black knit dress, washable. Black patterned tights, washable. Black boots, waterproof. Something tells me this is my new uniform. I can just be hosed down at the end of the day.

There's probably a special booth for that at O.

Alarm goes off at five a.m. I shower, find the hairdryer, blow my hair dry. Put on full makeup for the first time in months, eye shadow, mascara, red lips. The face looking back at me from the mirror looks both familiar and very strange.

Then Holly wakes up, and I can hear her over the baby monitor, cooing to herself. I go in to pick her up. She is laying on her back, touching her fingers together in wonder, perfectly happy. I appear in her line of sight and her face lights with a joyous smile of recognition, and now I am perfectly happy, too. But as I lean over the crib, her eyes—fixed on my face—go round with surprise and consternation. Her little face puckers. She begins to cry. I pick her up, but she is holding herself rigid and is now looking away from me, sobbing.

Noises in the kitchen tell me that Jemma has just arrived, and a few moments later she peeks in the room.

"Good morning, what's going on?"

"I think it's stranger anxiety. She doesn't recognize me with makeup."

"Give her to me. I always look the same." Jem takes Holly from my arms. "Go get ready."

By the time I gather up my bag and tote and put on my coat, Holly's sobs have reduced to just hiccups, but she still refuses to look at me. I hate leaving her this way. I kiss the back of her head and drag myself out to the car.

Peak commuter time, traffic stopped on the Mass Ave bridge to Boston. Traffic stopped in every direction, in fact. I am going to be late on my first day back. Everyone will already be at their desks, so they will all see me slouching in. Busted.

And I need to show them that nothing has changed. I can handle it all.

I reach the final intersection, only one car ahead of me now, when the light turns yellow. Shit! Another light cycle means seven more minutes sitting here. In a minor panic, I gun it and make the left turn just as the light goes red.

I'm about thirty yards down the street when I see another light in my rear-view mirror, very bright and flashing blue. Oh please, no.

Yep. Moving violation, $150. Pulled over for thirty-five minutes. The officer was unimpressed with my explanation.

By the time I pull into the parking garage where O reserves space for employees, I have been awake and trying to get here for four hours. I could have driven to Newark, New Jersey, in that amount of time. I approach my assigned space and just as I am turning into it, I see Carrie's red junker sitting there. I slam on the brakes just in time. The sudden stop propels my coffee out of the cup holder and across my thigh.

And still I do not cry.

I park behind Carrie's car and blot the coffee from my dress with a Pamper from the glove box. I knew washable was the way to go. I sling my tote bag over my arm and slide out of the car. That was no fun, but it's over. I'm here.

My professional day starts now.

I open the trunk to get the emergency umbrella I keep there— see? I am capable and prepared for any conditions. Except the umbrella is now buried beneath a collapsible stroller and a six-pack of paper towels, so I put down everything in my hands and unearth the umbrella. Load up again with tote bag, slam the trunk shut, and at the exact second I hear the car's automatic locks engage, I remember.

I set down the keys on the left side of the trunk. Inside it.

Channel Kelly Clarkson. What doesn't kill you makes you stronger.

As I am setting down my bag, Carrie bursts into my office, a look of horror on her face. "Chloe! I forgot you were coming in today! I'll move my car right away!"

"Good luck with that," is all I can muster. "Actually, could you please just get me some coffee?"

It's 9:20. I am exhausted.

"Yes!" she responds enthusiastically. "We have Grind It Fresh! now, did you know? It's changed my life."

"I don't think I can take any more life changes right now, Carrie. Just black coffee."

There is so much stuff piled up in my office, it's going to take me a month just to clear a space. I get started.

Open six envelopes, drink coffee—and it really is good coffee, wonder if Holly is taking her nap, check messages, return eleven emails, drink more coffee, wonder if Holly is up from her nap, break down and text Jemma:

All good?

Unsatisfying response: *All good :)*

Eat energy bar. It doesn't work. I am just so sleepy. And I'm not used to sitting still and, you know, focusing . . . Maybe if I open my office door, the air and outside sounds will wake me up?

As I'm swinging the door in, music comes on the PA system in the hall. That's new. We never had ambient music before. I pause, swaying to the infectious beat, and listen.

"Zion," by Lauryn Hill.

Henry appears around the corner. He is wearing grey yoga pants and a tuxedo jacket with a pink silk hanky in the breast pocket. No shirt. Must be a party in the spa this afternoon.

"Hey, girl," he says. "You gotta see this, come on." He grabs my hand and pulls me down the hall.

"Henry, what is it? I have so much to do! Have you heard from

Jemma today?"

"Zion" finishes and Natalie Maines starts singing "Godspeed."

He comes to a halt in front of the conference room and opens the door with a flourish. I look in.

The first thing I see is a banner that reads "O Baby!" There's a pile of gifts on the conference table, and a cake in the shape of a . . . is that a pink rabbit? The room is very crowded. I look at them, and they look at me, and suddenly they all start clapping. And whooping. A few whistles. I look at Henry accusingly.

"Don't blame me." He smiles.

Now, after baby tears and guilt, stress and traffic tickets and exhaustion, it's the show of love and support from friends that does me in. Tears fill my eyes. Something else spilling on this dress.

Carrie rushes up to me, wearing a pink feather boa and a huge smile. She hugs me and says, "Chloe, we wanted to do this before the baby came, but it all happened so fast, and then you were gone." She takes off the boa, wraps it around my neck, and leads me to the head of the table, where she pushes me into a chair.

She turns to the room and claps her hands. "HellO!" she calls. This is how our employee events typically open.

"HellO!" they call back.

It's kind of like elementary school, I know, but it works.

"Everyone pick up a gift," Carrie instructs them. "We'll open them one at a time. Chloe will start, and then we'll go around the room. When it's your turn, please read the card and tell us who the gift is from. At O, we share the love."

She winks. They hoot. Mousy Carrie has obviously been experiencing some professional growth while I've been gone. Also, the refreshments appear to include wine and beer.

She bends over and scoots a big, professionally-wrapped box toward my chair.

I open the card. "It's from Andrew McCormick," I read, "and it says 'Cheers from Anterdec!'"

I tear off the paper. It's a case of Dom Perignon. Oh my. The perfect gift for any occasion.

"Next!" Carrie announces.

Zeke is first on my left. "This is from the team in Accounting," he says. Pulling off the box lid, he holds up a garment, adult size. "Oh that's so sweet," Zeke comments. "It's something special for you, Chloe." Yards of cotton flannel spill out onto the floor. Zeke stands to display it better. It has long sleeves and a high neckline, and as he spreads the top across his chest, we all see that it features various slits and flaps on the bodice. There's also a pair of fuzzy slippers.

"I didn't realize you were adopting," Diane from Accounting says. "It's a nursing nightie."

"Thank you," I smile. "You can never have too many nighties."

Diane is next in line to open. "It's from Human Resources," she says, sounding puzzled. "The card says, 'We heard what Accounting was giving you.'"

She rustles the tissue paper and, with two fingers, lifts what appears to be a bright red chiffon bra. In her other hand is a matching lace thong. Diane's face is the exact same bright red color.

Zeke laughs so hard he falls off the side of his chair.

Hayley's next. She unwraps a package and reveals a soft plush baby doll, cute as a button. According to the box, it is from the "Girl Talk" line of educational toys.

"Wait," she says, examining it, "I think it talks!" She hunts around a bit and finds a button, which she presses.

"No means No!" the doll exclaims in a tiny, android voice. Hayley presses it again. "You'll have to buy me dinner first."

"Next!"

Next is Ryan, and his gift is from the staff at ONY. A Camelbak Antidote Reservoir, 100-ounce capacity. It's a backpack-type hydration unit for exercise, fitted with a small tube and a mouthpiece, hands-free. They must think I am a runner?

Ryan reads the card, written by Jack. "'We see the moms in Central Park wearing these all the time. Good luck!'" Ryan squeezes it. "It's filled with something." He opens the valve and takes an experimental sip. "Gin," he says, in a voice filled with admiration. "Hendrick's."

"Mommy juice," someone laughs, but I notice that Ryan tucks the box under his chair instead of putting it back on the table.

A sunbonnet from the skincare team is added to the pile. Marcy Silverman sent an envelope with a U.Fund College logo on the corner, but I said quickly that I would open it later.

Finally we come to the biggest box of all, which proves to be from Facilities Management. The card says, "Very popular in Cambridge!"

It's my very own MulchingMama. According to the instruction booklet, by using the enclosed sample diapers (refills sold online for $150 per case) and processing the soiled diapers through my MulchingMama unit, I can turn Poop to Profit. And potentially save the planet.

In my spare time.

Carrie begins slicing the cake and distributing plates and forks. At first, the cake appeared to be a big pink rabbit, but now that I have a chance to inspect it carefully, I see that it closely resembles a giant penis with long ears, a fluffy tail, and a smile made of M&Ms. I catch Carrie's eye.

She shrugs and whispers, "Catering. They did their best."

Henry, seated on my right, is last. He's not holding a gift. Standing, he picks up a bottle of Dom from the case, taps the side of it with his cake fork, and the room grows quiet. He clears his throat.

"You all may know that Chloe is a special friend of Jemma's and mine," he begins. "We go way back. And Chloe did us an enormous honor in giving our name to her beautiful daughter."

Tissues are being discreetly pulled out.

"It's an honor that can never be repaid, but can only be lived up to, lived into," he continues. Sniffles are audible. "As a sign of our commitment to our extended family, this artwork has been created.

It's forever."

He turns his back to the room and drops his tuxedo jacket. On his shoulder, the light catches a brand new tattoo: the leaves and berries of a holly branch.

There are a few seconds of silence, and then an explosion of applause, cheers, laughter, and joy. Over the PA, the playlist switches to Stevie Wonder's "Isn't She Lovely," and Zeke begins dancing with Diane, who looks like an uncomfortable robot.

As I am hugging Henry, he whispers in my ear, "Don't touch it, okay? It still hurts." At that moment, I see Jemma in the doorway, holding Holly.

And right now I understand that everything is going to be just fine, forever.

Nick

The texts are amusing.

And hot.

Sorry I fell asleep the other night, she texts. *Can I make it up to you?*

Attached is a picture of Chloe, wearing her power underwear, the bustier open and—

"Damn." Charlie draws out the word. "What's that porn site? I'd love to—"

My elbow "accidentally" connects with his jaw as I move the phone out of sight.

"Go away," I growl, feeling like a seventeen-year-old with an annoying little brother.

"Sexting?" His voice is filled with admiration. "Nice. I guess you *can* teach an old lap dog new tricks." He rubs his jaw and steps out of my reach. "Just don't send dick pics. Take my word for it. They end up on the internet, no matter what."

Something in his tone tells me not to ask.

Come over tonight? I text quickly, trying not to make typos.

Can't. Holly has a late pediatrician appointment, and I'm behind on work, she replies, adding a frowny face.

I'm frowning too, but it isn't with my mouth.

Tomorrow? she types.

I'm gone all the rest of the week, I reply. *LA for a design meeting. I'm back late Friday.*

When did life become so complicated? she answers.

Saturday? I ask.

Jemma and Henry are away for the weekend, so you'll have to date both of us, Chloe replies.

I look at the picture of Chloe.

I think about a "date" with Holly along for the ride. Expectations change when there's a teething baby in attendance. Can't assume sex. Or drinking to the point of lost inhibitions. Or a foreign film, or a good comedy set at Improv Boston.

But I get Chloe.

And Holly's not bad company, either.

Saturday, I reply back.

"Hot date?" Charlie asks, coming into the kitchen for a beer.

"Something like that."

"Now that the kids are all in college, isn't it great to do what you want, when you want?"

I stare at my phone screen.

"Yeah. It is."

CHAPTER TWENTY

Chloe

THERE IS A saying: space exists so everything doesn't happen in the same location.

Time exists so everything doesn't happen all at once.

Sometimes, though, time isn't enough.

Two important events coincide, and one has to yield.

This is what parenthood has done to me: forced the moment where I have to choose my job over my baby, even for a few hours. I knew this day would come, and here it is, two months into being back from maternity leave, and I am stuck.

It's not quite that stark, I remind myself as I fight tears, waking before sunrise and busying myself with showering and dressing, praying Holly stays asleep so I can pull on thigh highs with two hands like a civilized person. Last time she woke up while I was getting ready, I learned new yoga positions.

One-handed snake stuffer. Nylon rip asana. Skirt button warrior pose.

In the quiet, creepy dawn, I mainline coffee and hope I won't pass out at the last meeting of the day at two o'clock.

Three o'clock is a fine time to snooze on the plane, though. Eyes on the prize.

6:00 am. I need to be at the airport by 7:30. I hate to go so far away from Holly, even though I'll be home at the exact same time tonight as if I'd just been at the office. What if there's an emergency?

But I have to meet with the O NY staff, and we can't fly them all here to meet with me.

You know what would be great right now? One of those tanks from the Oxygen bar at O.

There may be no scientific evidence to support the claim, but a hit of pure oxygen, scented like gin and tonic, would really take the edge off my separation anxiety. Breakfast of champions, zero calories and no prescription required. Pricey, though.

Isn't the baby supposed to be the one with separation anxiety? Because she looks perfectly calm and composed. Enfamil is her drug of choice.

"Good morning!" Jemma calls, coming in the back door, bringing in a sprinkle of snow. It's the week before Christmas, and Thanksgiving was a blur of a feverish baby and a sleep-deprived mama. Baby's First Christmas is coming and so is my mother, Charlotte. Add in a last-minute business meeting to New York and call me Job.

I can't do pleasantries right now. I hand Jemma a document. Six pages, single-spaced.

The cover page is phone numbers: Holly's pediatrician, Children's Hospital emergency room, poison control center, Cambridge police, Boston Cab, O Boston, O NY, American Airlines, the car service in New York, the manager of my apartment building, Charlotte's cell, Howard's cell, Nick's cell, Carrie's cell, the electrician, the plumber, my cousin who lives in Newton, and the vet. Also health insurance info for Holly, and all my credit card numbers with PINs.

One page of infant CPR instructions, with diagrams.

Two pages of legal information, including Henry and Jemma's guardianship of Holly and my last will and testament.

Operating instructions and warranties for all the major appliances. And the coffee maker, which I certainly consider to be a major appliance.

Jemma flips through the pages.

"Poison control? Seriously? She can't even crawl yet, Chloe, how is she going to get *poison*? Roll to it?"

"Better to be safe than sorry," I mutter.

"I am here with Holly four days a week," Jemma says patiently. "I know her schedule. I know how to use the washing machine and the microwave. I have read *The Happiest Baby, Sh!t No One Tells You*, and *Pat the Bunny*."

"I know," I answer miserably, and gratefully.

"You are only going to New York," she continues. "For the business day. You could practically take a cab home. Now get your bag and go. We'll see you tonight, same time as always."

"Is Henry still planning to pick you up here after work?" I ask. Jemma and Henry are leaving immediately for her sister's wedding in Providence. The last-minute New York meeting put me into a tailspin. Jemma warned me months ago that she needed this day off for the wedding rehearsal and dinner. I've placed one of my best friends in a horrible position. She's split the difference for me, and I'm deeply grateful. Charlotte couldn't (wouldn't) come, and I haven't cultivated a relationship with any other caregiver for Holly.

I'm in a bind of my own making.

And it's killing me.

"Yes," Jem answers. "If we leave here by six thirty, we'll get to the rehearsal dinner in Providence by eight at the latest. We'll miss some of cocktail hour, but that's probably a good thing. It's going to be a long weekend with my family."

"And you're sure it's okay for the maid of honor to miss the rehearsal?" I ask dubiously.

"Yes, my sister the bridezilla walked me through it last weekend," she says. "As long as we get there sometime tonight, everything will be fine."

She looks back down at the pages in her hand.

"Hairball remedy?"

"For Minky," I explain. "Sometimes she chokes."

"GO," Jem says.

I pick up my leather bag and try to swing it over my shoulder, but it knocks into some of the supplies I have helpfully stacked on the island. Cans of formula and cat food, bottles of baby ibuprofen and Ipecac—just in case—fall and roll. The six-pack of Corona (for Henry) stands firm, but the lime rolls too.

"K bye," I call. If I start kissing Holly, I'll never leave. The sooner I go, the sooner I'll get home.

Or something like that.

♥ ♥ ♥

AROUND ONE P.M., in between meetings, I look out the window and see just a few glittery little snowflakes in the air. So pretty in the city. I hope it snows tomorrow night in Boston. It would be so romantic for my dinner with Nick.

Around two p.m., I look out the window and see . . . four inches of snow on the ground. At least, I can kind of see it. Visibility is about ten feet. Mostly I just see white. I should be heading to the airport in half an hour.

I pull out my phone to check for a text from the airline. And there it is. Flights to Boston Logan canceled.

Don't panic, Chloe. Do not panic. Breathe.

She doesn't pick up: "Jemma, it's me. My flight is canceled. Where are you? Call me."

I text her: *flight canceled call me!*

I email, and send a Facebook message. I resort to Twitter. I call Henry, whose phone goes directly to voicemail. He must be with a client.

Another deep breath. Another.

Solve the problem, Chloe. New York is not that far from Boston. I can get home somehow. Right?

I find Jack, the office manager, and ask him to call Amtrak for train reservations.

"Sorry, Chloe, they've canceled all trains to Boston. Looks like this is going to be a major blizzard. I'll find you a hotel room."

"No. NO! No hotel room. I have to get home." I am leaning over his desk. He leans away. "What about a car rental?"

"Chloe. It's a blizzard. We've had four inches of snow in an hour. You can't drive three hours in this! What if you get stuck on I-95? You could die!"

He's right. Shit.

Shitshitshit.

My phone rings, Jemma's ringtone.

"Chloe? Weather.com says you're going to get a snowstorm this evening. It's bypassing New England, but New York's getting whomped."

"Did you not see my messages?"

"No, we just got back from a walk. What did they say?"

"They said we are having a snowstorm!"

Heads pop up from cubicles all around me. I walk to a corner and lower my voice, cupping my hand around my phone.

"My flight is canceled. All flights are canceled. So are the trains. I can't get home."

"Well, that's just not possible," Jem says calmly. "I have to be in my sister's wedding. In Providence. You have to get home. In fact, we should probably leave sooner than we planned."

"How, Jemma? How am I going to get home? Teleport?"

Silence.

"Okay," she says slowly. "We need to figure this out. When do you think you can get here?"

"I don't know! Tuesday?"

Am I yelling? Jack has opened the door of an unoccupied office and is motioning me in.

"Hotel room?" he whispers.

I nod unhappily.

"I guess Henry could stay here with Holly," Jemma offers. "If you can get home tomorrow morning, he might even make the wedding." I hear the skepticism in her voice, though. Her sister's already pissed Jemma is missing the rehearsal. If Henry doesn't go, I could be the reason for a decades-long resentment that it's unfair to create for them.

"Oh Jem. That is so generous of you." They hate to be apart. "But I don't think Henry's interest in public health extends to wiping poopy bottoms. I wouldn't leave him alone with a baby for ten minutes."

I'm helping her save face.

"That's true. He's going to have to ease into fatherhood when we're ready," she says with a distracted laugh. "Besides, my family already doesn't like Henry. This could push them over the edge. If I go without him, it could get . . . bad." She sighs. "What about your cousin? The social worker?"

"In Florida. Visiting Charlotte. Who can't even fly up for an emergency now!" A little sob of desperation escapes from me.

My phone beeps. Another call coming in.

It's Nick.

"Jem? I'll call you right back. Two minutes."

"I just saw the storm reports," he says when I click over to his call. "How are you?"

"Panicked. Jemma and Henry have to go to Providence for her sister's wedding! I can't get home for Holly. I'm the worst mother ever!"

I start sobbing.

"I'm on my way to your place."

"What?"

"You're not going to get out of there tonight. You'll be lucky to be home tomorrow." He pauses. I don't know how to interpret it, but the silence makes me sit up, tears stopping. "I'll stay with the baby. Or bring her to my place. Something," he mutters.

There have been very few times in my life when I have literally been speechless. I cannot think of a single thing to say.

"Chloe? Are you there?"

"Yes! Did you just say . . ."

"I'll take care of Holly."

"No! It's too much to ask . . . I don't know what to say! Do you know how to change a diaper?"

He laughs. "Well, unless the whole concept has somehow changed, I think I can remember."

"It's a lot, Nick, and she doesn't know you that well. She's teething and gets cranky, and she might have another new tooth coming in . . ."

We both go quiet.

My call waiting beeps.

This is a very bad idea, but it's the only idea we have.

"Chloe."

His voice is so warm, like sunlight on sand. He doesn't need to say more.

"You're sure?"

"Chloe."

"I promise I will be on the first plane to Boston. Or train. Jemma will show you everything. And I'll be by my phone every second. And there's a list of emergency information—not that it was any use when this emergency came up—there's not much food in the house . . . oh Nick, I can't believe you're doing this!"

"Neither can I, actually."

I think that's what he says. The connection is breaking up.

I only hope *we* don't, after this.

I click over to Jemma, to give her the good news.

Good news. Ha.

Here it is. The moment everyone warned me about. I knew being a single mother by choice would be hard. I knew adopting would bring up my own adoption issues. Do mothers who aren't adoptees panic like this when it comes to an unexpected absence from their child? I don't have a barometer for measuring my own reactions against the norm.

I knew I'd need support networks and backup plans and that this fragile little life would depend on me in ways I never imagined.

But this—this isn't my fault.

So why do I feel like it is?

Nick

"I THOUGHT YOU said she wasn't my little sister," Jean-Marc grouses, looking at Holly like she's a rare animal in a zoo exhibit licking the window.

"She's not. Chloe's in a bind, trapped in a freak storm in New York. I'm watching her tonight." After talking a panicked Chloe down off her snow-covered ledge, I went to her house to find Jemma dressed in an elegant gown, Henry in black tie, and a thirty-page manual clearly written by Chloe, who should turn her talents toward writing pandemic preparation manuals for the CDC.

With assurances all would be fine, I sent them off.

Chloe's place is tiny, and all three of my kids are home for the beginning of winter break. It seemed easier to bring Holly here, along with half her baby gear, where the four of us can trade off child care. One seasoned father and three young adults should have no problem managing one teething infant.

Holly seems unimpressed by my townhouse, preferring to focus entirely on the button on my business shirt cuff as I hold her. Dark hair, straight and shiny like a wet seal, sprouts from her little head. Her birth mother is Asian and Holly's eyes are dark, but rounded. Chloe doesn't talk much about the birth father, but I'm guessing he wasn't Asian, given Holly's features.

For as serendipitous as the circumstances of Chloe's adoption of Holly are, she looks like Chloe. It's a strange—and beautiful—coincidence.

I'll have to ask about Chloe's baby pictures someday.

"Ay ya ga," Holly says, before dive bombing my thumb joint and clamping down like it's a chew toy.

I stare at the selection of baby toys I brought from Chloe's place and let her gnaw on me.

"Yeah. I got the last train out of town. A bunch of my friends are stuck in New York." Jean-Marc reaches for Holly's hand. She wraps a slick palm around his index finger. "Like Chloe, I guess."

"Urg," Holly says, grinning madly, a string of drool running down to their clasped hands.

Jean-Marc takes it in stride. "Babies are gross."

"So are teenage boys."

"It's not a competition, Dad."

I laugh. "No, it's not. But babies don't forsake paying to do laundry so they can spend more on entertainment." I look pointedly at his overstuffed duffel bag.

"I budget reasonably."

"That bag smells like a prison cell."

"DADDY!" Elodie walks in the front door, eyes like saucers, tossing her own bag of laundry on top of Jean-Marc's bag of shame. "Is that Chloe's baby?"

"Nah. Dad just decided to start a day care, El."

"Shut up."

She ignores me completely and smoothes back the tuft of hair on Holly's crown. It stubbornly sticks back up.

"Aren't you the sweetest!" she says, her voice full of sugar.

"Urg," Holly answers, opening her mouth and smiling with her whole face.

"Where's Chloe?" Elodie looks around wildly. "Have you reached the point where you're having the kids meet? Is it that serious, Daddy?" Her voice has dropped to a whisper.

"Why are you whispering?" Jean-Marc calls out from the kitchen, where he's digging in the fridge for leftovers. "It's not like the baby can't hear you."

"Because I don't want to be rude and say the wrong thing in front of Chloe!" Elodie shrieks. The sound could call dogs in battle.

Holly's happy countenance changes to surprise.

And then her face crumples into tears, her own shrieks

surpassing Elodie's as if this were, indeed, a competition.

"See what you did?" Jean-Marc shouts, irritated. "You made the baby cry."

Hands flying to cover her mouth, Elodie looks at me in horror. "I'm sorry!"

"Shhh shhh shhh," I say, bouncing Holly on one hip, focused on getting her to calm down. She's electric with fear, that full-body, full-throated screaming that babies have, where all the emotions pour out at once because there are no boundaries to contain them.

Within a minute, she's sniffling against my shoulder, body shaking with little sobs, and then a long, peaceful rattling sigh indicates that balance has been restored. I kiss her head and rub her soft scalp, smelling apricot and beeswax. She's deadweight in my arms now, most of her mass held up by my inner elbow, forearm up against her shoulder. Muscles I haven't used in years spring back to life with memory and I look at the last baby I held regularly.

Jean-Marc's holding a milk carton upside down and draining it. He looks like a young Charlie. He throws the empty into the trash, then searches the cupboards and finds a red can, shaking the remains of a Pringles tube into his open mouth.

Given that I don't eat those, Charlie's going to come home and be pissed that his mini-me has learned all his tricks and one-upped him in draining his inventory.

Elodie's studying me with narrowed eyes.

"You're really good with her," she says, with misplaced suspicion.

"Shhhhh," I soothe. I'd forgotten how babies change time itself. Minutes and hours telescope into a free-floating mode of being. You can't be in charge of a baby and have specific goals. You can try, and you can be fooled into thinking you're succeeding. Like poor Chloe.

All it takes is one freak surprise to make you realize you're not really in control.

"Where's Amelie?" I ask.

Holly's head pops up, as if to ask the same question. She looks around the room as if we're on the hunt.

"On her way."

"I really do get all three of you here tonight?"

She shrugs. "It's winter break. I'm not doing anything until Monday."

"And you said because I'm doing study abroad next year, you wouldn't pay for me to go anywhere," Jean-Marc grouses.

"You poor, suffering child. Would you like an extra serving of porridge to make up for it?" I ask dryly.

"So you get us all!" Elodie squeals, her face stretched into an overly happy expression as she taps Holly's nose.

Peals of laughter fill the room.

Bzzz.

Fumbling, I reach into my back pocket for the phone. It's an actual call.

"Nick? Nick? How is everything?" Panic fills my ear. "Is Holly okay?"

"Bop!" Elodie says.

Holly giggles.

"Is that Holly?" Chloe asks, the panic draining out of her voice.

I laugh, a deep sound that surprises even me in its purity. "Yes."

"Bop!" Elodie, encouraged by her audience's response, keeps going.

Giggle.

"It sounds—it sounds like you have everything under control," Chloe says, her voice filled with marvel.

"So far."

"Is she upset?"

"She's had her moments."

"What happened?"

"She got scared."

"She must be terrified! She's only ever been watched by me or Jemma. Is—should I talk to her? Can you Facetime?"

Chloe's words are blipping in and out. "Chloe? I think the connection's bad."

"I—but—can you Face—"

Signal out.

"Shit."

"Daddy! Don't curse in front of the baby!"

"It's fine. She can't really imitate words for another few months." I chuckle. "I remember when Amelie learned to say *merde*, though. Your mother said it one too many times around her when she was about fourteen months old and it stuck. Oh, man, was Simone pissed." I smile at the memory.

Holly smiles back.

Elodie and Jean-Marc share an intrigued look. "Really?"

"Except she said it like *mer*, so Simone convinced people she was just talking about the sea." My mind takes me back to a time when both twins were starting to walk and talk, when Elodie had long, crazy hair in a topknot and eyes bigger than her head. "But she said it whenever she was mad."

Elodie tilts her head as she watches Holly, brow knit. "What about me?" she asks softly.

"What about you?"

"Tell me a story about me as a baby."

My mind goes blank.

She waits, holding her breath.

"You were the sweetest baby. The easiest of the three."

Elodie reels back in shock.

"Maman says I'm the most stubborn of her children!"

"I said you were an easy *baby*. Not an easy *child*."

"What went wrong, Dad? When did she become such a pain in the ass?" Jean-Marc asks, crossing his arms, giving Elodie an amused chuckle.

"After I dropped her on her head."

"DADDY!"

"You were fluent in French before English," I say slowly,

remembering. "Which was strange, because Amelie and Jean-Marc learned English first. You wandered around like a little drunken toddler, mixing English and French all the time. At one point, Simone was worried you had a speech disorder. We finally had you evaluated when you were about two and a half and the specialist said you just had a unique way of learning."

"That's medical speak for *weird*," Jean-Marc interjects.

Elodie throws a sofa pillow at him. He ducks. It hits the empty Pringles can and sends it flying across the room.

Holly giggles.

We all laugh.

This is going to be a piece of cake.

Chloe

JACK HAS MANAGED to get me into an Anterdec reserved hotel room, which must be the only available room in the entire city. I sit on the edge of the bed and stare at my phone.

No messages of any kind.

I call Nick. Voicemail.

I call Jemma. Voicemail.

I call Room Service. "Yes, Ms. Browne?"

Thank god somebody picks up my calls. This was beginning to feel like a sci-fi movie.

"Could I please have a vodka martini with a twist? No, on second thought, two vodka martinis?"

It's not like I'm going anywhere. I look at the window. Whiteout.

"Yes, Ms. Browne. Anything else? We are serving a full dinner menu."

I'm a contentment eater, remember? And I am SO not content right now.

"No, thanks, just the drinks."

That first martini may be the best thing I have ever tasted. The second is pretty damn good, too.

"Yes, Ms. Browne?"

"Hi. Hi," I say softly, sweetly. "I was wondering if you could maybe send up another of these fantastic martinis? With lemon?"

"Of course. Will there be anything else? We're featuring tagliatelle pasta with a puttanesca sauce. It's excellent."

"Oh no, no, thank you. No pasta. Just the drink."

I have no clothes to change into, but there's a white robe in the closet. So much more relaxing than work clothes and stockings.

I should be giving Holly her bath right now. I can practically smell the lavender baby shampoo. What is happening there? Why is no one picking up my calls?

At last, my phone lights up:

Text from Nick: *She's crying. Been crying for about fifteen minutes, no sign of stopping. All 4 of us have tried everything. What does she want?*

All four of us? Huh?

Me: *I don't know, what's happening? Who's with you?*

Nick: *I gave her bottle, now crying. Me and my three kids here to help.*

Oh, they're all there? The bridge of my nose prickles with a rush of emotion, eyes filling. Nick managed to call in reinforcements. I couldn't find anyone, but he has this network.

I need a network.

I need *him*.

Me: *Did you try her binky?*

Nick: *What is binky?*

OMG! Does he not speak English? Should I check Google Translate?

Me: *Binky! Binky!*

Nick: *???*

I stare at the screen, thinking hard.

Pacifier, I type.

No dots. A very long minute goes by.

YES! appears in a grey bubble.

I fall backwards on the bed in relief.

Found it in cat litter box. Wiped on pant leg. She's sucking on it happily, he answers.

I burst out laughing.

If I weren't in your debt, you'd be dead, I reply.

You owe me? he types back. *That could get interesting.*

I'll be home first thing tomorrow, I tap out.

Doubt it, Nick replies. *There goes our date.*

Oh no no no, oh please no . . . I really need that date . . .

Facetime, I type.

Nick: *?*

If we can't be together, we'll Facetime our date.

Blank screen.

G2G need to rock her now chat later

Seriously? He needs to rock her? I need him to rock *me.*

Hello? I type. *Facetime date. I promise you'll have fun*

Sometime later, he responds: *;) Exhausted G'night*

I can't imagine why he's so tired?

I click on the TV and scroll through the offerings, which seem to be mostly described as 'Adult.' Which gives me an idea.

"THERE'S MAMA," I say, pointing to the iPad screen. Elodie's sharing hers with Holly so Chloe can "talk" to the baby. Chloe looks haggard and frayed, deep grooves of worry in the muscles of her face, but her eyes light up when we get Holly on screen.

"Hi, baby!"

Chloe promptly bursts into tears.

Holly tries to gum the corner of the tablet.

"She's fine," I soothe, at a loss. How do you comfort someone on Facetime? You can't hug the screen and have that count.

"I'm sorry," Chloe says with a sniffle. "It's just so good to see her. Thank you. How is everything going?"

"We want to babysit more!" Amelie chirps, half her face

coming into view from the left side of the screen. "Holly's a blast!"

"Hi Amelie!' Chloe says with a shaky smile. "Are you all there?"

"Yes!" Elodie says, waving.

"Hey," Jean-Marc grunts.

"You have four adults for one five-month-old. You've got this covered," she says, her voice filled with awe. It hits me. She doesn't have three people she can call for help. She has Jemma and Henry, but they're more like one person.

That's it.

I bounce Holly on my knee as she slimes the glass screen, trying to touch Chloe, who makes raspberries at the baby.

Chloe has Jemma and Henry.

And now she has me.

The kids talk to Chloe while I balance the baby, her hands sticky with saliva, little baby noises indicating happiness. Chloe's engaged in an intense discussion with Jean-Marc about the restaurants closest to her hotel in NYC as Amelie sneaks off to do her laundry. Elodie watches me.

I hope she can't see all the pieces of me, slowly falling to the ground, like a tree shedding fall leaves.

Free. For years I've spent so much time spinning my wheels, taking care of kids, building a business, finding stability, with my eyes on the prize. Not freedom.

No.

Family.

I look around the room, at Jean-Marc scavenging for food again, at Holly playing with my shirt button, at Elodie telling Chloe they're about to make a toy run for Holly and not to worry about BPA or red paint in any toys, and the concept of freedom turns to mist.

One gust of wind and it's gone.

One deep breath and it blends.

CHAPTER TWENTY-ONE

Chloe

DATE NIGHT.
11:00 p.m.
Showtime.

I've spent the day watching the snow pile up, plows rumbling by on the streets, small Bobcat vehicles clearing the sidewalks. Constantly checking *Weather.com* and the airline site doesn't seem to have any effect on accumulation. It just keeps relentlessly falling.

Twice today, I've tried Facetime with Holly. Nick has held the screen right in front of her, and I've recited *The Runaway Bunny* from memory. This was not as successful as I'd hoped, partly because every time I tried to say, *"If you run away,"* said his mother, *"I will run after you, for you are my little bunny,"* I broke down and sobbed.

Again.

And partly because Holly showed no interest in the screen whatsoever, other than using it as a chew toy. She patted it a few times, but then twisted in her high chair, reaching for Nick. I thought all children, no matter how small, adored technology? Clearly she is not destined for a career with Mark Zuckerberg. Damn.

I'm hoping that my appearance on screen tonight, just for Nick, will be more compelling.

To that end, I have carefully hand-laundered my black lace bra and thong from yesterday, and the dark grey thigh highs. I dried everything with the hotel hairdryer, which wasn't easy because it's one of those little ones mounted to the wall. These are not my absolute dead-sexiest pieces, but when I put them on yesterday morning, I wasn't planning on an audience. Still, they're La Perla. Nothing to be shy about.

Which is good, because tonight is not about shy.

I put my silk shirt from yesterday over the bra, leaving it half unbuttoned. Black heels. My hair is pinned up, makeup perfect, with red lipstick. It's not like I had anything else to do this afternoon. Plenty of perfume—he can't smell it, of course, but I can. After all, this is a date. I turn the lights on, but low, and set tonight's martini—dry, with a twist—next to my computer.

At 11:04, my phone rings, and I answer on the laptop. There he is, looking incredibly handsome. I love when he wears his glasses.

"Hey there." He looks a little more worn than usual. I hide a grin. Mr. "It'll Be Easy" is getting a refresher course in infants.

"Hey. Are you okay? Looks like you might get home tomorrow, snow's letting up."

"Thank god! What's happening there? Is Holly asleep? Are you exhausted?"

"She's asleep. The girls were here all evening playing with her. They just went into their rooms with their phones. It's so quiet."

"Oh, that's good. That means you can concentrate. Focus." I adjust the camera angle, moving it just a bit lower.

"Oh my," he breathes. "Look at you."

I take a sip of my drink. I move the camera lower. I say nothing.

I unbutton my shirt. Slowly. One by one.

Nick laughs quietly, a low sound of appreciation. "Even your pixels are gorgeous," he says.

I push open my shirt and slide my fingers under the lace of my bra, massaging. My head tips back.

And in a moment, I stand. Every movement is slow. There's no hurry.

Now he can see my thong, the lace tops of my stockings.

I turn my back to the camera, hook my fingers under my

thong, and slide it down. Slowly.

And then I turn back.

And I hear him—at a distance of two hundred miles—draw in his breath. I watch his face intently. Lifting one high heel onto the edge of the chair, I lick a manicured finger, and touch myself where I am yearning for his touch.

"Chloe . . . oh, my . . ."

I reach to the keyboard to increase the volume, wanting to hear his every sound. His excitement feeds mine.

And the screen goes black.

Shitshitshit!

What did I do? How do I undo whatever I did, *right now*? Where the hell is tech services when you really need them?

Frantically, I restart the computer, wait, enter my password, wait, reopen Facetime. The mood is evaporating with each lost second. I type Nick's number into the box, as I try to compose myself and recreate the hot scene I just disconnected. I stand, face the camera, position myself, take a deep breath.

And there on the screen is the devastatingly handsome face of . . .

Henry.

I shriek. He shrieks.

Jemma walks up behind him and shrieks.

We shriek in surround sound.

I sit down, fast.

"Chloe, what the fuck?" I didn't know Henry's voice could hit that register.

"I was calling Nick! I don't know what happened!"

"Henry, go in the other room," Jemma orders. "Chloe, what the hell?"

"I don't know! I was Facetiming with Nick, and my computer shut down, and I was calling him back! Why are you online, anyway? Aren't you supposed to be at the wedding?"

"I broke the heel on my shoe dancing. We just came back

to the room so I could get another pair. When did you get a full Brazilian?"

"Oh my god. Can we talk about this another time? I need to call Nick back. Is Henry going to be okay?"

"Are you kidding? In his line of work? Henry actually does know how to unsee things," Jemma says, clearly annoyed, but if she's making jokes, I know it'll be okay.

"I am so, so sorry!"

"All good, honey." She sighs. "But I am clearly going to have to up my game here."

Nick

I HAVEN'T GOTTEN that hard that fast since high school.

And now Chloe's gone.

What did I just see, and how can I see more of it?

I fiddle with my laptop keyboard, taking two seconds to read-just myself. It's late, Holly's asleep, and I'm in sweats.

Which means I can't stand up and go out into my own damn living room for a few minutes.

Laughter fills my chest, though I repress it. Don't want to wake the baby or draw attention to myself. Last thing I need is one of my kids coming in here when Chloe comes back on screen.

She *is* coming back on screen, right?

Coming . . . on screen . . . please . . .

Silence. One minute. Two. Three. The image of that lusciously hot position of hers, the wanton abandon, fills me with—

Damn it.

Hard again.

Bzzz.

My phone's on the edge of the desk and the vibration is just enough to put it over the edge.

Like me, in a moment.

I bend down, wincing, but grab it.

A text from Chloe.

Sorry about that.

Nothing 2B sorry about, I text back quickly. I'm desperate to have her come back on screen.

So desperate I'm using txtspeak.

I am so embarrassed, she replies.

Facetime with me, I urge.

Can't. I clicked over from you accidentally and, she texts.

Nothing.

Nothing.

Nothing.

Two minutes of silence.

I call her on Facetime. She doesn't pick up.

Sorry. I accidentally called Henry instead of you and he got a show, she finally explains.

I stare at the screen, jaw on my desk.

U wat? I text back.

OMG is this one of Nick's kids? she replies.

No. Sorry. I'm so shocked I reverted to txtspeak, I answer, jaw grinding. *Henry?* I add.

Yes. Sorry.

Make it up to me by going on Facetime again. In that exact same position, I reply, resisting the urge to add, That's an order.

Terrified. Mood gone, she answers.

Mood gone?

I look down at my groin.

My mood is definitely *not* gone.

Thank you, she adds. *And I'll make it up to you when I come home.*

I'm throbbing. I look like I have a joystick growing out of my sweats. Henry got to look at Chloe's naked, sprawling, hot show.

And this is where being a nice guy sucks.

But I do it anyway.

It's fine, I say, finding some mature part of myself I don't really like.

It's not fine, she texts. *None of this is fine. But you made it all safe. Thank you.*

I soften in more ways than one.

Any time, I reply.

I'd like that, she answers.

Like what?

To be with you any time.

Holly begins to squall and squawk in the other room. Damn. Timing is everything.

And babies are cockblockers.

I'd like that, too, I text back, with a silly little heart, as I stand and relax, back to being casual, practical Nick, and do what needs to be done.

CHAPTER TWENTY-TWO

Chloe

WHEN THE PLANE begins its descent into Logan, I signal the flight attendant. Of course it's a full flight. I have the window seat, about six rows from the back of the plane, so it takes her a few minutes to get to me.

"When we land, I have to get off the plane right away," I say urgently. "It's an emergency. My baby."

"I'm so sorry," she responds sympathetically. "I'll see what I can do. Do you need to get to the hospital?" Understandably, she looks around me, searching for, you know.

A baby.

"Oh, no, I have to get to my boyfriend's house."

She just looks at me.

"My baby's there. I was stuck in New York in the storm."

"And something happened to the baby?" she asks, still concerned.

"No, no, she's fine. But I'm sure she misses me, I've been gone since Friday morning."

The attendant has lost interest. In fact, that almost looked like a tiny eye-roll.

"We'll do everything we can to unload the plane quickly," she says. "I'm sure everyone is anxious to get home."

"But you *don't* understand!" I start, but she has moved off.

My seat mate looks at me. "You can go ahead of us, honey,"

she says. "Ours are teenagers. We're nothing but an ATM and tech support to them."

♥ ♥ ♥

I TEXT NICK when we land: *Landed*

I text him when the plane reaches the gate: *At gate*

I text him from the cab line: *In cab line*

He texts back: *We're fine, relax*

The cab pulls up outside Nick's house. I am so frantic to get out, I can't calculate the tip, and I'm not going to take the time to swipe my credit card and wait for it to go through. I hand the driver three twenties and pull my overflowing tote bag out to the curb.

By the time I make it up the front steps to the door, I am weeping with relief. My yearning for Holly is a physical ache. My yearning for Nick is not much different. A little different, but not much.

Okay, pretty different.

He opens the door, and I throw myself into his arms.

"I'm so glad to be home, I thought I would never get here, I'm so sorry, thank you so much, where is she?"

Nick laughs and holds me tight. "Take a breath, she's fine. You're so cold! Give me your coat." He yanks my bag into his foyer.

"Nick, where is she? She must miss me so much, and she doesn't understand why I've been away from her. Where's my baby? Did she eat anything?"

"She's right here," he says, taking my hand and pulling me down the hall. He stops at the doorway to the little sitting room off the kitchen, and motions to me to be quiet. I peek around the door frame.

There's Holly. There's my girl. My heart actually leaps. Holly is sitting in Jean-Marc's lap, although he's watching the football game on television and not paying much attention to her. Nick's girls are kneeling on the floor with puppets on their hands. Princess puppets, and a dragon. My baby girl has a teething wafer in one hand and

Amelie's long blonde hair wrapped around the other hand. She is enthralled.

I look at Nick, and back at the kids. Holly is wearing a little shirt I've never seen before. It's purple and has a big, sparkly pink sequin heart on the front. She is also wearing what appears to be a miniature pink tutu. There is a big satin bow somehow attached to the wispy hair on top of her head.

"The girls went shopping," Nick explains, stating the completely obvious. "They thought we needed a few things."

On the floor sits a stuffed toy lamb. Life size. Beyond it is a pile of alphabet blocks, and beyond those is some kind of round plastic table with a seat in the middle and toys attached to the tray. Nick's normally austere sitting room, with its black leather sofa and grey plaid carpet, is a sea of pink plush and purple plastic. On the cocktail table are the week's papers, buried under a stack of board books.

Holly looks up and sees me, and I'm across the room in an instant. I scoop her up and bury my nose in the sweet smell of her neck. The world falls back into place for the first time in days. Okay, *a* day.

Holly squirms in my arms, struggling a little bit to push back from my hug. She twists her little body around and leans down to Jean-Marc, holding her arms out to him.

Her face wrinkles up and she starts to cry. She kicks me. *Kicks* me!

I am horrified.

She has forgotten me. I left her, and now I am a stranger. I am a Bad Mother. She hates me.

Jean-Marc reaches up and takes her back. "Hey," he says to me, and "Sshhh," to Holly. She settles back down in his lap, quiet.

I am appalled.

The girls jump up. "She is SO sweet!" they are saying. "We had so much fun! Can she come back next weekend?"

Nick puts his arm around me. "Come on, we'll pack up her

things so you can get her home."

I follow him into the kitchen, looking back over my shoulder. I open the fridge to get her formula, and Nick hands me a tote bag.

Nick's refrigerator is usually pretty well stocked. Charlie makes sure of that. But pulling the door open now, I can't even see what's on the shelves. They are packed to overflowing. Baby yogurt, four six-packs. Fruit sauce in squeeze containers, a dozen flavors. A teething toy. Little yellow Cheerios containers.

Oh my god, a chocolate cupcake. With a blue frosting Elsa on top.

And several bites out of it.

Nick takes the cupcake out of my hand. "I couldn't resist," he says, not quite meeting my eye. "I love cupcakes."

Right.

"Did Holly eat this?" I ask. "Oh, Nick!"

I have lost control. I have failed to take care of my child.

"No," he admits. "That was me."

It's too much. I can't hold back the tears.

Nick pulls me into his arms. He kisses my tears and slowly, tenderly begins kissing my lips. The taste of him, the smell of his skin, make me respond in spite of my misery.

His hands move from my arms to my shoulders and slowly slide down my back. He presses closer, and I feel his growing hardness.

"I've missed you so much," he says in my ear. "And that call last night . . ."

"Well," says a deep male voice from behind me, "What's cooking in here?"

Charlie.

Nick turns, but keeps one arm tight around me.

"Hey, little brother," he says.

"Chloe," Charlie says, and kisses me on both cheeks, European-style. "I hear you had a relaxing getaway in New York."

For a moment, I am speechless.

"It was the worst weekend of my life," I sputter.

"Worse than when we borrowed Caroline Pressman's car and drove to Maine, but we only had sixty-five bucks between us, and her car broke down in Hampton Beach but we couldn't call our parents because we told them we were going to a choir retreat?" Charlie asks. "Worse than that?"

"Yes, it was worse than that!" I hear my voice rising. "I have a baby to take care of!"

"So did I," he chuckles.

He has always been able to get me going.

"And we had to stay in that thirty dollar no-tell motel, and you wouldn't let your bare feet touch the carpet?"

"That's enough, Charlie," Nick warns.

"And there was a vending machine for rubbers, so I had to keep asking for change at the front desk?"

"That is enough!" Nick says loudly.

From the other room, I hear Holly start to fuss.

"Time for us to go home," I say nervously, and reach for the half-packed tote bag.

"Stay for dinner," Charlie offers. "I'm roasting a chicken."

"Sounds great but I have to get Holly home to bed. Another time maybe."

Charlie looks abashed. "Was it something I said?"

He looks from me to Nick, and back to me.

"Look. I apologize," he says softly. "It's a weird situation. You were really important in my life, Chloe. I mean, you're both really important in my life. But we were just kids. And now we're grown up . . ."

"Some of us are," Nick mutters.

" . . . now we're all grown up, and you two seem like a pretty good fit. I love you both," he finishes. "But it's still weird."

This is so Charlie.

He opens his arms and hugs me tight, and I hug him back.

"Now how about that roast chicken?" he asks me.

"It's always been my favorite dinner."

"Wait till you taste mine. Better than Hamersley. Actually, it's his recipe. Garlic and lemon."

And thus we have dinner for six (mostly) adults, accompanied by one sleeping baby girl.

Family style.

Nick

"WHY," I ASK Chloe, my finger tracing the outer edge of her nipple, the skin curling up like a sweet blossom, "did you decide to stay the night?"

Holly is asleep in her Pack 'n Play in my den. Charlie is on the pull-out sofa. The kids are in their respective bedrooms. Chloe and I are in that lazy afterglow time in my bed, when minutes have no meaning and the outside world is there, but sex puts everyone else at a distance. Being naked together, body heat transferring without effort, lips and tongues and fingers all working their magic, makes the crazy hustle-bustle and stress of everyday life seem quaint. Cute.

Over *there*.

A thousand miles away.

"Who could turn down Charlie's roast chicken?"

I give her a pinch.

She squeaks.

She gives me a squeeze.

I fold in half.

"Hey!" I growl. "Precious cargo."

"It *is* of high value." Her hand shifts from violence to a stroke that makes me wonder what my refractory period is.

No one has tested it in a long time.

We can remedy that.

"Priceless," I murmur, closing my eyes, enjoying the attention. We made love quickly, the baby monitor on, worried Holly could awaken at any moment. The furtive sex quenched a thirst, but it didn't sate.

"What is this, Nick?"

I look under the covers. "That's my—"

She doesn't laugh when she interrupts. She lets go. "No. This. Us. What . . . what are we?"

We're in love.

I don't say it. The thought loops through my mind like a NASCAR race. Endless laps.

"What do you think we are?" I whisper, lobbing back the question.

"You first."

I pull back, watching her. Without contacts or glasses, she's blurry.

I need her to be clear.

Groping for my glasses on the nightstand, I fail to find them. Chloe hands them to me. The air between us is pregnant with questions.

I put the glasses on. Clarity achieved.

Visually, at least.

Her eyes search my face, sweet and loving, but there's a hesitation. A wariness.

Freedom. Family. Chloe's at the beginning of the race. I'm in my final laps.

Starting over seems foolish, on the surface.

But I was never a surface-level guy.

"I love you," I say, the words soft, like the fine hair that dots her arms, the little lashes on her lower lids.

Her wariness dissipates.

"I love you, too." She strokes my cheek, the back of her hand sliding down along my jaw. Stubble covers it, the sound of her movement like whispering sandpaper.

"Can love be enough?" I asked that question more than fifteen years ago, right before Simone left.

She told me *no*. Showed me, too.

"Of course," Chloe answers, her expression bemused. "How could it not be?" She frowns. "But love means something different now. It has to include Holly."

As if on cue, the baby monitor picks up the rustling of blankets and a baby's snurgle.

"I know."

"You want to start over? Really?" There's that wariness again.

"I want my freedom."

Wariness turns to alarm, and she stiffens.

"But freedom doesn't mean what I thought it meant."

She cuddles up again.

"What *does* it mean?"

"Being with you. Building a family. Blending families. Finding meaning. Loving you and my kids."

Holly kicks off her blanket, the movement caught in black and white on the video monitor.

Chloe gives me an *uh oh* look.

Time is precious.

"All my kids."

She jerks in my arms.

"However you want to define that."

"I'm a little old for you to adopt me, Nick."

I pinch her.

She squeezes me.

We make love again, quickly, before Holly wakes up crying.

But that's fine.

Because we made it.

Just in time.

CHAPTER TWENTY-THREE

Chloe

THESE DAYS, WHEN I have a date with my boyfriend, I stay home and my child goes out. Is that unusual? Tonight Holly has been delivered to Nick's house, where his girls will babysit. Nick and I then hightailed it back to my place. The logistics of my life would daunt an air traffic controller.

At least I don't have to pack very much for these visits. Holly has more toys and little outfits there than she does here, thanks to the twins. Like Charlotte, they seem to associate babies with shopping. Holly's first Christmas involved so many new toys and clothes that my condo looks like a Toys'R'Us bomb combined with a Hanna Andersson and Oilily fashion show.

Jean-Marc is less interested in accessorizing. His one notable contribution has been digging out their family copy of *Walter the Farting Dog*, which he reads to Holly with evident enjoyment whenever he is there.

If her first word is 'fart,' I am not going to be happy.

I'm standing at my sink, rinsing romaine and filling Nick in on the past few days. Although we work together pretty closely now, we try to keep it ultra-professional. No one at Anterdec knows we're dating. I'm pretty sure.

"They still can't officially tell me anything about Li, but our social worker manages to keep me updated. This week they thought they might have found her at a friend's, but when they got there, she was gone. Or she was never there." I sigh. "The adoption becomes final in ten days."

"Are you worried?" he asks. He's marinating the steak.

"No, not really. I mean, of course I'll be relieved when she's legally mine forever, but I don't think Li will try to stop it at this point, especially considering the police and social workers have never been able to locate her." I frown. He rubs my back, the gesture one of empathy. Li has no idea what a precious child she's brought into the world. I'm so grateful to be Holly's mother, but the fabric of our lives has this big loose end, and it's hard to accept. I hope Li is safe and in a good place. I can't help but worry.

"We need to celebrate the day the adoption is final. I'm declaring it a holiday . . . a Holliday." He chuckles. "We'll all go out for dinner, my kids and Henry and Jemma too."

"For Happy Meals," I add, laughing with him. "I love it. Let's invite Jessica Coffin."

Nick has put down the meat fork. He walks up behind me, and I expect to feel the warmth of his arms, but I don't. Instead, something lowers around me, and I look down.

He's fastening a delicate chain behind my neck. Suspended from the chain are thin circular bands of different colors of gold that interlock. I touch them gently. Spread out, they form a globe. A world.

Six bands of gold.

Tears fill my eyes and spill down around the necklace.

"You've become my world, Chloe," he says softly. "I want you to remember that every time you look at this necklace, or feel it against your skin. Especially at work, where I can't tell you myself. At least, not yet."

"Oh, Nick. It's beautiful." I hold the gold rings in my palm, like a talisman. Or a promise? I turn and kiss him, tears mingling with our lips.

He chuckles. "You rinsed the lettuce with tears. Not good. I'm trying to cut down on salt."

"I'm sorry," I sniffle. "Your blood pressure is very important to me."

"Especially in certain places," he smiles. "For dessert. In the meantime, I'm starving. Fire up the grill."

"Already nice and hot for you."

"Mmm, I like the sound of that," he says, giving me a kiss. Then he sets the steaks up nicely, with a flourish.

"If you were really watching your salt intake, you wouldn't have marinated the steak in soy sauce. Speaking of work, did I tell you that the new gO Spa vehicle is ready?" I help with dinner. I drink my wine.

Bzzz.

Nick groans and shoots me an apologetic look as he takes a call, walking into the living room. I walk outside and stare up at the dark night, thankful that in the ever-expanding universe somehow the two points of being called Nick and Chloe found each other.

Maudlin and a bit sappy, yes.

But also true.

"When's the maiden voyage?" he asks, his hands on my elbows, slipping around my waist from behind, cupping my belly where they link. I lean back into him, smiling.

"Scheduled to depart in two months, but we're having trouble arranging the delivery to New Orleans. We're going to have to delay. We need someone experienced on board, but O is too busy to spare any of the staff. Plus we need someone who knows how to handle a vehicle like that. We couldn't just hand Zeke the keys and send him off on the highway." I sigh against him.

"Right. Zeke's the one raised in England?"

"Yes. I think the only thing he knows how to drive is a Vespa, and even then he can't keep it on the right-hand side."

"I wish I could send Charlie on a long road trip. I could use some space every once in a while."

"Charlie's better at getting massages than giving them," I laugh as I turn in his arms, facing him. "A lot better."

Nick's eyebrows lower.

I shrug apologetically. "Oops. Sorry."

"I wish we could have that whole set of memories wiped out of your brain. Like on a computer. Highlight, delete, empty trash."

"It was a very long time ago. We were just kids. The only man on my mind is you."

He kisses me, a quick smooch that turns into something much slower, as he teases my lips with his tongue. Some part of me rises up, my body pressing into him, time elongating as the kiss makes that gentle pivot from a sweet connection to a deep anchoring. My fingers play with the fine hair at the nape of his neck, his mouth taking mine, my breath quickening until I don't know where his heat begins and mine ends.

And I am so, so glad.

His hands slide under my silk shirt, warm skin against mine, making me forget everything around me. Almost.

"The steak," I whisper. "I like mine rare."

"Damn!" He rushes out to the grill.

Overcooked.

But worth it.

"Go turn on the fireplace in the living room," Nick suggests after we finish the *very* well-done steak, the baby potatoes, the roasted broccoli, and a small plate of cheese and fruit. "I'll open another bottle of wine and be right in."

There was a time when I could not understand the appeal of a gas fireplace. No wood smell, no crackle? Then I bought this condo, flipped the switch on the wall, and beheld the roaring fire. Now I get it.

I curl up on the sofa, wrapping a soft mohair throw around my feet, and feel the room begin to warm.

Nick

Aside from destroying a beautiful cut of meat, the night's going as planned. Gorgeous woman with smiling eyes and fabulous conversation. Good food (steak excepted), gift bestowed, and happiness abounds. We're in that zone, the place where all the negativity of life washes away, and all that's left is the naked goodness of, well . . .

Being naked.

I struggle with the half bottle of Sauternes, the uncorking process more complicated than the Big Dig. Finally, it pulls free, with a lovely subtle pop. A few stragglers of cork float on top, mocking me.

Eh. That's what strainers are for.

I pour two glasses of wine, strain accordingly, and prepare to seduce Chloe.

"Here we are," I say, my voice low and—

She's asleep.

Blinking as if resetting my eyeballs will reboot the scene, I stare at her in repose, her head on the arm of the sofa, her legs curled under her. She looks like a kitten. Her breathing is steady and slow. Deep slumber.

I'm torn.

Angel Nick says, *Set down the wine, cover her with a blanket, and let her sleep. Go do her dishes.*

Devil Nick says, *Hey, dude. It's been a week since you got any. You know what to do. Blue is not your color.*

Devil Nick sounds a little too much like Charlie for my taste.

Sighing, I swig my wine, then gently pull up the mohair throw from Chloe's feet, covering her. The dishes won't wash themselves.

And besides, I realize, as I watch the fire glowing against the thin strands of the necklace I've just placed around her willowy neck, we have all the time in the world.

I met her just in time.

But I'll have her for the rest of my life.

Walking back into the kitchen, I start the hot water in the sink, going outside to grab the dirty grill grates. Setting them to soak in one half of the sink, I wash up all the rest of the dishes. I'm still figuring out the layout here at Chloe's place. Baby bottles and teething rings go in one cupboard.

Still don't understand the purpose of the wooden banana hanger.

I'm deep in my own head, scrubbing the grill insert, when I hear a sleepy gasp behind me. I turn around, hands filthy.

Chloe's there, blanket wrapped around her shoulders, rubbing her eyes.

"What are you doing?"

"Washing dishes."

"Why? We were—oh, Nick, I fell asleep, didn't I?" Her voice is filled with a panicked regret. She yawns, jaw popping from exertion, her shoulders rolling with effort.

"It's fine. I thought I'd get started on the foreplay without you," I joke.

She gives me a blank look.

"You know. Porn for women?"

Her eyebrows go up.

"Speak English."

"You still want to make love, right?"

She yawns again.

"Don't get so excited," I mutter.

"I'm going to need a lot of foreplay to get in the mood."

I scrub furiously.

"What are you doing?" she asks, laughing.

"Foreplay! Mari told me that men doing housework is an aphrodisiac for women."

"I can think of far, far better forms of foreplay," Chloe responds, her voice dropping to a familiar register that makes my blood quicken.

I wash my hands, abandon the rest of the dishes, and kiss her. As she steps into my arms, she pulls the blanket open, wrapping us in it. She's hot, a little sweaty at the neck, and she smells like a mix of faded perfume, well-seared steak, wine and musk.

She tastes like my future.

Breaking the kiss, she looks around. "You cleaned my kitchen!"

"Just wiped it down. Emptied the dishwasher. Soaked the grill plates and—"

This time, the kiss is like a burst of fireworks in a bonfire. Mari was right.

"You know, I clean a mean bathroom floor," I murmur in her ear, walking her backwards down the hallway to her bedroom.

She moans in ecstasy.

"And you should watch me scrub a toilet—"

Chloe's manicured fingers cover my lips. Our eyes meet.

"Stop while you're ahead there, mister."

"Not so arousing?"

A head shake greets me.

So does a lovely stroke over my pants.

"Chloe," I groan. Trying not to be obvious, I check the bedside clock. 8:19 p.m. We have more than an hour.

When I look back at Chloe, I find her watching the clock, too.

"Habit," we say in unison.

Then we laugh.

And then we most definitely stop laughing.

Chloe

MY BLACK VELVET pants, unzipped, drop to the floor, and my silk top slips off over my head. This leaves me wearing black heels, my new necklace, and perfume. Reaching for Nick, I unbutton his shirt, starting at the top, kissing and licking my way down, finding a new path. When I reach his belly, he moans. This man who is always so together, so in charge, can be utterly undone by my mouth on his skin. Amazing. I pull the clip from my hair and shake it loose.

My muscles are still cramped from sleeping curled up in one position on the sofa. When my ass hits the bed, I can't resist a full, luxurious stretch, arching my back and reaching over my head, eyes closed. But before I've completed it, I feel something more luxurious by far, as Nick's warm mouth covers me. His tongue starts slow, lazy circles, and I hear his quiet "mmmm" of pleasure as he senses my body's response. He knows what pleases me better than I know myself. How is that possible?

I relax completely, then begin to tense again, but in different places, pulsing with anticipation. The hands that I stretched over my head frantically seek something to grip tightly as Nick's lips and tongue move faster. There's never been a boundary between our bodies. My ecstasy is his and his is mine.

I cry his name as my orgasm begins to cascade. Seeing and hearing me come, tasting it, causing it to happen, makes him so hard that he plunges into me before I'm done. I want him desperately, and I know he feels the same. His moves become more urgent until his last powerful thrust, and I feel the hot flow of his climax. We finish together, my final shudders blending with his strong pulsing.

"My Chloe," he murmurs, almost to himself. I love hearing him claim me, when he's only half aware of his own words, lost in the golden moment. But a few minutes later, still inside me, as our breathing returns to normal, he says it again clearly: "My Chloe. My love."

I smile into his eyes, my palms on his scratchy face, but he looks back at me so seriously. With the fingers of one hand, he traces the thin chain of my necklace down to the interlocked gold rings of the pendant, warm now from our skin. He holds them up.

"You are my whole world. I love you. I need you."

My eyes fill with tears. "I love you, Nick. I've waited my whole life for you. It was worth every second."

And it was.

I waited years for Holly, knowing my life would never be complete without her, without a child to love. This mother's love is a fierce, protective force that flows in my veins. It was born when she was born, and will live inside me until the day I die. But I know it will evolve. My job is not just to love her and keep her safe, but to prepare her to find her own independent life, to fly from our nest someday on her own strong wings.

Just as Holly will do in her future, I've been living my own independent life. I've had happy times and sad times, successes and failures, with Henry and Jemma and Charlotte for support. I was doing okay. But it was chicken broth.

I start to giggle when I remember the saying: "Cooking is like love; it should be entered into with abandon or not at all."

Absolutely.

Then, like a horrible electric shock, my cell suddenly begins blaring "La Vida Loca." Dammit, Henry got to my ringtone setting again. As I reach for it, Nick's phone starts ringing, too.

"It's Elodie," I say, looking at the lighted screen. "How on earth does she know when we're . . . Hello?"

"Amelie?" I hear him say ominously into his own phone.

"Chloe? I'm really sorry . . ." Elodie starts, but I can't hear her over Nick yelling.

"I can't believe you girls are doing this! You are not ten years old anymore! You're not going to think it's so funny when I turn off your phone plan and you can only dial 911 and pizza delivery!"

"Shhhhhh! I can't hear her!" I hiss at him. "Elodie, what is it?"

"Hold on," Nick says furiously.

"Chloe, I'm really sorry!" Her voice breaks. "I hate to bother you, but we were trying to teach Holly to crawl and we were all on the floor and she picked something up and put it in her mouth and she swallowed it and we think it was a spider!" She's sobbing now. "And we don't know what to do!"

From Nick's phone, I hear the faint echo of " . . . what to do!"

I'm already standing, picking up my velvet pants from the floor and shaking them out. "We're on our way," I say. "Don't worry. Everything's going to be fine."

On his side of my bed, Nick is pulling on his shirt.

We're on our way.

We really are.

And everything's going to be *fine*.

Just fine.

THE END

♥ ♥ ♥

Thank you so much for reading *Our Options Have Changed*, the first in our On Hold of contemporary romances. Whether you like a little comedy with your romance, or some drama with your smiles, you'll find this new series to be just right.

Look for the next book in the series, *Thank You For Holding*, in 2017.

ABOUT THE AUTHORS

JULIA KENT

Text JKentBooks to 77948 and get a text message on release dates!

New York Times and *USA Today* bestselling author Julia Kent turned to writing contemporary romance after deciding that life is too short not to have fun. She writes romantic comedy with an edge, and new adult books that push contemporary boundaries. From billionaires to BBWs to rock stars, Julia finds a sensual, goofy joy in every book she writes, but unlike Trevor from *Random Acts of Crazy*, she has never kissed a chicken.

She loves to hear from her readers by email at jkentauthor@gmail.com, on Instagram and Twitter @jkentauthor, and on Facebook at *facebook.com/jkentauthor*

Visit her website at www.jkentauthor.com

ELISA REED

Elisa Reed is a journalist-turned-fiction-writer whose snappy, irreverent prose combines with an irrepressible zest for the simpler, and often intimate, pleasures of life to produce fun(ny) contemporary romance with a focus on second chances.

New England born and bred, Elisa Reed now lives, writes, and plays in New Orleans and along the sugar sands of the Gulf Coast.

You can find her on Facebook at: *www.facebook.com/elisareedauthor*

CPSIA information can be obtained at www.ICGtesting.com
Printed in the USA
BVOW01s2347260916

463395BV00001B/6/P